P. Wilson

Leaders in Literature

Being Short Studies of Great Authors in the Nineteenth Century

P. Wilson

Leaders in Literature
Being Short Studies of Great Authors in the Nineteenth Century

ISBN/EAN: 9783337204693

Printed in Europe, USA, Canada, Australia, Japan

Cover: Foto ©Andreas Hilbeck / pixelio.de

More available books at **www.hansebooks.com**

Leaders in Literature

Being Short Studies of
Great Authors in the
Nineteenth Century

By

P. Wilson, M.A.

Edinburgh & London
Oliphant Anderson & Ferrier
1898

To

MY WIFE

INTRODUCTORY NOTE

I VENTURE to publish these Studies in the sincere hope that they may become to the reader what they have been to myself,—a means of intellectual and moral stimulus.

Owing to the recent and exhaustive "Memoir" of the late Poet-Laureate, by his son, Lord Hallam Tennyson, I have refrained from submitting any estimate of mine of one who takes the first place in the Poetical Literature of the Victorian Era.

Although the Leaders in Literature referred to in this volume differ in many respects, they are nevertheless at one in dealing with themes ever interesting to the mind and heart of man.

P. W.

April 1898.

CONTENTS

RALPH WALDO EMERSON

"Man is a being of degrees; there is nothing in the world which is not repeated in his body; his body being a sort of miniature or summary of the world: there is nothing in his body which is not repeated as in a celestial sphere in his mind: there is nothing in his brain which is not repeated in a higher sphere in his moral system."

.   .   .   .

"All things ascend."—EMERSON, *Conduct of Life.*

"We wake and find ourselves on a stair: there are stairs below us, which we seem to have ascended; there are stairs above us, many a one, which go upward and out of sight."—EMERSON, "Essays."

RALPH WALDO EMERSON

I

EMERSON, leading easily in the Literature of America, takes a high place amongst the best Authors anywhere. In harmony with his own saying, that "great geniuses have the shortest biographies," the main facts of his life may be told in few words.

Born at Boston in 1803, he was about fourscore years old when he died. His forefathers were Puritan, many of them being preachers. Emerson, following in their footsteps, became minister in Boston of the Second Unitarian Church. After a pastorate of three years, 1829 to 1832, he resigned his charge, feeling, as John Morley puts it, "the bondage of forms and of public prayer." Thereafter, he took to Literature as his profession, choosing to utter his thoughts from a platform, and through the press, rather than from a pulpit.

It is easy to tell the story of Emerson's life, but it is not by any means so easy to grasp his thoughts, and it is as a great thinker that he ranks in Literature.

For one thing, he lives, moves, and has his being in a high and rare atmosphere; and for another thing, he is very sparing with his words.

Well has Emerson himself described his paragraphs as "incompressible."

To use a simile which he applies to Truth, it may be said that he is as difficult to catch as Light. If anything, so far as intelligibility is concerned, he ranks even worse than Hegel, the celebrated German metaphysician. Rumour has it that Hegel, on his deathbed, declared that there was only one man in Germany who understood his system, qualifying his admission by adding— *"and he doesn't."* But Emerson goes one more than the famous German philosopher, for he is frank enough to declare that he does not even understand himself. "I could not," he says, "give an account of myself, if challenged."

One of the peculiarities of a study of Emerson's writings is, that although the student cannot well tell what the gain has been, yet there is a latent consciousness that there has been a gain in the creation and increase of noble thoughts and moral impulses.

Whatever else Emerson's writings may be, they are genetic, and stimulating as mountain air.

It is not easy, as has been indicated, to say in a word what Emerson really is from a literary point of view. He is not a Poet, like Tennyson or Browning, or like his own countrymen, Longfellow or Lowell. His poetry is generally and justly acknowledged to be a failure. There are not more than a dozen living lines in all the verses that he has written.

He is not a Novelist, like Scott, or Thackeray,

or Meredith. In fact, he is no Novelist at all,
—looking with much scorn upon the whole of that
" juggling " tribe.

He is no Humorist, like Lowell or Mark Twain.
He has indeed an Essay on the Comic, but it is, if
anything, the dullest and saddest of all his Essays.
He is no Art-critic, like Ruskin.

One of the happiest descriptions of Emerson
is that of John Morley, who calls him " A great
interpreter of life."

In our opinion he is well characterised when
he is called *a Moralist*, for such he is, and that
of the intensest order. He glorifies two things,
and two things only — Intellect and Virtue.
Without agreeing with him in his isolation of
Virtue, we most cordially agree with him in his
praises of it. Here he is always right and strong.
Whenever he comes to treat of Virtue his pen
runs, and his words are like thunder-peals from
Sinai.

Writing of Napoleon, he says that although
Napoleon did all that in him lay to live and thrive
without moral principles, yet he was ruined by the
eternal laws of man and of the world. As with
Napoleon, so, writes Emerson, is it with all like
him—" where there is no moral principle, riches
will leave them sick ; there will be bitterness in
all laughter ; and wines will burn the mouth."

Emerson never for a moment loses sight of the
transcendental importance of morality. He is
neither dazed nor dazzled with our so-called
Civilisation. In the presence of the vital refine-

ments of moral and intellectual steps, it is, he
thinks, frivolous to insist on the invention of
printing, or gunpowder, or steam-power, or gas
light, or percussion caps and rubber shoes. Vastly
before all these, he sets the appearing amongst
men of the Hebrew Moses, the Indian Buddha,
Socrates and Zeno, and the advent of Jesus. These
persons represent " causal facts," which carry forward
races to new convictions, and elevate the rule of
life.

II

So far as Religion is concerned, the present
writer does not, and cannot, sail in the same boat
with Emerson. Not that his writings do not deal
with this great subject, for they are simply full of
it. It would, indeed, have been very surprising if
a writer like Emerson, a man of utmost sincerity
and intensest thought, had not written much on
the all-absorbing theme of Religion. He has,
however, very much to say here ; thereby putting
himself into line with the great writers of all the
ages. Nay, on his own principle, " *that all things
ascend*," he has reserved his last word for this great
theme.

Although it is difficult to define Religion, perhaps
we are not far wrong in considering it to be man's
relation to the Highest. We somehow think that
Emerson himself would agree to such a definition,
although, amongst the many definitions of Religion
which he has given, the above does not find a place.
The definition of Religion just given is very simple ;

and yet it leaves room for variety of opinion as to what the Highest may be with which a man must be related if he be religious.

If it be possible to put a great matter like this into a nutshell, we would say that Emerson differs in his religious views from most, inasmuch as he holds that the Highest is not personal, but impersonal. Most people believe that Religion means a personal relationship to a Personal God. Emerson, however, believes that Religion means a personal relationship to the Impersonal as the Highest; or indeed, for he varies, a relationship to *one's own self*. For reasons, which he considers sufficient, he rigorously excludes from Religion the element of the Personality of the Highest.

We do not remember if Emerson, anywhere in his writings, calls himself a Pantheist; and yet we do not think that he is wrongly named when he is named so, as he oftenest is. Many a time he emphasises the Impersonal as the Highest, and many a time he insists upon trueness to one's self as the very essence of all Religion worthy of the name.

In one of his Essays he writes of a distemper called Chorea, in which the patient keeps spinning slowly on one spot. We do not object to make Religion the spinning round one centre, but we do object to making this one centre that spot which is called *man's own self*. In a single word, we consider that the one grand defect in Emerson's Scheme of Religion is his leaving out the element of the Divine Personality, and man's relationship to a Personal God.

2

It is because he has made the Impersonal the Highest, or has made man's own self the centre in Religion, that he falls out of rank with such great teachers as Browning, and Ruskin, and Tennyson, and even with Thomas Carlyle. Browning claims to be written down as one who "believed in soul, and was very sure of God." We gladly write down Emerson as one who believed in soul, and that with an intense belief; but we cannot claim him as one who believed in the God of Browning, the God of the Bible, or the God of the Christian Church.

Lowell speaks of him as having a Greek head screwed on to Yankee shoulders, and such a description agrees well with actual facts, for Emerson is more distinctively Greek than Christian.

As has just been said, he is very liberal in his definitions of Religion—they are indeed as plentiful as blackberries in Autumn. Perhaps he never came nearer a truer conception of Religion from the practical side than when he wrote of it as the " doing of all good ; and, for its sake, the suffering of all evil."—Souffrir de tout le monde et ne faire souffrir personne. Here are some of his definitions of Religion :—" Man's public nature "; " the moral sentiment "; " the flowering of human culture "; " the introduction of ideas into life "; " putting an affront on Nature by declaring, as its first and last lesson, that the things which are seen are temporal and the things which are unseen are eternal."

We are quite sure that we do him no injustice

when we represent him as maintaining that Religion is faith in Laws—for he is a great believer
in Laws.   Once he cries out, with all the passion
of a devotee, " Law prevails for ever and ever."
Believing in cause and effect, he thinks that scepti-
cism justs means unbelief in this principle.   A
passage like the following will indicate, better than
any words of another, what Emerson believes :—
" A man does not see that as he eats so he thinks ;
as he deals, so he is, and so he appears.   His son
is the son of his thought, and of his action.   His
fortunes are not exceptions, but fruits, and what
comes out, that was put in.   As we are, so we do ;
and as we do, so is it done to us.   The dice are
loaded ; the colours are fast ; the globe is a battery,
because every atom is a magnet."

Following hard upon his Religion comes his
Creed.   Emerson believes in the centre ; he loves
man ; he venerates the saints, although he is glad
that the old pagan world stands its ground, and
dies hard.   He believes in a Divine Providence ;
he believes in the Immortality of the soul ; he
believes in thought, in intellect, in ideas.   Once—
we think only once—he cries, " Oh, brethren, God
exists ! "   It may be, as he himself has said, that
we are wiser than we know.

Morley has said that Emerson has not founded a
Church.   And very likely he has refrained from
doing so, for the very good reason that one cannot
make bricks without straw.   We can well excuse
him for not attempting to build a Church, whilst
we thank him with our whole heart for the good

work which he has done in the world,—work that moves on lines which are moral rather than ecclesiastical. Although we cannot claim him as in harmony with those who regard Religion as a personal relationship to a Personal God, it is well to recognise that he is helpful in many ways to those who have come to believe after this manner.

III

Emerson helps the cause of true Religion by his Idealism. He is an out-and-out Transcendentalist. He is no Materialist, professing to discover in matter the secret of the universe and of man,—will not allow, indeed, the Materialist to find a rest for the soles of his feet in those atoms which are the Materialist's unwise ultimate, for Emerson insists that the atoms are not idealess, but, on the other hand, that power and purpose ride upon each of them.

Not only is he no Materialist, but he turns the tables against the whole school. He is a great believer in soul—in soul, first; in soul, second; and in soul, ever more. He believes, not that matter generated, or generates mind or soul, but that mind generates matter, that the soul makes the house, that the world, indeed, is but the externisation of soul.

Napoleon believed that the world was moved by the pit of the stomach: Emerson looks in quite another direction for the secret of the world's government. He is sure that the world is moved

not by the pit of the stomach, but by the power of
Ideas and of Thought.

The grand old Book says, " In the beginning,
God———" and Emerson would, we think, say
" Amen," if allowed to define God in his own
way. He is inexorable in his insistence on the
priority of Intellect ; the priority of Soul. Somewhere he says that the key to every man is his
thought, and would lend all his weight to the
doctrine, that a thought lies behind every thing.

One of his peculiar, and at the same time stimulating, doctrines, is that of the Over-Soul—that
Unity—that Common Heart—that great Nature in
which we rest, as the earth lies in the soft arms
of the atmosphere—that unseen Source, whence
flows that wondrous river which brings to men
their best thoughts.

There need be no surprise that Emerson, living,
moving, and having his being in Idealism, is such
a worshipper of Plato—that to him Plato is philosophy, and philosophy is Plato. Neither should
there be surprise that he is in such sympathy with
the Idealism of Berkeley, and that he holds in still
greater admiration what he calls the Idealism of
Jesus, inasmuch as both Idealisms testify to the
fact, that all Nature is but the rapid efflux of
goodness executing and organising itself,—not only
that God is, but that all things are shadows of
Him.

True to his Idealism, Emerson is not carried
away with the material display of a much-vaunted
Civilisation. Like Ruskin, he sets store on things

better and deeper, questioning, indeed, whether people are better, or wiser, or happier, for all steam appliances and electrical apparatus. He would prefer to have worse cotton and better men.

That our age is so non-idealistic is, to Emerson, one of its worst signs. Quoting, with approval, the saying of Carlyle, that "that is bestial which rests not on the Invisible," he greatly deplores the fact, that whilst there is so much faith in chemistry, meat, wine, wealth, machinery, steam engines, galvanic batteries, turbine wheels, sewing machines, and public opinion, there is none in the intellectual and moral world, and in Divine causes.

A clear article in his Creed is that true manhood lives, moves, and has its being in another current than the merely mechanical one. He regrets that in our large cities the population is so Godless and materialised,—not men indeed, but hungers, thirsts, and fevers, — held together, after their pepper-corn aims are gained, by the lime in their bones, and not by any worthy purpose. He does not forget that Columbus discovered the New World in an undecked boat, and that Plato and Newton were great men, even before the discovery of the electric telegraph.

Emerson also helps the cause of true Religion by his firm belief in the Immortality of Man. Were we to put on record what we admire most in his writings, we would single out his Essays on "Compensation," on the "Over-Soul," and on

"Immortality." His Essay on "Immortality" proved especially helpful. When Carlyle and he —the brightest stars in the literary firmaments of two great countries, met together at Craigenputtock; after a walk over the long hills, they sat down within sight of Criffel, and talked of the Immortality of the soul. Very touching are the words of Carlyle on that occasion, "Christ died on the tree—*that* built Dunscore Kirk yonder, *that* brought you and me together. Time has only a relative existence."

Any writer who helps to a belief in the great triad of subjects—God, Freedom, Immortality, or to a belief in any one of them, helps immensely the cause of true Religion. We deeply regret that Emerson fails, so far as the belief in a Personal God is concerned. We have a partial regret that he makes so little of Freedom, and so much of a crushing Fate. Yet we are grateful to him, and greatly so, for his contribution on the fundamental truth of Man's Immortality. Here, he is clear and sure as Tennyson; clearer, indeed, than Browning on natural grounds.

Without entering into anything like a full consideration of the details in reasoning which led Emerson to his conclusions on Immortality, it may be said that whilst he maintains that this belief cannot be proved by any kind of syllogism, he yet holds that it cleaves so to the constitution of man, that whenever we whisper his name we invariably associate with it this immense belief in Immortality.

Amongst other arguments advanced by him on

behalf of Immortality, we have been struck with the way in which he represents the unreasonableness of thinking that a being, for whom so much has been done, and on whom so much has been spent, should pass into nothingness—should drop, to use the words of Tennyson, " into vacant darkness and cease to be." There is something irresistible in the way in which Emerson puts this thought in the concrete.

Nature, he says, does not, like the Empress Ann of Russia, call together all the architectural genius of the Empire to build, finish, and furnish a palace of snow, to melt again to water at the first thaw. Will you, he asked, with vast cost and pains, educate your children to be adepts in their several arts, and as soon as they are ready to produce a masterpiece call out a file of soldiers to shoot them down? Only one answer can be returned to such a question, and Emerson presses home the argument, that our destiny may be inferred from the preparation.

When dealing with this great theme of Immortality, he presents with power such facts as these—that the soul does not age with the body; that we are just ready to be born when we come to die; that this world is for our education; that everything is prospective.

We have been much impressed with his assurance that the " Creator keeps His word with us."

Not less convincing is his reference to our delight in immense Time, and our devotion to the Gracious Infinite—that " Flying Ideal " which ever leads onward and upward.   Significant, in this respect, are the words of the late Poet-Laureate, as the shadows were gathering about him, proving how the great thinker and the great poet are at one in their belief in the Immortality of man—

> "When the dumb hour, clothed in black,
>   Brings the dreams about my bed,
>   Call me not so often back,
>   Silent voices of the dead,
>   Toward the lowland ways behind me,
>   And the sunlight that is gone ;
>   Call me rather, silent voices,
>   Forward to the starry tracts—
>   Glimmering up the heights beyond me—on, and always on."

Very helpful, too, in the cause of true Religion, is the Individualism which permeates all his writings.   If he has missed the Personality of God, —and how he has missed it we fail to see, he has certainly not failed to do justice to the personality of man.   This he acknowledges to the full, and emphasises abundantly.   He is quite sure that "you are you, and I am I."   Souls, he declares, are not saved in bundles.   The Spirit saith to the man, "How is it with thee ?—thee personally ?—Is it well ? is it ill ? "   One would fancy that these are not the words of Emerson at all, but of some red-hot gospeller—so germane are they to ordinary religious teaching and language.

And very helpful, too, is his enthusiasm for Virtue.   We say enthusiasm, for Emerson's love of Virtue could not be described by any weaker word. If, on the one hand, he has glorified Intellect, on the other hand, he has glorified Virtue. In this utter devotion to Virtue he is more like a Hebrew prophet than a Greek sage. He speaks of that "grand word 'ought,'" and makes as surely in intention for righteousness as the arrow for its mark. Whatsoever things are true, honest, just, pure, lovely, and of good report, find through him ample acknowledgment and encouragement.

Meditating on Virtue, he cannot contain himself, and exclaims: "When one loves the Right; then is Truth beautiful within, and without, for ever more. Virtue, I am thine: save me—use me. Thee will I serve day and night, in great and in small, that I may be, not virtuous, but Virtue."

We claim him as an ally in the cause of true Religion, when we remember his conception of Human Life. Morley calls him "A great interpreter of life"; and to a certain extent he deserves the description given of him by one of his greatest admirers. He is no Pessimist. To him life is no vulgar joke. Holding life sacred, not cheap— he is terribly in earnest about it. He would have people write on their hearts, that every day is the best day, that every day, indeed, is doomsday. "It is a gay and pleasant sound," he says, " to hear the whetting of the scythe in the mornings of June; yet what is more lonesome and sad than the sound of a whetstone or mower's rifle, when it is too late in the season to make hay?"

He believes that life may be lived nobly, although it be lived in poverty. He does not forget that the Gods have come to earth in the lowliest of guises, and quotes with approval the words of Milton, that the epic Poet, he who shall sing of the gods, and their descent unto man, must drink water out of a wooden bowl."

Measuring life by its depth, rather than by its length, he looks more up than down, more to the end than to the beginning. One of his favourite thoughts is " that all things ascend "— that we are on a stair,—stairs below us, and stairs above us. To his credit, he thinks most of all of the stairs which go upward and out of sight.

Meanwhile, " we are only half human; there is no animal which has not got a footing in our nature, and there is often an ebbing of the soul downward into the animal nature." And so, like Tennyson, he calls upon man, as with the blast of a trumpet, to " work out the beast, and let the ape and tiger die." The population of the world —a conditional population, is not at its best. " There shall be a better, please God."

Still another thing, helpful to the cause of true Religion, is his unsparing criticism of what often passes for Religion. Here he plays the part of the candid friend. Churches and Ministers come under his lash. So far as we remember, he has not one good thing to write either of the one or the other.

When in Scotland, he was impressed with the

insanity of dialectics among the intellectual. "By taste, ye are saved"—is his summary of the Gospel of the Church of England. Everything and everybody seemed in a bad way. He heard Ministers who could not preach, and Ministers who could not pray; Ministers who were ashamed to plead for Missions, and to urge to a godly life; Ministers who were ashamed to rebuke blasphemies, and so on.

The Church was tottering to its fall; Faith was dead; Religion was almost gone. Instead of sucking at the roots of right and wrong, the Church almost encouraged a divorce between Religion and Morality. And then he takes notice of such a levity in all the creeds. "Witness," he writes, "the heathenisms in Christianity — the periodic "revivals"—the Millennium mathematics — the peacock ritualism—the retrogression to Popery, etc. . . . Not knowing what to do, the Churches stagger backward to the mummeries of the dark ages."

It is well to see ourselves as others see us, and in so far as the lines in the picture drawn by Emerson are true to fact, they deserve the most careful attention; and yet we may be allowed to say, that there are lines awanting which ought to have been in—lines there which ought never to have been, and lines which are all too dark.

In all conscience, the religious world is bad enough, and yet we venture to think that it is not anything like so bad as he makes it. There are Ministers who can preach and pray, who are

as real as the "snowstorm," to which he so
graphically refers, Ministers who are not ashamed
to do each and all of the duties referred to in
his criticism.   We are not aware that the right
kind of Religion has ever sought to proscribe
intelligence, or prevent the human mind from
orbing out.   The Book which is the Supreme
Standard says—"If ye will enquire, enquire ye."

IV

Whilst there is much in Emerson's writings
helpful to the cause of true Religion, we are
bound in all honesty to state that there is likewise much that is hurtful.

Perhaps the very head and front of his offending
lie in his notion of the Impersonal.   The soul, he
writes, knows no persons; it invites every man
to expand to the full circle of the Universe.
Persons themselves acquaint us with the Impersonal.   In all conversation between two persons,
tacit reference is made to a third party, as to a
common nature.   That third party is not social:
it is Impersonal, it is God.   When Emerson utters
his last word on the great theme of worship, he
says that the new Church will be founded on
moral science—without shawms, or psaltery, or
sackbut, having science for symbol and illustration.
The nameless Thought, the nameless Power, the
superpersonal Heart,—man shall repose alone on
that.   The Laws are his consolers—those simple
and terrible Laws.

And he has the courage of his opinions. All through his writings his tendency is to rest in Fate, in Duty, in Law, in Intelligence, in the full circle of the Universe, in the Over-Soul. It is this which makes him so ill at ease with the prominence given by Christians, and in the Christian Faith, to the Person of Jesus, leading him to write of it as a " noxious exaggeration," and giving him the hardihood to declare that the Person of Jesus will yet retire before the sublimity of moral laws.

We have no hesitation in saying that a theory of the Universe, ending with such impersonal entities, comes short of what is highest and best, even in ourselves. In this he is the type of that large class of theorists whose ultimate is not a Personal God, but a World-Order, or Infinite Substance, or a Persistent Force, or a Power, not ourselves, that makes for righteousness. All such theories are smitten with the unreasonableness of maintaining that a thing is more than a thought, and that a thought is more than a thinker.

We are aware that many shrink from accepting the idea of a Personal God, because they think that in doing so they would limit that which ought to be Infinite, and also through a dread of Anthropomorphism. As for the fear of limiting the Infinite by ascribing to Him the element of personality, it is surely well not to forget that there may be degrees of perfection, in this very matter of personality, ranging from the finite to the infinite, and that we are warranted in concluding that God has absolutely that which man possesses but imperfectly. As Lotze writes: " Perfect personality is in God only; to all finite minds there is allotted but a pale copy thereof."

And then, regarding the dread of Anthropomorphism, a ghost which many a philosopher calls up from the vasty deep, it is well to remember that a man may as easily seek to escape from his own shadow as escape from being anthropomorphic in his conceptions of the Universe and of God. There is indeed no choice, for Emerson is as anthropomorphic when he speaks of the Over-Soul, as any ordinary Christian is when he speaks of " our Father in Heaven."

Having accepted the impersonal as the ultimate, we are not surprised at his antagonism to Prayer, although we deeply regret it. Remembering how he puts it on record that these words were written on the gates of Busyrane—" Be bold "; and on the second gate—" Be bold, be bold, and ever more be bold "; and then again at the third gate—" Be not too bold "; we venture to say that Emerson is too bold in entering, as he does, into that Holy of Holies called " Prayer." He utters many a word on the duty of self-reliance, but never a word on the duty of God-reliance, the very soul of prayer.

Are not these words a travesty of this sacred exercise ? And yet they are Emerson's own words : " Prayer is the contemplation of the facts of life, from the highest point of view. It is the soliloquy of a beholding and jubilant soul—the Spirit of God pronouncing His works good. To

work is to pray.   The prayer of the farmer kneeling in his field to weed it, the prayer of the rower
kneeling with the stroke of his oar,—these are true
prayers heard throughout nature."

We are startled at definitions like these, but we
are shocked when he writes about prayer as a
means to effect a private end as neither brave nor
manly,—as vicious, as meanness and theft,—as a
disease of the will, etc.

Where now, we ask, are the oft-repeated counsels
which he gives, " Obey your own heart," and " Be
true to yourself " ?   We believe, most assuredly,
that instead of Prayer being a " disease of will," there
is nothing more natural to the human heart all the
world over, and in all ages.   We regret to utter it,
but utter it we must, that in so far as Emerson is
antagonistic to Prayer, he has failed sadly to fulfil
the function ascribed to him of being a " great interpreter of human life," and has thereby cut himself
off from the company of the great revealers of the
human heart.   In this he is quite at variance with
his adored Shakespeare, as he is also at variance
with those other poets who have laid bare human
nature as a nature which moves as readily to Prayer
as doves fly to their windows.   Mrs. Browning
excels Emerson as an interpreter of life, and gets
nearer the true nature of our humanity when she
writes in " The Cry of the Human "—

" 'There is no God,' the foolish saith—
      But none, There is no sorrow.
And Nature, oft the cry of Faith
      In bitter need will borrow :

Eyes, which the preacher could not school,
   By wayside graves are raisèd,
And lips say, 'God be pitiful,'
   Which ne'er said, 'God be praisèd.'
     Be pitiful, O God."

Like many others in the present day, Emerson maintains that Divine Revelations are still going on—that God's Bible is not closed, that vision and prophecy are not sealed. An opinion like this can, of course, be very easily tested by taking the contributions of a writer like Emerson himself to the world's volume of wisdom. What new light, it may be asked, has dawned upon the world since he has come and gone ? And what is the answer but this, that no new light has dawned upon the world through Emerson's advent. He has restated with power some few, precious, moral and spiritual truths, but he has not originated any.

There is nothing new in telling people to be true to themselves, in preaching a gospel of work, or falling in love with Love. It is true that he maintains, that the visible rests on the invisible, that the soul is infinitely precious, and that duty is a noble thing; but we have heard all this before.

We are deeply indebted to him for recording his assurance of man's Immortality, but we have the conviction, that had not this truth shone so clearly on another Page, and in another Place, it would not have shone so clearly in the writings of Emerson. It is the Divine Word alone that prevents us writing again to-day the " IF " that was written on

the portal of the Temple at Delphi, and that prevents multitudes from saying with the dying Rabelais,
" I am going to see the great Perhaps."

Emerson relates a very touching anecdote about
two Materialistic Senators of the American Con-
gress, who, whilst attentive to the ordinary routine
of public duty, were yet deeply concerned with
such questions as the Immortality of the soul.

These friends, after being separated from each
other for some five-and-twenty years, met at a
crowded reception at the President's house, Washington.   Their first words were questions: " Any
light, Albert ? "   " None," replied Albert.   " Any
light, Lewis ? "   " None," replied Lewis.   They
looked *in silence* in each other's eyes, gave one
more shake each to the hand he held, and thus
parted for the last time.

We do not tarry to consider Emerson's denunciation of Dogma and the Worship of the Past.   If
Dogma be, as we think it is, religious truth stated
as scientifically as possible, then we fail to see how
anyone, more especially a writer like Emerson, is
entitled to speak so bitterly against it.   It has
been said that " Athanasius defined, because Arius
shuffled."

As for the Worship of the Past, making Religion
a quotation, as Emerson says so many do,—never
thinking our own thoughts, nor uttering our own
words, nor going our own ways,—all that we
have to say is this, that we are ready to change
our worship of the Past to a worship of the

Present, when it has been shown that the Present is superior to the Past in wisdom or in worshipfulness.

We do not blame him for his devotion to Plato, but we question his right to blame anyone for devotion to Jesus. Emerson sat at the feet of Plato, because Plato was to him the incarnation of Wisdom; and we sit at the feet of Christ, because He is to us, not only greater than Plato, but has a Name which is above every Name.

Emerson hits out vehemently at some person whom he calls the "vindictive theologian." And when the matter is narrowly looked into, it does not amount to much after all; turns out, indeed, to be another instance of the "Idolon Fori"—the writer being the victim of a word. We acknowledge that the word "vindictive" sounds badly, carrying along with it the idea of revengefulness and malice. But, we ask, is there such a Theology, or such a Theologian?

Emerson fastens this name upon the Theologian who maintains that there comes a time when the heart of the sinner is so hard, the conscience so seared, the character so confirmed, that his destiny is fixed, and that for ever; and fixed for ever, because it is impossible to lead him to repentance and conversion. But surely it is possible for a Theologian to maintain such opinions without being at all "vindictive."

And here an appeal must be taken from Emerson unwise to Emerson wise. It so happens, there is no other writer who has preached with more

earnestness and clearness the fearful doctrine of
Retribution.

If ever there was one who believed with his
whole heart and soul, that a man shall reap what
he has sown, that writer is Emerson.   He believes,
with an intense belief, that what comes out is that
which was put in ; that for each offence there is a
several vengeance, that reaction is the rule of the
universe,—that every secret is told, every crime
punished, in silence and certainty ; that crime and
punishment grow out of the same stem ; that you
cannot do wrong without suffering wrong; that
where there is an inlet of crime there is an outlet
of suffering.

Surely it ill becomes one who preaches Nemesis
after this fashion to fling stones at the Theologian,
who simply declares that character may be irre-
vocably fixed, that sowing the wind ends in reaping
the whirlwind, that sin is followed by punishment,
and eternal sin by eternal punishment.

V

We regret that Emerson did not say less or say
more about the Founder of the Christian Faith.
Honest enough, he does not withhold his tribute
of admiration for the character of Christ.   He
considers that Jesus was both good and great,
worthy to be classed with the good and great of
Greece, and Rome, and Egypt, and Persia, and
India.

He speaks of Him as that sublime spirit,—that

noble and good heart, as one who has not written but ploughed His Name into the history of the world.

We do not quarrel with Emerson, in so far as he, a Unitarian, did not acknowledge the Deity of Christ; but when he says that we are afraid to speak of Christ as a man, lest we degrade His character, we have to say that our fear is not to degrade His character if we speak of Him as a man, but lest we take His character quite away—*Si non Deus, non bonus.*

It will scarcely be believed that Emerson considers that Christ did not preach the personal Immortality, and it will scarcely be believed that when he handles the question of the Resurrection, whilst telling people to go and read Milton and Shakespeare, or any truly ideal Poet—to go and read Plato or any seer of the interior realities— to go and read St. Augustine, Swedenborg, and Immanuel Kant, he deliberately refrains from advising his readers to go to the Gospels, so full of the words of Eternal life.

It is a remarkable fact, that whilst he often refers to Christ as a Teacher, as One who had a deep insight into the soul, and into the essential worth of man, he never once, so far as we remember, refers to Christ as a Saviour. And yet why should we be surprised at this omission, when we discover that he has entirely omitted any reference to the terrible fact of sin. If there be no disease, there is, of course, no need for a Physician. It is, however, surely a matter for wonder, how anyone can either pose or be called " a great interpreter of

human life" who is blind, at once to the deepest
and most awful fact of human existence and to the
gladsome truth that the Healer has come. Sings
Dora Greenwell—

> " He didn't come to judge the world, He didn't come to blame,
> He didn't only come to seek, it was to save He came ;
> And when we call Him, Saviour, then we call Him by His
> Name."

VI

Emerson's sayings are like bits of broken glass.
His style has been called a "difficult staccato."
He is nothing if not epigrammatic. He is oracular,
and is so purposely. Let the following suffice as
illustrating his tendency to Epigram :—

> "Everyone can do his best things easiest."
> "Right Ethics are central, and go from the soul outwards."
> " We must not be sacks and stomachs."
> "Life is a sincerity."
> "Great is Drill."
> " Hitch your waggon to a star."
> "Difference from me is the measure of absurdity."
> "Every hero becomes a bore at last."
> "You are you, and I am I, and so we remain."
> "Plato is philosophy, and philosophy is Plato."
> "All things are double, one against another."
> " The Devil is an ass."

VII

Emerson's works are full of thoughts on all sorts
of subjects. He has a delightful page on the
interesting and imperious ways of babies, and on
the charm of a schoolgirl's love. He tells of a
mistress who was in a sad plight because of her two

maidens ; one of whom was absent-minded, and the
other absent - bodied.   He was, upon the whole,
favourably impressed with the people whom he saw
in England.   He thinks that the Englishman, of all
men, stands firmest in his shoes ; and that by comparison, the American is a bag of bones.   The
women in England are the finest in the world.
The English people are characterised by common
sense and thoroughness.

He quotes a story, which he says he heard every
day, about an Englishman and a Frenchman who
fought a duel, and who agreed to fight it in a dark
room so as to reduce the chance of fatality to the
minimum.   The Englishman, in his magnanimity,
fired his pistol up the chimney, and brought down
the Frenchman who had fled there for refuge.

The English, he says, have a passion for utility.
The Frenchman invented the ruffle, but the Englishman added the shirt.   The English kiss the dust
before a fact, have a terror of humbug, and pay an
absolute homage to wealth.

It will be a surprise to some to know that he
even sets himself up for an authority in matters of
Etiquette.   A gentleman, he says, makes no noise ;
a lady is serene.   A gentleman gives the law where
he is.   He out-prays the saints in the chapel, out-
generals the veteran in the field, and outshines all
courtesy in the hall.   He quotes approvingly the
words of Talleyrand : "Above all, gentlemen, no
heat."   There should be no loud laughter, no call
beyond ten minutes, no exaggeration.   We are to
beware of jokes, and never name sickness in society.

VIII

His mode of using scientific data is not only striking, but even startling. The unity of the whole is a favourite idea of his. Perhaps he would not go as far as to say that there is natural law in the spiritual world, but he does go as far as to say that natural law has its counterpart in the spiritual world, or, as he himself puts it, the " laws above are sisters to the laws below."

He has borrowed from Swedenborg the truth, that nature exists entire in leasts, and that the mind is a finer body. There are, he says, no straight lines in nature. Everything there goes by indirection.

He refers to the agitation of Newton when his hand so shook and the figures so danced, on the verge of his great discovery of the Law of Gravitation, that he was forced to call in an assistant to finish the computations. And Emerson asks, Why so agitated ? and answers himself by saying— *Why ?* but because Newton saw in the fall of an apple to the ground, the fall of the earth to the sun, the fall of the sun, and all suns, to the centre. His perception was accompanied by the spasm of delight, by which the intellect greeted a fact more immense still—a fact really universal—holding in intellect as in matter, in morals as in intellect—" that atom draws to atom throughout Nature, and truth to truth throughout spirit."

One of his most suggestive chapters is a chapter on " Circles," and one of his most suggestive statements is, that " around every circle another one can

be drawn "—a fact, used by Emerson, to indicate
the expansiveness of the human mind. He quotes
Augustine's definition of God as a " Being whose
centre is everywhere, and whose circumference is
nowhere "; and we think that he would define man
as a being whose centre is here, but whose circumference extends everywhere.

IX

Although Emerson quotes Talleyrand to the
effect that he finds nonsense singularly refreshing,
there is little of this in his own writings. Now
and again he is merciful enough to introduce an
incident or two fit to provoke a smile. His description of the atmosphere of London has the brevity of
wit—" On a fine day it is like looking up a chimney,
and on a foul day it is like looking down one."

He tells of the poor woman who came from her
wretched garret for the first time to the seashore, and
was greatly delighted that for once in her life she
had seen something of which there was enough for
everybody.

He quotes the wise word of an Indian Chief, of
the Six Nations of New York, to one who was complaining of the shortness of time,—" Well," said Red
Jacket, " I suppose you have all there is."

X

We are not surprised to learn that Emerson
has much to say on Development—that idea

which so holds the field in modern thought; only, his eye is fixed on man's goal, rather than on man's starting-point. Of course, as an Idealist, he has no sympathy whatever with those who look for man's start in frog's spawn. When Emerson begins, he begins with mind, with soul, with God.

He does not account for soul by matter, but rather accounts for matter by soul, and sees opening out before man an endless vista for progress.

He writes of the " Flying Ideal," and adopts Swedenborg's forms, to the effect that the mental series tallies with the material series; that the circular is the perpetual-angular; the spiral, the perpetual-circular; the vortical, the perpetual-spiral; the celestial, the perpetual-vortical; and the spiritual, the perpetual-celestial. According to Emerson, all things ascend—everything in nature climbs to a higher platform. Conscious of our insatiable demand for more, and of our enormous ideal, he encourages a Divine discontent.

He is sure that in presence of that Ideal, which he calls the Gracious Infinite, we can never be content with either things or persons. There is no such critic and beggar as our own terrible soul. Genius, counting all its miracles poor and short, is never able to execute its own ideas. The Iliad—the Hamlet—the Doric column—the Roman arch — the Gothic minster,—when they are ended, the master casts them behind him.

Here we find the cue to that Optimism which is so happily characteristic of him, and of his best teaching, so far as life is concerned. He is passionately on the side of the higher nature.

He is a strong advocate of Education, looking upon it, we fear too hopefully, as the Panacea for all the ills of life. The best heads take, he says, the best places.

Like Carlyle, he preaches incessantly and earnestly the gospel of Work. " I say it," he writes, " but Nature says it oftener, ' Work ' "—" Stick to one business, young man." He has a crown for the head of him of whom it can be said that he " toils terribly." He quotes what a brave painter once said to him—" There is no way to success in our art but to take off your coat, grind paint, and work like a digger on the railroad, all day and every day."

His sympathies are altogether on the side of Freedom—with man's heaven-born right to get on. He regards self-government as the best of all governments, as the true end, indeed, to which all civic government should tend.

> " God said, I am tired of Kings,
>   I suffer them no more ;
> Up to my ears the morning brings
>   The outrage of the poor.
>
>   .   .   .   .   .
>
> I will have never a noble,
>   No lineage counted great ;
> Fishers, and choppers, and ploughmen
>   Shall constitute a State.
>
>   .   .   .   .   .

My angel—his name is Freedom—
  Choose him to be your King.
He shall cut pathways, East and West,
  And fend you with his wing.

    .   .   .   .   .

And ye shall succour men ;
  'Tis nobleness to serve.
Help them who cannot help again,—
  Beware from right to swerve."

CARLYLE AND EMERSON:
A COMPARISON

"There is in man, a Higher than Love of Happiness ; he can do without Happiness, and instead thereof find Blessedness."

. . . .

" Love not Pleasure; love God. This is the *EVERLASTING YEA*, wherein all Contradiction is solved : wherein whoso walks and works, it is well with him."—CARLYLE, *Sartor Resartus*.

" Virtue, I am thine : save me : use me : thee will I serve, day and night, in great, in small, that I may be not virtuous, but Virtue."—EMERSON, " Miscellanies."

CARLYLE AND EMERSON:
A COMPARISON

I

In one of his books, Lowell comes down very heavily upon Carlyle for his deep disdain of human nature and his Literature of Despair. In estimating these two great writers, Carlyle and Emerson—the greatest of two great continents, Lowell not only places Emerson superior to Carlyle, but insists that Emerson should be compared, not with Carlyle, but with Plato.

As the present writer felt aggrieved at this estimate, on the score of a first love, and also on the score of simple justice, he was constrained to look into the matter a little more closely, and has ventured to express his opinion on this subject.

There is much to be said in defence of Lowell's partiality for Emerson, and his severity towards Carlyle. As is well known, Lowell was a passionate friend of the slave, and did much by his eloquent and humorous pen to set the enslaved free. And, alas! Carlyle cannot be called a friend of the slave. He was all wrong on the Nigger Question, and took the wrong side in the American War. One is shocked to read that he believed that the black

gentleman was born a slave by appointment of God
Almighty, and therefore that slave he ought to be
to the end of the chapter.   Of all heresies this is
surely the rankest, setting at defiance both of God's
Bibles; that Bible which we call Humanity, and
that other Bible which we call the Book of God.
There is little wonder that Lowell, the friend of the
slave, did not take kindly to Carlyle, who was no
friend of the slave.

And then, Lowell was devoted to America; and
thought there was no land in the world to be compared with it.   Valuing its political independence,
he was as keen for its literary independence and
glory.   This being so, we need not be surprised
that he was inclined to minimise a writer like
Carlyle, who was honest enough to say that he set
little value on America, or anything in it.

Carlyle   acknowledged,   without   worshipping,
America's cotton crops, and Indian corn, and dol-
lars;   and   it   must   have   sorely   vexed   Lowell's
patriotic soul to read how Carlyle declared that he
knew of no great thing that ever came out of
America—no great thought, no great soul.   America's
vast population—eighteen millions of people—were
contemptuously spoken of by the Sage of Chelsea as
"Eighteen millions of the greatest bores in all God's
universe."

We are constrained, however, to reverse Lowell's
conclusions; and, as the outcome of what we believe
to be a just comparison, to give Carlyle the superior
place.

With a single exception, we consider Carlyle to

be a greater man than Emerson—greater in genius, in intellect, in force, in scholarship, and in influence. We say, with a single exception, and that exception is, that Emerson is much more optimistic than Carlyle. He is sunny and cheerful, clinging to the thought of melioration. Things may look bad, but they shall be better, please God.

It would not be true to call Carlyle an out-and-out Pessimist, for he is not that; although, especially in his latter days, his outlook was very gloomy. He was fond of quoting his master, Goethe's poem, ending with the words, "Work, and despair not." His parting counsel to the students of Edinburgh University was the word, "We bid you be of hope."

And yet, these are but gleams in a great darkness. Carlyle's picture of the age is painted in blackest hues. He heaps words upon words, to tell of its shams, and unveracity, and hypocrisy,—an age without God, without Soul, and without Religion —an age of Flunkeyism, and Mammonism, and Dilettanteism — an age of Scoundrelism — an age of Ballot-Boxes, and Counting Heads—an age of Shooting Niagara. The whole head is sick, and the whole heart is faint.

There is much that is wrong, says Carlyle, with the Body Aristocratical. He is dissatisfied with our Lords and Dukes, who care for nothing so much as Game-preserving and Partridge-shooting. He would have these gentlemen remember their duties, as well as their privileges. There has been a French Revolution; there may be a British one as well.

4

There is much that is wrong with the Body Ecclesiastical. Carlyle considers Bishops as but poor Overseers of souls. This is No. 51, in his brief Catechism, in Jesuitism, one of the *Latter-Day Pamphlets* :—" 'What are Bishops ? '—Overseers of Souls. 'What is a Soul ? '—The Thing that keeps the body alive. 'How do they oversee that ? '—They tie on a kind of Apron, and publish Charges."

He comes down heavily upon Bishops, and spares not Ministers of any degree. Whilst he acknowledges that it is a good thing to have a person set apart to speak on spiritual things, he thinks that Ministers have wandered terribly from the point.

And there is much that is wrong with the Body Social. The age is too Democratic. The Suffrage is too universal. There's too much counting of heads,—Judas Iscariot is considered to be as good as Jesus Christ. There's too much beer and balderdash. There's too much talk—the whole regiment, indeed, has gone to drum.

There can be no doubt that Carlyle is pessimistic, and that his pessimism is in contrast with Emerson's optimism.

Of Carlyle's pessimism, this, however, must be said, that he is at least sincere in his mood. If he were pessimistic, it is because the burden did indeed lie heavily on his soul. No one will question this, who remembers his portrait of later times— the face like that of Dante—" the mournfullest face that ever was painted."

With this single exception, that Emerson is more optimistic than Carlyle, we are constrained to place Carlyle superior to Emerson, and that all along the line.

II

Perhaps the greatest difference between Carlyle and Emerson is to be found in their political views, meaning by that, their views regarding the best form of National Government.

If we accept Abraham Lincoln's definition of Democracy, as " Government of the people, by the people, and for the people," we may regard Emerson as favouring Democracy upon the whole; although he had the strong conviction that the less Government the better. Emerson endorses the saying of Fisher Amos, that Monarchy is a merchantman which sails well, but which will sometimes strike on a rock and go to the bottom; whilst Republicanism is a raft which will never sink, but then your feet are always in the water.

Carlyle's views of the best form of National Government are not very clear to the reader, very likely because they were not quite clear to himself. One thing, however, is certain, that, like the Irishman, he was " Agin' the Government."

He is terribly severe against Downing Street— against that talking apparatus called Parliament —against game-killing Dukes and Lords—against miraculous Premiers—against Ballot-Boxes and Universal Suffrage—against Democracy in general.

He is especially severe against Universal Suffrage

—counting of heads, as the way of getting the ablest and wisest as Governors of the nation. He would give the Suffrage to some—to how many we don't know—and he would give to the others a dog muzzle, and plenty of water on a summer's day.

He cannot believe that out of our " Twenty-seven millions, mostly fools," we can get any good thing. He cannot believe that out of unwisdom we can get wisdom, any more than we can get gold out of the Thames mud.

Carlyle favoured an Aristocracy rather than a Democracy as the best form of National Government,—the right kind of Aristocracy, however; not an aristocracy of King's clothes, but of Kings inside the clothes—real Kings, and not sham ones—real Captains, not phantom ones.

He believed that we should be governed by the ablest—that is, by the wisest—a belief to which all will say Amen. The difficulty is how to get hold of them. A favourite illustration with Carlyle is a ship sailing round Cape Horn; and he reminds his readers that all the voting of all the crew will never take that ship round Cape Horn,—that only one thing will take that ship round Cape Horn, and that is the wisdom that lies in the head of the Captain. That, and that alone, and not voting this way or that, will be of any avail when the icebergs begin to come dangerously near, and the storms begin to blow.

But Carlyle has not solved the Government difficulty, with his illustration of the wise Captain who alone can take the ship round Cape Horn, for the difficulty of getting the good Captain still remains. Very obviously, just as the owners of the ship selected the Captain, so the owners of the nation should select their Governor or Governors. Carlyle simply says, they can't do it. To which the remark may be made, the sooner they are helped to do it the better.

In other words, the principle of a Democracy is one which is sound and just, only all lovers of their country should see to it that the Democracy is the best that can be—educated, sober, wise, moral, and religious.

One is somewhat surprised that Carlyle, who came himself from the people, should be so severe on Democracy. Surely a source that has given to the world such an one as Carlyle himself has in it marvellous possibilities of good government, and of good everything.

His little plan of securing the ablest as Governors of the nation would vest in the Queen the power to select the wisest of the land, and to say to this wise man here, and that wise man there, "Come thou, and thou, and govern, and help me to govern, this great Empire."

No doubt Carlyle had the notion lying somewhere in his head, that the Queen could have found at least one to help her in the government of this great Empire,—one who lived not far from Cheyne Row, Chelsea.

And yet, things are better as they are. It was better for this land and for all lands, for this age and for ages to come, that Carlyle toiled away at his desk in Cheyne Row over his *French Revolution*, and his *Frederick the Great*, or even his *Latter-Day Pamphlets*, than that he should have passed his time drafting Parliamentary Bills. Although he may have thought otherwise, Carlyle was more profitably engaged writing his books, than if he had been a Privy Councillor to her Majesty the Queen.

III

Whilst we consider Carlyle to be the greater of the two, there are many interesting points of resemblance.

Carlyle and Emerson are much alike in their pious ancestry and upbringing. We have not so many details of Emerson's forebears as we would like to have, but we know that he came of a good Puritan stock. He was the son of a Unitarian Minister, and was for a while a Unitarian Minister himself.

On the other hand, there is perhaps no celebrated person of whom more is known than of Thomas Carlyle. He had a good father and a good mother, members of the Burgher Kirk in Ecclefechan. Of that Kirk, the Kirk of his childhood, Carlyle thought much,—thought more, indeed, of that humble Meeting-house, thatched with heath, than of the biggest Cathedral. There were " tongues there of authentic flame."

He was proud of his peasant father ; would not have exchanged him for all the Kings ever known to him.   If anything, he was prouder of his mother, who, although neither rich nor learned, was one whom he loved and revered—"best of all mothers," as he calls her.

After all that has been said of Carlyle's Religion, we cling to the hope that, as he himself has said, his Religion and that of his mother were essentially one.

Both Carlyle and Emerson had thoughts of the ministry as their profession.   Emerson was for a time a Minister, and Carlyle was on the threshold of the ministry.   He was a Divinity student at Edinburgh University, but turned back because of " grave prohibitory doubts," but not before he had preached a sermon from the text, " Before I was afflicted, I went astray."

Both became preachers; and let it be added, good preachers too, because preachers of Righteousness.   It is true that they did not wholly find their texts in that Book which we call the Bible. They got texts elsewhere—in the great books of Nature—the human heart—conscience, and history. Their books are their sermons, and their congregations are the peoples of every land, wherever English Literature is known.

They were much alike in their resilement from Creeds and Formulas.   Emerson gave up his position as a Unitarian Minister because of his uneasiness under the bondage of Forms and of Public Prayer; and Carlyle, as we have just said, drew back from the ministry because of his " grave prohibitory doubts."

Both Carlyle and Emerson deal hard blows against Creeds and Formulas, and against those who favour them. Mirabeau, one of Carlyle's heroes, was, as he reminds us, a "Swallower of Formulas."

All readers of Carlyle are familiar with his abhorrence of "Cant," and we take the liberty of remarking that this wholesale denunciation of all Creeds makes one fear that Carlyle and Emerson can "cant" with the worst. There are Creeds and Creeds. It is indeed impossible to do without a Creed of some sort or another. The Atheist and the Materialist are on the same footing here with the Calvinist. It may be granted that the Universe is not constructed altogether in accordance with the Westminster "Confession of Faith," but the Universe is constructed in some way; and it is surely the part of a wise man to see to it that he has got some idea of how this matter stands. Carlyle has a Creed, and Emerson has a Creed, and everybody has a Creed. Nay, everybody who is sincere considers his Creed the right one. Orthodoxy, says Carlyle, means my Doxy, and Heterodoxy means your Doxy.

Very likely, what Carlyle and Emerson mean to insist upon is just this, that one's Creed should not be a something that we put on and off, as we do our clothes, but that it should be what one does really believe,—what one does really lay to heart about the world and the Maker of it, and our duties and interests here.

Emerson's greatest Commandment is, "Obey

your own heart"; and Carlyle never ceases insisting on a life-and-death certainty,—on a belief which is at least genuine.

As Carlyle reminds us, the Romans believed in Jupiter, and the Greeks believed at least in the fact that all crimes against the law of God are most certainly and awfully punished. And Oliver Cromwell, Carlyle's greatest hero, was what he was, and did what he did, because he believed in God.

Carlyle and Emerson are alike in their gravitation to Literature. All the fame which has come to both has come to them from their books, from books dealing with the same kind of themes, and with themes which lie close to the human heart.

They treat of Freedom, Duty, Obedience, Work, Religion, and of God. Carlyle quotes a saying of Novalis, that "Philosophy cannot bake bread for us," but that it can bring to us God, and Freedom, and Immortality. And it may truly be said, that although we do not learn from the works of those two great Authors how to bake bread, we learn therefrom much about some of the greatest subjects that can occupy the human mind, or influence human hearts.

Carlyle thinks that the best University is a collection of good books, and declares that all the University did for him was to teach him to read books, in various languages.

It is encouraging for many a youth to remember that Carlyle rose to the highest pinnacle of literary fame from the very humblest position—from running about, a barefooted lad, in the streets of Ecclefechan. Perhaps his portrait has never been better painted than in the words of Miss Welsh: " He stood there as he had made himself, a peasant's son who had run about bare foot in Ecclefechan streets, with no outward advantage, worn with many troubles, bodily and mental. His life had been pure and without spot—an admirable son — a faithful and an affectionate brother; with splendid talents which he felt rather than understood—determined to use them well, as a trust committed to him, and never never sell his soul by travelling the primrose path to wealth and distinction."

We know that he determined he would never sell his soul to the Devil—never speak what he did not wholly believe, and never do what in his inmost heart he did not feel to be right.

Carlyle and Emerson were contemporaries. They corresponded as friends, and have enriched Literature by the publishing of their correspondence. When Emerson came to this country for the first time, beyond meeting with such celebrities as Wordsworth and Coleridge, he was anxious to meet with Carlyle. They did meet at Craigenputtock, and, as has been already noted, after their walk on the long hills they sat down in sight of Criffel, and talked about Immortality, and Carlyle, pointing to Dunscore Kirk, said, " Christ died on the tree— *that* built Dunscore Kirk yonder, *that* brought you and me together."

Not only were Carlyle and Emerson writers of books, but it is simple justice to observe that both have written their books well. There is no trace anywhere of " shoddy." So far as we remember, there is not a slovenly sentence in all " Emerson." Nor in all " Carlyle." Carlyle put his life into his books. As he told the students of Edinburgh University, in his address to them as Lord Rector, he never wrote a book " that did not make him ill."

He gave, as we know, fourteen years of his life to his *Frederick the Great.* The labour spent on *Oliver Cromwell* and the *French Revolution* is Herculean. He had to see the thing, cost what it might.

Both toiled terribly at their work, and they have had great reward.

They are also alike in their universal sympathies. They are men of colossal build—large-minded and large-hearted, intermeddling with great problems— with what concerns Man, the Universe, and God.

Were the present writer to express what he owes most to Emerson, he would say that he is most indebted for help received on the great theme of Immortality, especially for the way in which Emerson has deciphered the handwriting on this great thought in the book of Human Nature.

And were he to sum up in a word his indebtedness to Carlyle, it would be to make mention of moral stimulus received from him. Carlyle is, indeed, what Goethe called him long ago, a " Moral Force." No one can read his writings sympathetically without rising from the study of them a better moral man, dowered with his scorn of scorn, his hate of hate, and his love of love,—his hate of all that is false, and insincere, and low, and his love of all that is virtuous, and true, and noble. In one of his letters he writes : " Train little Jane to this, as the corner-stone of all morality, to stand by the truth,—to abhor a lie, as she would Hell-fire."

IV

These writers differ widely in style. Emerson leaves upon his readers the impression that he paid a great deal of attention to style, whilst one is led to think that Carlyle did not care a brass farthing for what Purists consider a literary style. With him, the great matter seems to be to get something to say, and then to leave the saying of it very much to itself.

We are of the opinion, that Carlyle would with great wisdom reduce all rules of literary style to these two—First, Get something to say ; Second, Say it in your own way. He says somewhere that every man has his own style, like his own nose, and so be it is his own nose, and not any other body's, no person has a right to amputate it, although it were as long as the " nose of Slawken-bergius himself."

Emerson's style is one of condensation. He courts the abstract. He writes as if he were writing telegrams. He abounds in terse sentences, and rarely condescends to the concrete. He favours thoughts, ideas, contrasts, summaries.

It is this abstract, condensed style that makes

him so tough to read, and so difficult to understand. Lowell declares that Emerson " begins nowhere, and ends everywhere."

Carlyle's style, on the other hand, abounds in the concrete. He loves men and delights in incident. The minutest incident does not escape his attention. He does not forget the vein on Mahomet's brow,— does not forget that all the powder had been rubbed off the wig of Louis XVI., on the side on which he had been lying during a snatched sleep in the awful time of the Reign of Terror. He excels in description. There are passages in his writings unmatched for vividness in the whole range of Literature. He saw it all, and he makes us see it too.

And then, we ought not to forget that Carlyle has in abundance what Emerson almost completely lacks, and that is humour. Emerson is barren in this respect, as flat as a bottle of soda-water long uncorked. He is stern, almost severe. There is not a laugh, scarcely a smile in him, from beginning to end.

It's all so different with Carlyle. There's humour everywhere, even in his bursts of cynicism. He puts things so amusingly, makes jokes even of his wretched dyspepsia, telling us how he had, like Ramdas, " too much fire in his belly."

We recall his description of the Dandiacal body, " elegant vacuum,"— and of the man who was deemed respectable " because he kept a gig." He brings his great work, the *French Revolution*, to a close by declaring that all " respectability and

collected gigs " were ordered thereby to take themselves off the face of the earth.

V

Carlyle and Emerson resemble each other as
Philosophers and Moralists. Both were Idealists
or Transcendentalists in Philosophy. The latter is
a great admirer of Plato, and the former of Immanuel Kant. The foundation-stone of their
Philosophy was the priority of intellect, of idea—
the priority of God.

And so, both went dead against all Materialism
and Atheism. To them it was a " frightful theory "
to hold that mind and soul are generated by matter.
They maintained the very reverse to be the truth.

At anyrate, soul must be first. Emerson is a
great believer in soul. It is first, soul; second,
soul ; third, soul,—soul for ever more. So also is
it with Carlyle.

According to Sceptics, when you come to the last
box of the Universe, you will find there—nothing.
According to Materialists, when you come to the
last box of the Universe, you will find there atoms
—atoms of matter.

But according to both Carlyle and Emerson,
when you come to the last box of the Universe, you
will find there Mind, Thought, Law, Soul.

It is surely a great gain to our age to have the
two greatest of its thinkers and writers on the
side of Spirit as against Matter, of Freedom as
against Necessity, of God as against Chance.

And both Carlyle and Emerson excel in the sphere of a pure, lofty, uncompromising Morality. Emerson has glorified Virtue, and Carlyle has done likewise. According to Carlyle, right is right and wrong is wrong, and are so eternally, because made so by the Maker of the Universe and of Man. These are not compatible, but are separate from each other, as Heaven is from Hell. He quotes with appreciation the well-known words of Kant, that of all things in the world he is taken most with " the starry Heavens above him, and the Moral Law within him."

It is not difficult to give in a sentence or two the essence of Carlyle's Moral Philosophy. To him this is the conclusion of the whole matter,— " The Universe has Laws—these Laws are there by the Maker of the same. If you obey these Laws, it shall be well with you ; and if you don't obey them, it shall not be well with you."

We need not therefore be surprised that Carlyle is very severe, not only on Materialists in Thought, but also on Utilitarians in Morals. By Utilitarians he means those who would whittle down the eternal distinction between right and wrong, and substitute what is known as the " Greatest Happiness Principle,"—whose one dictum in morals is, " Act so that you may be happy."

It would be hard to say whether Carlyle's wrath or scorn is greater. Advising all to leave happiness on its own basis, many a time he reminds his readers that the Maker of the Universe means His creatures to aim at something else, and something better, than simply being happy. According to his reading of history, the lives of the gods have been a sublime sadness, and there was One whose crown was a Crown of Thorns. Soul, he declares, is not synonymous with stomach. His Everlasting Yea is, " Love not pleasure, love God."

Although his Pig's philosophy may be somewhat coarse, and has greatly offended a Moralist like Herbert Spencer, it is well to be reminded that, however it may be with pigs, men and women ought to realise their Paradise in a somewhat different way than in an unlimited attainability of pig's wash.   Carlyle and Emerson would substitute for this Greatest Happiness Principle a Greatest Nobleness Principle ; and in doing so, they strike into the Eternities.

We are convinced that Carlyle is misunderstood when he is represented as believing more in mights than in rights.   The fact of the matter is, in his scheme of thinking these are one and the same. Carlyle insists again and again that a person is strong, and invincibly so, as his strength rests upon what is just and right.   The strength on which he insists so much is not brute strength, nor purse, nor army, nor even intellectual strength, but always moral strength.   And so he declares that at the Diet of Worms, Luther, the miner's son, was really stronger than all the Dignitaries of the Roman Catholic Church, with all their thrones, and tiaras, and wealth, and learning, and position.   This one man was stronger than they all, simply because he took his stand on Justice—on Reason—on Conscience—on Truth—on the Word of God.

VI

Carlyle and Emerson closely conform in their Religion, and by Religion we understand what they did really believe, and lay to heart about God, the Universe, and Man. We accept Carlyle's saying, that Religion constitutes the most important factor about any person. Although they had their own way of thinking and expressing themselves on this all-important subject, it is only fair to state that they were both deeply and earnestly religious. If it be necessary to designate Emerson from a religious point of view, he may be called a Pantheist. He did not believe in a Personal God, maintaining rather that the impersonal was higher than the personal. He believed in the Over-Soul, in Law, in the sublimity of Moral Principle. Having discussed this matter in a previous paper, we are only concerned here and now to state the fact.

As for Carlyle, we think that he has a tendency towards Pantheism—but only a tendency. It is true that he dwells much on the Immensities and the Eternities. He writes often about the Ultimate Power, all-wise, all-just, all-beautiful. Like Emerson, he makes much of the Laws of the Universe, but, unlike him, he also makes much of the Maker of these Laws, and thereby saves himself from a thoroughgoing Pantheism.

In a well-known passage Carlyle has himself

described his religious position. " Personal God—Impersonal God—one—three—what meaning can any mortal attach to these in reference to such an object. I dare not and do not. Finally, assure yourself, that I am neither Pagan, nor Turk, nor circumcised Jew, but an unfortunate Christian individual, residing at Chelsea, in this year of grace, neither Pantheist nor Pot-theist nor any Theist nor -ist whatsoever, having the most decided contempt for all such names of system builders, or sect founders, feeling well beforehand that all such are and ever must be wrong. By God's blessing one has got two eyes to look with, also a mind capable of knowing and believing. That is all the creed I will at this time insist on."

From this and other passages we gather that, in his opinion, God is so great, that all naming of Him by creatures such as we are, comes far short of that great Reality of Realities—that great Fact of Facts —which we call God. Carlyle cries out with Faust, " Why durst name Him ? "

Here we would simply ask, if it be a matter of naming God, why not name Him by the best of names ? Carlyle himself names Him, Power—Reality—Fact—All-wise—All-just—All-beautiful. Why not also name Him, as the Christian Religion has taught us, by the name of *Father*, the best of all names ?

We fear that we must come to the conclusion that we can claim neither Carlyle nor Emerson for the Christian Religion as ordinarily understood.

There are, indeed, some passages of Carlyle's

writings in which he scarcely does justice to the
genius of the Christian Faith.   There is, for
example, that notable passage in his famous Inaugural Address to the students of Edinburgh
University, in which he refers to the Three Reverences in Goethe's *Wilheim Meister*, one of the most
remarkable bits of writing, as he says, that ever
was written.   In fullest sympathy with Goethe,
he speaks of the Reverence for what is above us
as the soul of the Pagan Religion—the Reverence
for what is around us as the soul of Culture—and
the Reverence for what is beneath us as the soul of
the Christian Religion.   He justifies this reference
to the Christian Religion from the fact that Christianity has discovered a blessing in sorrow—in loss
—and in contradiction.

We venture to question the above as a fair
description of the Christian Faith.   The Christian
Faith has certainly the Reverence for what is
beneath us, but it has also as clearly the other two
Reverences, and ever so much more besides.

If we understand Carlyle aright, he chafes under
the Particularism or narrowness of the Hebrew
presentation of the Eternal Realities.   He wants
to see a Heaven which is more than three ells broad.
He wants to get rid of the Hebrew " Old clo'
business."   He wants an Exodus from Hounds-
ditch.

The Bible is to him neither final nor satisfactory.
He wants something broader, more rational, more
universal.   And to their credit for boldness, both
Carlyle and Emerson have tried their best to give

us a new Bible. Honesty, however, forces the confession that they have made nothing of it. "The old is better."

Heaven is broader far, and more beautiful by far, in the old Hebrew Bible, than it is in that new book called Bible, written by the sages of Boston and Chelsea.

It is only just, however, to observe, that whilst we cannot claim either Carlyle or Emerson for the Christian Religion, we do not find that either of them has written a single word against the Christian Religion, or against Him who is its Author. The very reverse, indeed, is the truth. To Carlyle, the Christian Religion is the highest ever attained; from which man cannot retrograde; and Christ is God, and Godlike—the greatest Genius—the Divine Sorrow—the Martyr Hero—the Noble Labour—the Revealer of the silent expanses of Eternity. And Emerson, too, casts his crown at the Master's feet.

And although we cannot claim these two great writers as clearly Christian in their Religion, it is a matter for thankfulness that the whole trend of their writings is to strengthen religious foundations —to lead back to God, to Soul, and to Religion. To Carlyle, God is not like a clockmaker, who makes the clock, and then allows it to go as it pleases; neither is the Soul "so much wind contained in a capsule." He does not believe in Puseyism, nor in kissing a closed Bible, nor in the gospel of MacCroudy, nor in the cash-nexus between man and man. Whatever Religion is, Re-

ligion at least is not that.   Religion is work; it
is reverence; it is morality; it is obedience.

There is a splendid robustness about Carlyle,
which braces the soul like the blast of a nor'-
easter.

We respect the Sage of Boston, as we would a
beautiful Greek statue, but we love the Sage of
Chelsea as we love a grand mountain, or a bold,
free, flowing river.

He is so thorough and so human, at times grim
and fierce, and yet withal so good, and true.   Very
readily do we grant what he himself has claimed,
that he has not been an " unworthy labourer in the
vineyard."

We conclude with words which have come to us
as his own.   " And this is what we have got to,
all things from frog's spawn—the gospel of dirt
the order of the day.   The older I grow, and I
now stand on the brink of eternity, the more comes
back to me the sentence in the Catechism which I
learned when a child, and the fuller and deeper it
becomes, ' What is the chief end of man ? '   ' To
glorify God, and to enjoy Him for ever.' "

JAMES RUSSELL LOWELL

"Though we break our father's promise, we have nobler duties
    first;
The traitor to Humanity is the traitor most accursed;
Man is more than Constitutions; better rot beneath the sod
Than be true to Church and State, while we are doubly false
    to God."

                    LOWELL, "Capture of Fugitive Slaves."

        "Nothing pays but God."
                        LOWELL, "The Cathedral."

        "Ez for war, I call it murder,—
        There you have it, plain and flat."
                        LOWELL, *Biglow Papers.*

JAMES RUSSELL LOWELL

I

" WHO reads an American book ? " so once asked
Sydney Smith.   Lowell, an American to the core,
stung to the quick, called this a scornful question.
Such a question would not be asked now, for the
readers of American books are many, and are
increasing in number.   As Lowell himself would
have us consider, it is scarcely fair to expect so
much in the way of Literature from a new country
like America, as from an old country like our own.
People there are so busy making their Iliad, that
they have not as yet time to sing about it.   In
America there is an Apotheosis of Work, and if
there be any Poetry, it is " like the waste of water
over the dam."

> " Those horn hands have as yet found small time,
> For painting, and sculpture, and music, and rhyme ;
> These will come in due order ; the need that pressed sorest,
> Was to vanquish the seasons, the ocean, the forest."

The first thing that brought Lowell into notice
was the publication, in 1848, of the First Series of
the *Biglow Papers*.   In these papers, altogether
unique in Literature, Lowell, in Yankee dialect, and
with great humour, expressed his indignation at the

Mexican War, which had arisen in the interests of the slave-holders. Not only did these Papers make him famous; they also made him a factor of the greatest importance and power in the political and social life of his country. By means of them he set the heather on fire.

They had an enormous circulation; were recited in the homes and workshops of the people, and determined elections. These Papers were published as Letters and Poems sent to the *Boston Courier* and other newspapers, "By Mr. Hosea Biglow, Jaalam, and Mr. Bird O'Freedom Sawin, Private in the Massachusetts Regiment, and all under the careful supervision, with elaborate annotations, of the Rev. Homer Wilbur, A.M., Minister of the Independent Chapel, at Jaalam." There was, for a time, considerable controversy regarding the author of them, Lowell himself having once heard the matter discussed, and the conclusion come to, that whoever the Author might be, "it was not that fellow Lowell," who, in the estimate of the speaker, was quite unequal to their production.

For twenty years Lowell was Professor of Modern Literature and "Belles Lettres" in the University of Harvard, succeeding his friend, the Poet Longfellow. Afterwards he was appointed Minister of the United States, proceeding first of all to Madrid, and afterwards to London. He died in 1891.

It might be said of Lowell, as he himself said of Agassiz, "His magic is not far to seek; he is so human." "*He is so human*"—here, in a single sentence, lies the secret of the charm, as well as of

the characteristics of Lowell's life and writings.
He can be written down as "one who loved his
fellowmen,"—perhaps, after all, the highest tribute
that can be paid to a human being.   It is this
enthusiasm for humanity which explains, as we
think, the whole trend of Lowell's life—his anti-
pathies, conflicts, and successes, his Essays, Poetry,
Politics, and Religion.   "There is," he writes, "one
institution to which we owe our first allegiance,
one that is more sacred and venerable than any
other, and that is the soul, and constitution of
Man"—

  " Though we break our father's promise, we have nobler duties
      first ;
    The traitor to Humanity is the traitor most accursed ;
    Man is more than Constitutions ; better rot beneath the sod
    Than be true to Church and State, while we are doubly false
      to God."

Touring in Italy, Lowell declares that his
favourite gallery was just the street, the men
and women with whom he came into contact.
These he found to be always entertaining at least.
When in Edinburgh, at the Tercentenary of the
University, he was most deeply interested in "dear
old John Brown," the author of *Rab*.
    We must not regard Lowell as a great genius,
scarcely, perhaps, as a genius at all.   He is not an
Essayist like his own Emerson, nor a Poet like his
own Longfellow.   He is neither a Thinker nor a
Moral force, like Carlyle, lacking, as he does, that
genetic faculty which goes along with genius of the
first order.

There is, however, much in Lowell's life and writings that is pure, noble, and admirable.

Perhaps he attempted too much, and would have done more if he had done less.   It is by no means easy to succeed as Poet, Critic, Essayist, Editor, Politician, Professor, Diplomatist, and also as Man of the world; and Lowell in his day played, as best he could, all these parts.

II

We have the impression that, from whatever source Lowell's fame comes, it does not come from his Essays in Literature, and these are plentiful. With the exception of our own countrymen, Scott and Burns, there is scarcely a great name in the Literature of any age which has not furnished a theme for his pen.

There are Essays on Dante, Lessing, Rousseau, Shakespeare, Pope, Dryden, Milton, Emerson, Wordsworth, and Carlyle.   These essays—pedantic and prolix—lack the hall-mark of lucidity insisted on so much by Matthew Arnold.   Lowell's fame comes rather from his Poetry.   His *Biglow Papers*, and a few of his Poems, must be classed with those words which men will not willingly let die.

A well-known modern journalist records that over against one of Lowell's poems, the poem entitled "Extreme Unction," he wrote these words when quite a young man—"This poem changed my life."

There can be no doubt that every word of this

Poem is worthy of being written in letters of gold,
quivering, as it does, with moral earnestness and
noble purpose. It is a poem fit, we should say,
to take its place side by side with Longfellow's
" Psalm of Life," or Browning's " Rabbi Ben
Ezra."

But not only does Lowell get the credit of
changing, and having power to change, a life for
good, he also gets the credit of being the Author of
what is known as the " New Journalism." This
" New Journalism " is said to be the fruit of seed
sown by Lowell, who insisted strenuously that the
Press should now take the place of the Pulpit, and
the Modern Editor become true preacher and
prophet. It may be well to give in full the Pious
Editor's Creed, as it appeared in the *Biglow Papers*,
and which is said to have borne such fruit.

" Ordinary clergymen are twitted as walking off
to the extreme edge of the world, and throwing
such seed as they have clear over into that darkness, which they call the ' Next Life.' . . .

" So it has come to pass that the preacher, instead
of being a living force, has faded into an emblematic
figure at christenings, weddings, and funerals, or if
he exercise any other function, it is as a keeper and
feeder of certain theological dogmas, etc. . . .

" Meanwhile, see what a pulpit the Editor mounts
daily, sometimes with a congregation of fifty thousand
within reach of his voice, and never so much as a
nodder amongst them.

" And from what a Bible he can choose his text,
. . . the open volume of the world, upon which,

with a pen of sunshine or destroying fire, the inspired Present is even now writing the annals of God.

"Methinks the Editor, who should understand his calling, and be equal thereto, would truly deserve that title ποιμὴν λαῶν which Homer bestows upon Princes. He would be the Moses of our Nineteenth Century; and whereas the old Sinai, silent now, is but a common mountain, stared at by the elegant tourist, or crawled over by the hammering geologist, he must find his Tables of the New Law, here, amongst factories and cities, in this Wilderness of Sin, called Progress of Civilisation, and be the captain of our Exodus into the Canaan of a truer social order."

These wise words, clearly written in a vein of humour, although true, are by no means new. We have the very same thought expressed with more earnestness and force in the pages of our own Carlyle, who would resolve Universities and Churches into Literature. "Books," writes the Sage of Chelsea, "pamphlets, papers,—these are your true University, true Church."

Now that we have had some experience of the New Journalism, we are coming to see that there is room for all—for the University and the Church as well as for the New Journalism, and room for the New Journalism as well as for the University and the Church. Nay, we may go as far as to say, that after seeing the new Moses, our reverence for the old Moses has increased—as well as for the old Sinai, and for the old Way, through the old Wilderness, into the old Canaan.

III

Almost all Lowell's writings manifest a distinctly religious spirit, and are pervaded by a reverence for sacred things. Even the *Biglow Papers*, full as they are of drollery, are by no means irreverent, not even the well-known couplet, "An you've gut to git up airly, ef you want to take in God."

We regret that we have to except from this commendation two of his poems, "Fitz Adam's Story" and "Burns' Centennial," in which he has handled the themes of Hell and of Heaven in a way, as seems to us, verging on blasphemy.

In one of his most thoughtful and carefully constructed poems, "The Cathedral"—a poem suggestive of Browning's intellectual introspectiveness, Lowell speaks out clearly on the importance of personal Religion. Setting his seal on Spencer's dictum, that "whilst Religions perish, Religion lives," he teaches that man's chief difficulty does not lie in being religious, but in deciding to become and remain irreligious.

"Man cannot be God's outlaw if he would,
    Nor so abscond Him in the caves of sense ;
    But Nature still shall search some crevice out,
    With messages of splendour, from that Source,
    Which, dive he, soar he, baffles still, and lures."

In that same poem Lowell declares that, although he has become wearied of the forms of a traditional Faith, yet he is not recreant to the Faith itself—

"I, that still pray at morning, and at eve ;
    Loving these roots that feed us from the past,
    And prizing, more than Plato, things I learned
    At that best Academe—a mother's knee."

Amongst other personal experiences in the all-important matter of Religion to which reference is made in "The Cathedral," he expresses his abhorrence of those who cruel-kind would turn him out naked into speculation's "windy waste," and obscure—

> "With painted saints, and paraphrase of God,
>   The soul's east-window, of divine surprise."

He tells us how more than once he has felt that "perfect disenthralment, which is God."

Like Tennyson, he rather welcomes than frowns upon honest doubt, sure that—

> "Perhaps the deeper faith, that is to come,
>   Will see God, rather in the strenuous doubt;
>   Than in the creed, held as an infant's hand,
>   Holds purposeless, whatso is placed therein."

In every sense Lowell's poem entitled "Extreme Unction" is noble,—throbbing through and through with moral earnestness. The following extract may give an idea of how vividly, how awfully, indeed, the Poet gives voice to the irrevocable misery and absolute loss which awaits unimproved opportunities—

> "God bends from out the deep, and says,—
>   'I gave thee the great gift of life.
>   Wast thou not called, in many ways?
>   Are not my earth and heaven, at strife?
>   I gave thee of my seed, to sow,
>   Bringst thou me an hundredfold?'
>   Can I look up with face, aglow
>   And answer, 'Father, here is gold.'
>
> Men think it is an awful sight,
>   To see a soul just set adrift,
> On that drear voyage, from whose night
>   The ominous shadows never lift."

But 'tis more awful to behold
A helpless infant newly born,
Whose little hands, unconscious, hold
The keys of darkness and of morn.

Mine held them once ; I flung away
Those keys—that might have open set
The golden sluices of the day,
But clutch the keys of darkness yet ;
I hear the reapers singing go
Into God's harvest ; I, that might
With them have chosen, here below,
Grope shuddering at the gates of night."

When we say that Lowell was an out-and-out Humanitarian in his Religion, we express at once his excellency and his deficiency in this respect. There is excellency inasmuch as he lays so much emphasis on the human and practical side of Religion, a side unfortunately too much overlooked. There is deficiency inasmuch as he is so blind to the doctrinal and Godward side.

Whilst there is a tendency to separate what God has put together, there can be no doubt that a perfect Religion, such as the Bible reveals, includes both sides. Although we consider Lowell and the school to which he belongs to err by deficiency, we cannot but thank him for what he has written on the manward side of Religion, and could have wished that he had written as much and as well on its Godward side. With great power he exalts, emphasises, and enriches the fact, that no one is worthy of being called religious in any sense, or a follower of Christ at all, unless, like the Master, he is rich in humanity, going about like Him doing good.

6

Tired of discussions about Apostolic Succession, Sacraments, and Religious Dogmas, he is keenly alive to the Christianity that shows itself in deeds of beneficence. He has a deep insight into the far-reaching power of the Christian Faith, or perhaps we should rather say, into the influence of Christ Himself. In the new life, and the new ideas of the New World, he sees the incarnation of truths uttered centuries ago by the Great Teacher.

The Spirit that brought about the overthrow of the terrible curse of Slavery, was but the Spirit of Christianity,—"Elastic as air, penetrative as heat, invulnerable as sunshine, against which creed after creed had measured their strength and been confounded,—a restless Spirit, which refuses to be crystallised in any sect or form, but persists as divinely commissioned, radical and reconstructive, in trying every generation with a new dilemma, between ease and interest on the one hand, and duty on the other."

Here is a verse or two from " The Parable "—

" ' Have ye founded your thrones and altars then,
  On the bodies and souls of living men ?
  And think ye that building shall endure
  Which shelters the noble and crushes the poor ?

  With gates of silver, and bars of gold,
  Ye have fenced My sheep from their father's Fold ;
  I have heard the dropping of their tears,
  In heaven, those eighteen hundred years.' "

Lowell is a firm believer in Retribution, on the largest and smallest scale, as a law holding true for an empire as for an individual. "Where empires

towered that were not just, lo, the skulking wild fox
scratches in a little heap of dust."

This is from one of his Sonnets — " The
Street "—

> " They trampled on their youth, and faith, and love ;
>   They cast their hope of human-kind away,
> With Heaven's clear messages, they madly strove
>   And conquered—and their spirits turned to clay.
>
> . . . .
>
> Alas ! poor fools, the anointed eye may trace
> A dead soul's epitaph in every face ! "

Lowell preaches, and preaches earnestly, devotion
to duty, self-sacrifice, and consistency in life and
religion. He is of the opinion that more harm has
been done to the Christian Faith by inconsistency
than by anything else ; declaring that whilst no
human device has ever prevailed against it—no
array of majorities or respectabilities ; yet neither
Cæsar nor Flamen ever conceived a scheme so
cunningly adapted to neutralise the powers of the
Christian Religion as the fearful compromise " which
accepts it with the lip and denies it with the life,
which marries it at the altar and divorces it at the
church door."

The present writer does not at all see eye to
eye with Lowell in his poem entitled " Bibliolatres,"
opening with the words, " Bowing thyself in dust
before a Book." If we make out his meaning
aright, he seeks to teach that the Canon of the
Book of God is not yet closed, and that God is still
revealing Himself to men, and sending new messages through His prophets.

" Slowly the Bible of the race is writ,
  And not on paper leaves nor leaves of stone ;
  Each age, each kindred adds a verse to it,
  Texts of despair, or hope, of joy, or moan.
  While swings the sea, while mists the mountain shroud,
  While thunder's surges burst on cliffs of cloud ;
      Still at the prophets' feet, the nations sit."

This certainly sounds well, but we are of the opinion that there is not so much in it as many might suppose.

We ask, for example, what new verse Lowell himself has added to the old Book, after all his thinking and writing, extending over half a century ? As has been said already, the highest tribute that can be paid to him is to write him down as "one who loved his fellowmen," and yet there is nothing new in such a praiseworthy attitude. His message, " Love thy neighbour as thyself," is indeed a great message, and yet, as everyone knows, this is not a message which can be called new.

The conviction indeed deepens, that not one of our ablest thinkers or best singers has added one iota in the moral and spiritual sphere to what has been revealed in the Bible. Nay, it may be said that our thinkers and singers only think and sing to purpose when they are in touch with the thoughts which breathe and the words which burn in that old Book, to which we cannot yield too great a homage, either of head or heart.

IV

Lowell's *Biglow Papers* demand more than a passing attention. It has been said, and it is surely

a marvellous tribute to the might of the pen, that
to the influence of these papers "eighty thousand
slaves owe their freedom, and twenty millions of
his fellow-citizens, their conscience." They consist
of two Series, of which the First, the better by
far, was written in connection with the outbreak
of the Mexican War in 1846, and the other, in
1864, in connection with the war of Secession
between the Northern and Southern States of
America.

He espoused with his whole soul the cause of the
North—the cause of Freedom. The *Biglow Papers*
were written in Yankee dialect, and Lowell is
anxious that his readers should know that this
dialect is not at all slang, and that he does not put
on the cap and bells of the jester. He is giving
voice, in the language of the people, to views of the
people on such things as War, Slavery, Candidating,
etc. The three characters that figure in the Papers
are the Rev. Homer Wilbur, M.A., Minister of the
Independent Chapel of Jaalam; Hosea Biglow, a
talented Parishioner; and Mr. B. Sawin, a Private
in the Massachusetts Regiment; and these three
imaginary persons are intended to be representative,
—the Rev. Homer representing the cautious and
pedantic element in Yankee character; Hosea Biglow representing plain common-sense; and Mr. B.
Sawin representing drollery.

These Papers are full of good things. Here, for
example, is one of them, so far as Literature is concerned: "Mister Wilbur, sez he to me, onct, sez he,
'Hosee,' sez he, 'in Litterytoor, the only good thing

is Natur'. It's amasin' hard to come at,' sez he, 'but onct get it, and you've got everythin'.' "

And this is how Hosea Biglow puts the matter of War—

" Ez for war, I call it murder,—
    There you have it, plain and flat ;
I don't want to go no furder,
    Than my Testyment, fer that ;

God hez sed so, plump an' fairly ;
    It's ez long, ez it is broad ;
An' you've gut to git up airly,
    Ef you want to take in God.

        .   .   .   .   .

Ef you take a sword, and dror it,
    An' go stick a feller thru,
Guv'ment ain't to answer for it—
    God'll send the bill to you.

Wut's the use o' Meetin'-goin'
    Every Sabbath, wet or dry,
Ef it's right to go amowin'
    Feller-men, like oats an' rye.

I dunno but wut it's pooty,
    Trainin' roun', in bobtail coats ;
But it's curus Christian dooty,
    This 'ere cuttin' folks's throats."

Well, yes, this cutting of folks' throats is curious Christian duty. Ruskin says that if our soldiers were dressed in black like other executioners, instead of in scarlet, the army would not be so attractive.

Mr. B. Sawin, Private in the Massachusetts Regiment, sends home a letter, in which he says, amongst other things—

> " This sort of thing aint *jest* like that,
>   I wish that I wuz furder ;
>   Ninepence a day fer killing folks
>   Comes kind o' low, for murder."

> " It's glory—but, in spite o' all my trying to get callous,
>   I feel a kind o' in a cart a-riodin' to the gallus."

Hosea adds as P.S.—"Ef anythin's foolisher, and moor dicklus than militerry gloary, it is milishy gloary." And the Rev. Homer Wilbur inserts a very wise reflection to the effect, that we ought to fill our bombshells with copies of the Thirty-Nine Articles, and to wrap up every cannon ball in a leaf of the New Testament.

Here is a description of General C., a War candidate—

" General C. is a dreffle smart man :
    He's ben on all sides that give places or pelf ;
But consistency still wuz a part of his plan,—
    He's been true to *one* party—an' that is himself,—
            So John P.
            Robinson he,
        Sez he shall vote for General C.

General C. he goes in for the war,
    He didn't vally principle more'n an old cud.
Wut did God make us raytional creatures fer,
    But glory an' gunpowder, plunder and blood,—
            So John P.
            Robinson he,
        Sez he shall vote for General C.

.   .   .   .

Parson Wilbur sez *he* never heard in his life
    Thet the Apostles rigged out in their swaller-tailed coats
An' marched round in front of a drum an' a fyfe,
    To get some on 'em office, and some on 'em votes,—
            But John P.
            Robinson he,
        Sez they didn't know everything down in Judee."

It is the *Biglow Papers* that has given us the couplet that has become so familiar, especially in Political circles—

> " A marciful Providence fashioned us holler,
>   O' purpose that we might our principles swaller."

There is also much worldly wisdom in the following—

> " I'm willin' a man should go tollable strong,
>   Agin' wrong in the abstract, for thet kind o' wrong
>   Is ollers unpop'lar, an' never gets pitied,
>   Because it's a crime no one ever committed,
>   But he musn't be hard on partickler sins,
>   Cos then, he'll be kickin' the people's own shins."

The opposition candidate speaks as follows—

> " Ez to my principles, I glory
>   In hevin' nothin' o' the sort ;
>   I ain't a Whig, I ain't a Tory ;
>   I'm jest a candidate in short."

V

Although the prevailing note of Lowell is his earnestness, yet he is largely endowed with humour ; not the grim humour of Carlyle, nor the laughter-producing humour of Dickens, nor the genial humour of Scott, but a humour of such a peculiar kind that for want of a better name it may be called American. It is smart—saying well a good thing.

" Hez the bell fell yet ? " was the first question which the farmer asked when he arrived, breathless, on the scene, and saw the church on the hill wrapped in flame.

Lowell tells of a deacon, very accommodating in

the matter of the apples which he sold. "Well, deacon," asks A., "have you any sour apples?" "Well, no," says the deacon, "I haven't any that are exactly sour; but there's the bellflower apple, and folks that like a sour apple generally like that." Exit A. Enter B. "Well, deacon, have you any sweet apples?" "Well, no," says the deacon, "I haven't any that are exactly sweet; but there's the bellflower apple, and folks that like a sweet apple generally like that." Lowell calls the deacon's apples "Laodicean," because they were neither one thing nor another.

He tells of a Scotch gardener whom he knew, Fraser by name, and who now and then got sublimed into a poet by means of whisky. He had been an old soldier, and it seems that when the whisky had warmed him up he was in the habit of telling bloody histories of the "Forty-Twa," and showing an imaginary bullet, sometimes in one leg, sometimes in the other, and sometimes at nightfall in both.

Describing a corps of volunteers, the Harvard Washington Corps, he mentions that, after being royally entertained by a maiden lady in the town, they entered in their orderly-book, a vote that Miss Blank "was a gentleman." "I see them now," says Lowell, "returning from the deadly breach of the law of Rechab, unable to form other than the serpentine line of beauty, while their Officers, brotherly rather than imperious, instead of reprimanding, tearfully embraced the more eccentric wanderers from military precision."

Writing of the Italians, he says that they quarrel as unaccountably as dogs who put their noses together dislike each other's smell, and instantly tumble one over the other, with "noise enough to draw the eyes of a whole street." He describes Italian beggars as presenting a withered arm to you as a highwayman would a pistol,—a goitre is a life annuity; a St. Vitus dance is as good as an engagement as Prima Ballerina at the Apollo; and to have no legs at all is to stand on the best footing with fortune.

One of his friends gave a very tiny coin to an old woman who was begging, and the old woman delicately expressed her resentment, by exclaiming, "Thanks, Signora, God will reward even you."

Lowell makes a slight alteration on the well-known lines: "One impulse from the vernal wood will teach us more of man," etc., by suggesting that it would be wise to substitute "birchen" for "vernal,"—all, of course, in the purest humour.

VI

Lowell is American from head to foot,—proud of his country, proud of its institutions. According to him, it is the country of the future. Next to the fugitives whom Moses led out of Egypt, that little shipload of outcasts who landed at Plymouth two centuries and a half ago is destined to influence the future of the world. He sums up the creed of America, not in Thirty-Nine Articles, but in Three —Faith in God, in Man, and in Work.

"It is a New England and a better,—no nobles, either lay or cleric,—no great landed estates,—no universal ignorance, as a seed-plot of vice,—an elective magistracy and clergy,—land for all who would till it,—reading and writing, will ye nill ye,—honest dice, uncogged by prerogative, patricianism, or priestcraft."

He sums up the characteristics of the American as a certain capacity for enthusiasm, a devotion to abstract principle, and an openness to ideas. The American goes by Intuitions rather than by Syllogisms, and has a positive preference for the bird in the bush—an excellent quality of character, adds our Author, before you have your bird in hand.

He feels keenly that Americans should be called "vulgar"; that it should be said that although they are in the West, they by no means form the West end of the world. So far as he can see, the only reason why they should be called vulgar is that they vent their ideas through that organ by which men come to be led, rather than take the place of leaders. He acknowledges that the War had done them good. Before it, as a nation, they were a little loud and braggart, but the War sobered them somewhat, making their thoughts, policy, and bearing a little more manly.

"By God's grace," he says, "we are resolved to Americanise you; and America means, education—equality before the law, and every upward avenue of life, made as free to one man as to another."

He refers with a justifiable pride to the fact, that one of the characteristics of his fellow-countrymen is the custom of giving away money during their lifetime, and giving it away to such good purposes as the foundation of Colleges and the erection of Libraries.   There is, he writes, no country in which wealth is so sensible of its obligations as America.

Often Lowell lifts up his voice to emphasise the fact that the true greatness of a country is moral rather than material,—is to be measured not by its square miles, its number of yards woven, its hogs packed, and bushels of wheat raised, not only by its skill to feed and clothe the body, but also by its power to feed and clothe the soul.

If all nations have their messages, the message of the American nation is to preach and practise before all the world the freedom and divinity of man—the glorious claims of brotherhood, and the soul's fealty to none but God.

He has an intense admiration for Abraham Lincoln, "the first American"—new birth of a new soil. Nothing of Europe here, he says; a man "whom America made, as God made Adam—out of the very earth,—unancestried, unprivileged, unknown; to show us how much truth, how much majesty, how much statecraft await the call of opportunity in simple manhood, when we believe in the justice of God and the worth of man."

And Lowell had also an intense admiration for the Puritans, who were the founders of New England; drawing a very sharp distinction between the original Puritanism and the Puritanism which has become traditional. Speaking of the latter, he

says, that it translates Jehovah by "I was" instead
of "I am." The Puritanism of bygone days meant
something when Captain Hodgson, riding out to
battle through the morning mist, turns the com-
mand of the troops over to a Lieutenant, and stays
to hear the prayer of a Cornet—"There was so much
of God in it."

He distinctly traces the great stream of social,
political, and religious life in America to the
Puritan fountainhead. The English Puritans pulled
down Church and State to rebuild Zion on the
ruins; and all the while it was not Zion but
America they were building.

The Puritans, he thinks, had their faults. They
did not understand the text, "I have piped to you,
and ye have not danced," nor consider that the
saving of one's soul should be the cheerfulest, and
not the dreariest of businesses. And their preachers
had a way, like the painful Mr. Perkins, of pronouncing that word "Damn" with such emphasis
that it left a doleful echo.

Touching on the charge of intolerance and
narrow-mindedness, which is levelled against the
Puritan Fathers, he justly declares that these men
can scarcely be called narrow-minded, who gave
every man the chance of becoming a landholder,
who made the transfer of land easy, and put knowledge within the reach of all.

They were perhaps intolerant, but, Lowell asks,
Of what?—and answers, "What they believed to be
mischief, or dangerous nonsense."

He is, of course, a strenuous upholder of Democracy, and writes clearly and wisely on this subject. Democracy, he reminds us, does not attempt the impossible—making one man as good as another, but rather the making of one man's manhood as good as another. Democracy is the establishment of the divine principle of authority, on the common interest and the common consent, making a contribution from the free will of all a power which should curb and guide the free will of each for the general good.

But Lowell is wise enough to know that, as a form of Government, Democracy is no better than any other form of Government, except, and in so far as, the virtue and wisdom of the people make it so. He reproduces the memorable definition of Democracy given by Abraham Lincoln: " The Government of the people, by the people, and for the people." He also quotes the saying of Theodore Parker, that Democracy does not mean, " I am as good as you are," but " You are as good as me." He remembers that Christ Himself was the first true Democrat that ever breathed, just as the old dramatist Dekker said, " That He was the first true gentleman."

Lowell is, of course, dead against Slavery. Recalling the awful decision of the Supreme Court in America, " That negroes are not men in the ordinary meaning of the word," he utters for himself and for his countrymen this other word, as high above the decision of the Supreme Court as the heavens are above the earth, " *We shall count the negro a man.*"

There is, he writes, no question of white or black, but simply of man, and the only way to get rid of the negro is to do him justice. When the question is asked, " Will you confer equality on the negro ? " the answer is, " Equality cannot be conferred upon any man, white or black; if he be capable of it, his title is from God, and not from us."

One of Lowell's ambitions, with which we do not at all sympathise, was to create a Literature in America which should be independent of Europe. One would have expected from such a thorough-going Democrat a more hearty recognition of the great Republic of Letters, in which all should be equal, and all welcome who are loyal to the Good, and the Beautiful, and the True.

He rates his countrymen roundly for having a mental as well as a physical stoop in the shoulders. He tells them that they steal Englishmen's books, and think Englishmen's thoughts. America's wild eagle is caught by their salt—" on her tail."

" Though you brag of your New World, you don't half believe
    in it,
And as much of the Old as is possible weave in it."

We are astonished to find him counselling Americans to

" Forget Europe wholly, your veins throb with blood
To which the dull current in hers is but mud."

It is this partiality for whatever is American that explains to a large degree his scornful attitude towards Carlyle, and his intense admiration for Emerson. Emerson and Lincoln are his gods.

" Emerson," he says, "awakened us, saved us, brought us life, gave us ennobling impulses. He has a Greek head on right Yankee shoulders. . . . He is a Plotinus, a Montaigne."

VII

Many of Lowell's utterances are proverbial, full of uncommon common sense. Here are a few proverbs, picked out of his writings :—

" One learns more Metaphysics from a single temptation than from all the Philosophers."

" It needs good optics to see what is not to be seen."

" All Deacons are good, but there's odds in Deacons."

" To be misty, is not to be a mystic."

" Clerical unction in a vulgar nature easily degenerates into greasiness."

" The world never neglects a man's power, but his weaknesses, and especially his publishing them."

" Real sorrows are uncomfortable things, but purely æsthetic ones are by no means uncomfortable."

" Truth is the only unrepealable thing."

" Treason against the ballot-box, is as dangerous as treason against a throne."

" The foolish and the dead alone, never change their opinion."

" The only argument with an east wind, is to put on your overcoat."

" It is cheaper in the long-run to lift men up, than to hold them down."

" Don't never prophesy, unless you know."

" That is best blood that hath most iron in't."

" A world, made for whatever else, not made for mere enjoyment."

" Nothing pays but God."

VIII

If Lowell live, he will live, as has been said, because of his Poetry. He has written a great deal —wrote, indeed, more or less for nearly fifty years. Some of his poems, notably " The Changeling," are very sweet, reminding one of Mrs. Browning in her tenderest mood. And many of them are like trumpet calls; they are so earnest. He has nothing but scorn for the bard environed with his silken proprieties; for "the empty rhymer" who lies with idle elbow on the grass. He wants the soul to break out in music-thunders, and the song to rush forth "like molten iron, glowing."

There are, we think, about a dozen of his Poems worthy of Immortality. Perhaps the first place ought to be given to his " Extreme Unction."

There is the right Democratic ring about "The Heritage," in which the Poet sides so heartily with the " poor man's son," justifying one of his own sayings elsewhere, that the chief concern in social life is not where a man goes in, but where a man comes out.

In "The Parting of the Ways" he takes the side of Duty against Pleasure. These lines may suffice as a specimen of the good things which abound in "The Cathedral," the most thoughtful, perhaps, of all his poems—

" And find out, some day, that nothing pays but God,
Served whether in the smoke-shut battlefield,
In work obscure, done honestly, or vote
For truth unpopular, or Faith maintained,
To ruinous convictions, or good deeds
Wrought for good's sake, mindless of Heaven or Hell."

In the three poems, "The Search," "A Parable," and "The Vision of Sir Launfal," we have the expression of the Poet's mind regarding a genuine Christianity.

In the first, he tells us how he found the "Christ," for whom he searched, neither in Nature, nor in the world, but by following in the footsteps of Love, which he knew to be the footsteps of the Lord—

> "I followed where they led,
> And in a hovel rude,
> With naught to fence the weather from his head,
> The King I sought for meekly stood;
> A naked, hungry child
> Hung round His gracious knee,
> And a poor hunted slave looked up, and smiled,
> To bless the smile that set him free.
>
> .   .   .   .
>
> I knelt, and wept—my Christ no more I seek,
> His throne is with the outcast and the weak."

In "The Parable" he gives voice to the thought that genuine Christianity is absolutely inconsistent with the neglect of the poor, the oppressed, or the weak. "The Vision of Sir Launfal" teaches that the "Holy Grail" is to be found at our very door, in the act of kindness to the poor and needy, in a Christian and sympathetic spirit. In the "leper" Sir Launfal saw the "Christ"—

> "The leper no longer crouched at his side;
> But stood before him glorified,
> Shining and tall and fair and straight."

The following words embody at once the spirit of the Poet in his humanism and the spirit of the

Christian Faith in its genuine love for man, as the outcome of a genuine love to God.   The voice that was " calmer than silence " said—

> " ' Lo, it is I, be not afraid !
> In many climes without avail
> Thou hast spent thy life for the Holy Grail ;
> Behold, it is here—this cup which thou
> Didst fill at the streamlet for me but now,
> This crust is my body broken for thee ;
> This water—His blood that died on the tree ;
>
> .   .   .   .   .   .
>
> The Holy Supper is kept, indeed,
> In what—so, we share, with another's need ;
> Not what we give, but what we share,—
> For the gift without the giver is bare,—
> Who gives himself, with his alms, feeds three,—
> Himself, his hungry neighbour, and Me.' "

GEORGE ELIOT

"Conscience goes to the hammering in of nails."
GEORGE ELIOT's "Gospel. '

"Men do not want books to make them think lightly of vice, as if Life were a vulgar joke."—GEORGE ELIOT, *Romola.*

"I am poor like you. I have to get my living with my hands, but no lord or lady can be so happy as me, if they havn't got the Love of God in their souls."—GEORGE ELIOT, Dinah Morris in *Adam Bede.*

GEORGE ELIOT

I

For the last forty years the name of "George Eliot" has been amongst the best known in general Literature. Her novels justly occupy the foremost place in fictional writings, and maintain to this day their supremacy.

Since her life has been written with so much fulness by Mr. Cross, and all her books published, we are in a favourable position for forming a right estimate of George Eliot, both as a woman and as an Authoress.

George Eliot was a *nom-de-plume*. She selected this name because "George" was the Christian name of Mr. Lewes, with whom, unfortunately, she lived as wife for over twenty years ; and she selected "Eliot" because it was a good, mouth-filling, easily pronounced name.

Her own name was Mary Ann Evans. Born at Arbury Farm, Warwickshire, in 1819, she spent twenty-one years of her life at Griff, a house on the Arbury estate, where her father was agent.

It is remarkable—peculiar, indeed, that we learn next to nothing about her mother. George Eliot seems to have known nothing of a mother's loving care, a fact which may help somewhat to account for her rather masculine traits of character.

Her father seems to have been an uncommon person, somewhat after the type of "Adam Bede" and "Caleb Garth"—a Tory who had not exactly a dislike to innovations and Dissenters, but a slight opinion of them, as persons of ill-founded self-confidence.   As with the father, so with the daughter.

Her own childhood was far from being a happy one; and very rashly she ventures the assertion that it is so with all childhood.   Instead of childhood being the beautiful and happy time with which it is associated in contemplations and retrospect, it is full, she declares, of deep sorrows, the meaning of which is unknown.   What with colic, and whooping-cough, and ghosts, and Hell, and Satan, and an offended Deity in the sky, "who was angry when she wanted too much plumcake," young Mary Evans seems to have had quite a bad time of it.

A most talented girl; clever, indeed, at most things, she excelled in English Composition.

In one of her letters she says, "I love words."

Very early Miss Evans manifested those traits of character which deepened as life went on—the religiousness of her nature, sympathy with moral beneficence, and intellectual strength, feeling within her "A man's force of genius!"

In her early womanhood, so far as Religion was concerned, she was ultra-evangelical; her manners were ascetic, and she delighted greatly in Hannah

More's Letters, "longing to do something for the re-generation of this groaning and travailing creation."

All through her life she was an enormous reader,—tackling books of the severest type, and in many languages; taking a dose of Mathematics every day to prevent her brain from becoming quite soft. Her motto was, *Certum pete finem.*

Mr. Cross says that the most important event in her life was her union with Mr. Lewes. We are rather of the opinion that the most important event in her life took place when she changed her religious beliefs.

This disastrous change was due to a book written by her friend Mr. Charles Hennell, entitled, *An Inquiry concerning the Origin of Christianity.* After the reading of this Rationalistic book George Eliot changed in many ways. We do not say that she ever got rid of the religiousness of her nature, or her sympathy with the good, and the true, or her interest in unseen spiritual realities; but this has to be said, that after this she cut herself adrift from the anchorage of the Christian Faith, and so went sadly and aimlessly on the *mare magnum* of uncertainty, and on what was worse.

If after this she had any Faith at all, it was only a faint Theism, or a kind of Eclecticism. She never, however, became a scoffer at the Christian Faith. She went to church and continued the practice, loving her Bible as very sacred and precious. The translating of Strauss's *Leben Jesu* made her sick, and only the sight of the Crucifix on her study desk enabled her to endure it.

It is not easy to discover, in addition to her antipathy to the miraculous, what George Eliot objected to in the Christian Faith. Very unwisely, she seemed to have longed for a certainty in Religion, corresponding to that which prevails in Mathematics, heedless that such a certainty would prove the very death of the religious spirit.

And, then, in her opinion Christianity was not final. She thought that something better, something higher, was forthcoming,—a something that would express less care for personal consolation, and a more deeply awing sense of responsibility to man, springing out of sympathy with that which of all things is most certainly known to us, the difficulty of the human lot.

She distinctly disclaimed any desire for Negative propagandism, was horrified, indeed, at the thought of being supposed to rob any man of his religious beliefs, knowing the special blight that followed no faith.

Instead of sympathising with Free Thinkers, or being antagonistic to religious doctrine, she only cared, she said, to know, if possible, the lasting meaning that lies in all religious doctrine, from beginning to end.

We are of the opinion that this talented woman parted from the Christian Faith without fairly and fully understanding what this Faith really is. We take the liberty of saying that the heart and soul of the Christian Religion does not lie, as George Eliot thought it did, in a fear of vengeance; eternal gratitude for predestined salvation, and a revelation of future glories as a reward. Two of these Doctrines may be found on the fringes, but they do not make up the pure and beautiful garment of the Christian Religion.

We have said that George Eliot's perversion from the Christian Faith changed her in many ways. For one thing, it determined her towards pessimistic views of life, and gave to her own life and writings that profound sadness with which they are charged. She gives her address as "Grief Castle, River of Gloom, Valley of Dolour."

And for another thing, it introduced her to new and strange companionships. Her first literary work thereafter—as usual, done thoroughly—was Strauss's *Leben Jesu*. By and by she translated Spinoza, and was busy with Voltaire. In course of time she became Assistant Editor of *The Westminster Review*, and helped largely to make that Magazine the most important means of enlightenment of a literary nature then existing.

It was while she was connected with *The Westminster Review* that she became acquainted with the leading intellectual celebrities of the age, notably with Herbert Spencer and with Lewes.

Here we must refer to George Eliot's relationship to Lewes, which she herself calls, one that was "profoundly serious." It was so, in all conscience. There is, we think, only one word that can describe it, and that is the word "*immoral*," for it was an immoral relationship—grossly so. George Eliot's behaviour in this Lewes business shows how easy it is to drift from the anchorage of ordinary morality, when one has drifted from the anchorage of the Christian Religion. So far as we know, George Eliot nowhere expresses regret for her conduct, but rather seeks to defend it; and, if we mistake not, we come upon the shadow of her defence in the words and conduct of some of the characters in her novels.

It would be treachery to truth and morality to palliate or condone this distressful side of George Eliot's life. We frankly acknowledge that she almost worshipped "George"; and we as frankly recognise the literary industry of both to keep, at the outset, the wolf from the door—and yet the blot remains, black as ever.

On the death of Mr. Lewes she was married to Mr. Cross, who has written her life. After a married life of seven months she died suddenly, December 1880; her spirit, as her biographer puts it, "joining that choir invisible, whose music is the gladness of the world."

II

As an Authoress, George Eliot is known in the literary world as Essayist, Poetess, and Novelist. There is nothing immortal about her Poetry or her Essays. As an Essayist, she is perhaps at her best in her last published volume, *The Impressions of Theophrastus Such*, a work characterised as usual by great intellectual ability, but at the same time very uninteresting, and full of a caustic spirit.

Her fame rests on her Novels, and is, we think,

secure on this basis. A well-known authority, Scherer, has said that for George Eliot was reserved the honour of writing the "most perfect novels yet known."

Of these, the most popular, and perhaps on the whole the best, is *Adam Bede*. Adam Bede is supposed to be a reproduction of her father; whilst Dinah Morris is like an aunt of the writer, a Methodist, who told her how she once attended in prison, and accompanied to the scaffold in a cart, a poor girl who was condemned for child murder. This incident supplied the germ of the novel, and of poor "Hetty" as a character.

Romola was the novel which took most out of her; and she herself says that she could put her finger on this book as marking a well-defined transition in her life. "She began it a young woman, and finished it an old one." She was offered some ten thousand pounds for this novel.

The names of other novels are—*Scenes of Clerical Life, The Mill on the Floss, Felix Holt, Daniel Deronda, Silas Marner,* and *Middlemarch.*

A marked characteristic of her style as a Novelist is her thoroughness. In every one of her books she acts out what is to her a gospel, that conscience should go to the "hammering in of nails." She not only grasps the character, but also the medium in which the character moves.

Readers of *Romola* will not be surprised to learn that the writing of this book so ploughed into her, —for everything in it is so thoroughly delineated, indicating a deep study of life in the city of

Florence, from an intellectual, artistic, religious, and social point of view.

Believing in details, every scene in her novels is minutely painted. George Eliot does not consider it enough to tell the reader that the room was furnished; the reader is also told the colour of the carpet and curtains, the number of the chairs and how they were placed, and all about the statuary and painting. She is not content with saying that " Dinah Morris " had a very interesting face. She describes Dinah's eyes, and cheeks, and mouth. Hetty's beauty was like that of kittens, or " very small downy ducks, making gentle rippling noises with their soft bills, or babies just beginning to toddle. Hetty's cheek was like the rose petals. Dimples played about her pouting lips, whilst her large dark eyes hid a soft roguishness under the long eyelashes. . . . She was a Springtide beauty."

Another characteristic of her novels is the variety of life which they represent. George Eliot has more than one string to her bow. She is equally at home with the Aristocrat of the Grandcourt type, and with the Radical like Felix Holt. We take very kindly to that shaggy-headed, large-eyed, strong-limbed person, Felix Holt, " without waistcoat or cravat, who, as his mother said of him, ' Used dreadful language, called most folks' Religion rottenness, and even said his dead father's medicines were good for nothing.' "

In *Felix Holt* we have a characteristic interview

between Harold and the Rector on the subject of
Radicalism.

The Rector: "Calling yourself a Radical, I've
been turning it over in after-dinner speeches, but it
looks awkward; it's not what people are used to.
It wants a good deal of Latin to make it go down.
You'll not be attacking the Church, and the institutions of the country; you'll be keeping up the
bulwarks, and so on."

Harold: "I shan't attack the Church, only the
incomes of the Bishops, to make them eke out the
incomes of the poor Clergy."

The Rector: "Well, well, I've no objection to
that,—nobody likes your Bishop, he's all grab and
greediness, too proud to dine with his own father.
You may pepper the Bishops a little; you'll respect
the Constitution, you'll rally round the Throne."

Harold: "Of course, of course, I am a Radical;
I only root out abuses."

"That's the word I wanted, my lad," said the
Rector, slapping Harold's knee. "That's a spool to
wind a speech on; *abuses*,—that's the very word."

Felix had very strong views about most things.
"You believe in conversion?" said the Rev. Rufas
Lyon to Felix. "Yes, verily," said Felix. "I was
converted by six weeks' debauchery. I have looked
life fairly in the face, to see what can be done
with it, and I have made up my mind that the
world shan't be the worse for me, if I can help it."

Felix had not very much faith in Phrenology.
A Phrenologist in Glasgow told him once that he
had large veneration, but one there, who knew

him, laughed, and said "that Felix was the most blasphemous Iconoclast living."

"That," said the Phrenologist, "is because of your large Ideality, which prevents you from finding anything perfect enough to be venerated."

Felix hated your "gentlemanly" speakers, declaring that they shoot with boiled peas, instead of bullets.

He favoured independence, even in Congregational singing, regarding with satisfaction the way (as he puts it) that old-fashioned Presbyterians in Glasgow do. The preacher gives out the Psalm, and then everybody sings a different tune, as it happens to turn up in their throats (*sic*). It's a domineering sort of thing, according to Felix, a denial even of private judgment, "to set a tune and expect everybody to follow it."

Mike declared that Felix went "uncommon against drink, and pitch-and-toss, and quarrelling, and sich, and was all for school, and bringing up the little chaps."

There are also in George Eliot's novels samples of Doctors and Lawyers: the Lydgates, and Wakems, and Matthew Germyn.

"Matthew" is described as a "fat-handed, glib-tongued fellow, with a scented cambric handkerchief; one of your educated, low-bred fellows, a foundling, who got his Latin for nothing at Christ's Hospital; one of your middle-class upstarts, who want to rank with gentlemen, and think they can do it with kid gloves and new furniture. Matthew

chose always to dress in black, and was especially
addicted to black satin waistcoats, which carried
out the general sleekness of his appearance; and
this, together with his white, fat, beautifully shaped
hands, which he was in the habit of rubbing
gently as he entered into a room, gave him very
much the air of a lady's physician."

George Eliot excels in her description of child
life. Readers will recall Totty, Mrs. Poyser's child,
Maggie Tulliver, Tom, and Bob Jakin. Totty " was
seen arduously clutching the handle of a miniature
iron with her tiny fat fist, and ironing rags with
an assiduity that required her to put her little red
tongue out as far as anatomy would allow."

Maggie Tulliver's father said of her, " I don't
like to fly in the face of Providence, but it seems
hard as I should have but one gell, and her so
comical."

Tom's opinion was that Maggie was a silly little
thing; all girls were silly; " they couldn't throw
a stone so as to hit anything "; couldn't do anything with a pocket-knife, and were " frightened
at frogs."

As for Bob Jakin, Maggie felt sure that Bob
was wicked, without knowing very distinctly why.
Bob's trousers were always rolled up at the knee,
for the mere convenience of wading on the slightest
notice.

Neither does George Eliot forget animal life.
She doesn't forget the dogs. Readers will re-
member Adam Bede's " Gyp," also " Yap " and
" Mumps." " If Gyp had had a tail, he would

8

doubtless have wagged it, but being destitute of that vehicle of emotion, he was, like many other persons, destined to appear more phlegmatic than nature had made him." "Yap, Yap," says Maggie, "Tom's come home"; whilst Yap danced and barked round about her, as much as to say, if there was any noise wanted, "he was the dog for it."

Church and Dissent come in for a good deal of attention. There is much of the "Rector," and also of the "Methodist." Upon the whole, the sympathies of the Authoress are with the Rectors; although she has atoned for much of her contempt for Dissenters by the introduction of Dinah Morris, the female Methodist preacher, one of the most exquisite characters that has ever been portrayed in fiction, and, in our opinion, the gem in portraiture of all George Eliot's writings.

If well bred, the Clergy are often dull. It is unfortunate that Dissent is almost always held up either to ridicule or contempt. Dissenters are sure to be in the chandlery business, or are handloom weavers, or miners. "They say folks always groan when they's harkening to the Methodys, as if they was bad in the inside; I mean to groan like your cow, and then the preacher'll think I'm all right."

George Eliot makes the Rev. Rufas Lyon, Minister of Malthouse Yard, altogether too silly, with his little legs and his large head, whom the boys in the street called "Revelations," and who, in reply to questions about the weather, remarked on the course of Providence, and "that remarkable incident mentioned in the life of that eminent man, Richard Baxter."

It was this same Rev. Rufas who rebuked his servant, Liddy, by saying, "If you are wrestling with the enemy, let me refer you to Ezekiel xiii. 22, and beg of you not to groan." It is a stumbling-block of offence to my daughter,—"She would take no broth yesterday, because she said you had cried into it."

And yet, as we have said, much in this line may be forgiven to George Eliot, seeing she has given to us that beautiful character, Dinah Morris. Ben Cranger said that "it would be a good while before his head was full of the Methodys." Nay, said Adam Bede, it's "often full of drink, and that's worse."

"Come," says Seth, "and hear Dinah; you might get religion, and that would be the best day's earnings you ever made." And Seth sums up the whole matter well, by saying to Adam Bede, "Thee doesn't believe but what the Dissenters and Methodys have got the root of the matter, as well as the Church folks."

As for Art, it may be truly said, that it is of itself quite an education to read George Eliot's *Romola.*

It goes without saying, that the passion of Love is to be found in all George Eliot's novels. There is but one tune played with many variations—the course of true love never does run smooth. If

one, indeed, were to take the cue from the story
of the heroes and heroines who figure in these
novels, where it is so very difficult to get married,
and where married life is such a very uncertain
state of bliss, then, like Felix Holt, it were wisdom
to resolve never to get married at all.

Felix, however, broke through his own resolution,
as do so many, notwithstanding all that has been
written, said, or done.

III

Although there is a tone of sadness running
through George Eliot's works, it is only fair to
state, that there is also much humour, not, it may
be, of the side-splitting type, yet very pleasant, and
closely allied to wit.   Mrs. Poyser, old Tulliver, and
Mrs. Cadwallader are her chief humorists.

Mrs. Poyser is not afraid to speak to her servants,—"Why," she says, "you'd leave the dirt
in heaps in the corners; anybody would think
you'd never been brought up as Christians."   "You
are never easy until you get some sweetheart, as
is as big a fool as yourself; you think you'll be
finely off when you're married, I daresay, and
have a three-legged stool to sit on, and never
a blanket to cover you, and a bit of oatcake for
your dinner, as three children are a-snatching at."

It is Mrs. Poyser who says that folks must
put up with their own kin, as they put up with
their own noses,—"It's their own flesh and blood."

As for farming, "It's putting money into your

pocket with your right hand, and fetching it out with your left."

"To see substantial-looking Ministers in the desk o' a Sunday is," according to Mrs. Poyser, "like looking at a full crop of wheat, or a pasture with a fine dairy o' cows in it—it makes you think the world's comfortable-like."

It was Mrs. Poyser who remarked about Craig, the Scotch gardener, "I think he's welly like a cock as thinks the sun's rose i' purpose to hear him crow." And Craig himself said not a bad thing about Frenchmen, when he remarked, "They pinched themselves in wi' stays, and it's easy enough, for they've got nothing i' their inside."

It was said that the two little Poysers looked as much like old Poyser as two small elephants are like a large one.

Old Tulliver was very hard upon Lawyers,—believing that rats, weevils, and Lawyers, were created by Old Harry. He wouldn't make a downright Lawyer of his son Tom, whom Mrs. Tulliver declared to be "such a boy for pudding" as never was, for he should be sorry for him to be a raskill, but he would like to make him a sort o' engineer, or a surveyor, or a valleyer like Riley, or one of those smartish businesses as are all profits and no outlay, only for a big watch chain and a high stool.

He would like Tom to know figures, and write like print, and see things quick, and know what folks mean, and how to wrap up things "in words that aren't actionable."

It was Tulliver who said that "an over-cute woman's no better nor a long-tailed sheep, she'll fetch none the bigger price for that."

Simple Mrs. Tulliver cried out once, "Maggie, Maggie, you'll tumble into the water and be drownded some day, and then you'll be sorry you didn't do as mother told you."

Mrs. Tulliver never quarrelled with her sister Glegg, any more than a waterfowl, who puts out its leg in a deprecating manner, can be said to quarrel with a boy who throws stones.

Aunt Pullet's cleanliness, so hateful to Tom, may be guessed from the fact, that, when on a visit, Tom had been compelled "to sit with towels wrapped round his boots."

IV

There can be no doubt that the prevailing tone of George Eliot's works is one which is healthy and pure. At times she puts into the mouths of her characters, words expressing principles of conduct based more upon the lower than upon the higher nature, and depicts scenes which had better been left undepicted; and yet we have no hesitation in saying, that the tone of the whole is morally good. Her chief characters, Adam Bede, Felix Holt, Daniel Deronda, Romola, Savonarola, Silas Marner, and Dorothea, are distinctly of outstanding goodness.

Dinah Morris, who has already been referred to as the gem of all her characters, her Koh-i-noor, is more than moral: she is a Christian woman of the best sort. Mrs. Bede said that she had a face like a lily; Mrs. Poyser declared that Dinah was never easy but when she was helping somebody. George Eliot says, " her face was one of those faces that make one think of white flowers, with light touches of colour on their white petals." And Dinah is made to speak of herself thus: " I work in a cotton mill; I am poor, like you; I have got to get my living with my hands, but no lord or lady can be so happy as me, if they haven't got the love of God in their souls.

" Think what it is, not to hate anything, but sin ;— to be full of love to every creature, to be frightened at nothing, to be sure that all things will turn to good, not to mind pain, to bear it because it is our Father's will, to know that nothing, nothing, can part us from God who loves us. All my peace and joy have come from having no life of my own, no wants, no wishes for myself, and living only in God, and those of His creatures whose sorrows and joys he has given me to know."

" I can," she says to Mrs. Poyser, " no more help spending my life in trying to do what I can for the souls of others, than you can help running if you heard your little Totty crying at the other end of the house."

We take the liberty of giving a bit of her sermon to the villagers on the common. Turning to poor Bessie Cranger, Dinah said: " Poor child, poor child, He is beseeching you, and you don't listen to Him. You think of ear-rings, and gowns, and fine caps. You never think of the Saviour who died to save your precious soul. Your cheeks will be shrivelled one day, your hair will be grey, your poor body will be thin and tottering, then you will begin to feel that your soul is not saved; you will have to stand before God dressed in your sins.

" Ah, poor child, think if it should happen to you as it once happened to a servant of God in the days of her vanity. She thought of her lace caps, and saved all her money to buy them; she thought not of the clean heart and the right spirit, but one day when she looked into the glass, when she had put on her new cap, she saw a ' Bleeding Face, crowned with thorns.' That Face is looking at you now,— tear off your follies; they are poisoning your soul; they are dragging you down to the bottomless pit, where you shall sink for ever, and for ever, and for ever, farther away from the light of God."

The darling virtues in George Eliot's code of morals are Duty and Self-sacrifice. Duty she somewhere calls the " Love of law," and she adorns all her chief characters, notably the women, with self-sacrifice, that grace of graces. Esther renounces Harold Transome, with all his great estates, to marry Felix Holt, who has just come out of prison. " Could you share the life of a poor man, Esther ? " " If I thought well enough of him," she said, her smile coming again with the pretty saucy movement of her head. " Have you considered well what it would be—a very bare, a simple life ? " " Yes," said Esther, " without Attar of roses."

Self-sacrifice, too, was the grace of Romola ; and

it will be remembered how Maggie Tulliver found so much peace, at least for a time, in the adoption of this same moral principle.

Maggie had been panting for happiness, and she became ecstatic because now she thought she had found the key of it.   Her three chief books were the Bible, *Thomas à Kempis*, and *The Christian Year*.

There is nothing more striking than George Eliot's use of the great Law of Nemesis.   Somehow or another, it seems to have got burned into her mind, that it shall be ill with the wicked. Most certainly, she allows none, or next to none, of her wicked characters to escape a frightful ending. The Furies may walk with leaden foot, but they strike with iron hand.   That clever sinner, Mrs. Transome, has to exclaim, that "for more than twenty years she has not had an hour's happiness."

George Eliot seems very fond of finishing many of her characters by drowning them.   So she rounds off Grandcourt, and Tito, and Dunstan Cass; and so, too, unfortunately, she ends Maggie and Tom Tulliver.

As illustrating the use she makes of Retribution, there is the sad end of Gwendolen, and the tragic history of Hetty Sorrel, who was ruined by Captain Donnithorne.

Poor Hetty Sorrel soliloquises at the edge of the pool, whither she had gone to drown herself because of her coming shame, and could not.   "She set her teeth, and cursed Arthur, wishing that he too might know desolation and cold, and a life of shame, that he dared not end by death."   After the trial,

Hetty was condemned to death for the murder of her child. The judge said, "Hester Sorrel"—at the words, "and to be hanged by the neck till you be dead," a piercing shriek rang through the hall. It was Hetty's shriek. Adam started to his feet, and stretched out his arms towards her, but his arms could not reach her.

In strict justice, George Eliot causes Captain Donnithorne to suffer misery as well as Hetty, whom he has ruined. "It was all wrong," he says, "from the very first, and horrible wrong has come of it; God knows, I'd give my life if I could undo it."

V

Another characteristic of George Eliot as a Novelist is her marvellous epigrammatic power. Her writings are well mixed with Attic salt. We close with some of them :—

"A woman's hopes are woven of sunbeams ; a shadow annihilates them."

"Miss Jermyn is vulgarity personified, with large feet, and the most odious scent on her handkerchief, and a bonnet that looks like the fashion printed in capital letters."

"Esther went to meet Felix in prison; they looked straight into each other's eyes, as angels do when they tell the truth."

"I like to differ from everybody ; I think it is so stupid to agree."

"He was short, just above my shoulder, but he tried to make himself tall, by turning up his moustache, and keeping his beard long."

"You let the Bible alone ; you have got a jest-book, haven't you, as you read, and are proud on,—keep your dirty fingers to that."

"To hear some preachers, you'd think that a man must be doing nothing all's life but shutting's eyes and looking what's a-going on inside him. I know a man must have the love of God in his soul, and the Bible's God's word, but what does the Bible say, it says that God put His sperrit into the workman as built the tabernacle, to make all the carved work, and things as wanted a nice hand ; this is my way of looking at it. There's the sperrit of God, in all things and all times, weekday as well as Sunday, and in the great works and inventions, and i' the figuring and mechanics."

"I'll stick up for the pretty woman preachers ; I know they'd persuade me a deal sooner than ugly men."

"I am afraid the drink helped the brook to drown him."

"Both the sisters were old maids, for the prosaic reason that they had never received an eligible offer."

"Two things cannot be hidden, love and a cough."

"If I am not as wise as the three kings, I know how many legs go into one boot."

"Savonarola tells the people that God will not have silver crucifixes and starving stomachs."

"If you want to step into a round hole, you must make a ball of yourself."

"As Voltaire said, 'Incantations will destroy a flock of sheep if administered with a certain quantity of arsenic.'"

"Upon my word, I think the truth is the hardest missile one can be pelted with."

"Men do not want books to make them think lightly of vice, as if life were a vulgar joke."

MRS. BROWNING

"Let us love, let us live,
For the acts correspond."
MRS. BROWNING,
"A Rhapsody of Life's Progress."

"'Glory to God—to God!' he saith :
'KNOWLEDGE BY SUFFERING ENTERETH,
AND LIFE IS PERFECTED BY DEATH.'"
MRS. BROWNING, "A Vision of Poets."

"The truth which draws
Through all things upwards—that a twofold world
Must go to a perfect Cosmos."
MRS. BROWNING, "Aurora Leigh."

MRS. BROWNING

I

WHEN we remember that in the Victorian era more than forty names of women are considered worthy to rank as Poetesses, it may be well said of this era, as Mrs. Browning said of the Elizabethan, that its "Poets are as plentiful as birds in summer."

And yet, of all the Poetesses of the Victorian era, Mrs. Browning is far and away the greatest. It would not, indeed, be too much to say, that of the women who have ever sung songs, there is no one to place beside her, with the exception, it may be, of the ancient Sappho.

Almost all the interest that gathers round this gifted woman comes from her poems.

Born in 1805, she spent her childhood near Ledbury, Herefordshire, the country seat of her father, who was a wealthy Indian merchant. Along with her brother, she received a superior classical education from an excellent tutor. Never of robust health, she was for many years a confirmed invalid, almost confined to her room through an injury to her spine.

The most important and romantic event in her life took place in 1847, when, without either her father's knowledge or consent, she was secretly married to the celebrated Poet, Robert Browning, subsequently escaping with him from her father's house to the Continent, and settling finally in Florence. It was a love marriage of the purest kind. As Mrs. Browning herself has said, " I was constrained to act clandestinely, and did not choose to do so. God is witness, and will set it down as my heavy misfortune, and not my fault."

There is something romantic in the story of her flight,—she stole away from her father's house, attended by her maid and her dog, whilst the family were at dinner. The only difficulty was lest the dog in barking should betray the situation. Mrs. Browning, taking the dog into her confidence, said, " Oh Flush, if you make a sound, I'm lost." Flush understood, and crept after her mistress in silence. That same night Robert Browning and she took the boat to Havre, on their way to Paris.

It is not without interest, as explaining the shadows which abound in Mrs. Browning's life and poems, to remember that her father never forgave her for marrying Robert Browning, and remained, to her great sorrow, unreconciled and irreconcilable to his dying hour.

She died in 1862, leaving behind her one son, and only child.

Mrs. Browning's appearance is disappointing. We would have expected a more beautiful face, to correspond with the soul of one of the greatest " prophets of the beautiful." It is rather an earnest, calm, sad, intellectual—almost a masculine face.

But if the face cannot be called beautiful, the soul shining through the eyes certainly can be called, as it has been, "crystalline" in its beauty.

Mrs. Browning has realised in her own life what she devoutly desired for that large-brained woman and large-hearted man, George Sand, "The angel grace of a pure genius sanctified from blame."

It is to the undying honour of Mrs. Browning that she has never written a word, and never suggested a thought, which the purest of women could wish unwritten or unsuggested. Larger in brain, and larger in heart than George Sand, she was what George Sand was not, pure in soul as the Alpine snows.

Her Poetry not only makes the heart beat fast, and that is much: it makes the heart beat pure, and that is more.

Good, and good only, comes from the study of Mrs. Browning's poems. Such a study may not put more money into the pocket, nor make one hold one's sides with laughter, nor add anything at all to the stores of useful knowledge, and yet it will do much good. One cannot walk long or far in company with such a pure and lofty soul without having "the smell of thyme upon the feet."

There is much in her Poetry to lift above the enslaving Materialism of the age, and keep the roads open between the seen and the unseen. There is much to draw closer to the world of Nature and of man, to awaken a deeper interest in life and Art, and, what is perhaps best of all, to confirm in the Christian Faith.

II

It is no easy task to characterise Mrs. Browning's Poetry. For one thing, there is plenty of it. Had she written nothing but "Aurora Leigh," there would have been material enough for our study, and for her fame; but "Aurora Leigh" fills but one of six volumes of her poems.

There are amongst her poems, good, better, and best. The present writer prefers her Sonnets, including her "Sonnets from the Portuguese," her "Casa Guidi Windows," and, of course, her "Aurora Leigh." It is likely that she will be remembered longest by the last-named poem. She herself tells us that she has put all her strength into this work, and that it embodies her maturest convictions on life and Art. "Aurora Leigh" is the ripe fruit of her genius, and of her life's experiences.

Altogether it is a remarkable book, to be read and reread, always yielding literary, intellectual, and moral profit.

George Eliot has said that her Religion went to "the hammering in of nails," and Mrs. Browning has been religious, in George Eliot's sense of the word, in the writing of her books. She has put more than Religion into "Aurora Leigh": she put herself into it, "fertilising every leaf of it with her life's blood." There is no scamping of work here. Every word is selected with the utmost care. Every simile, and they are plentiful as stars, is wrought out with marked brevity, and yet with the happiest of insight. It is a book aglow with poetic fire, abounding with epigrams which have passed into current coin, and teeming with wisest lessons on the most pressing problems of our age.

We do not, of course, consider " Aurora Leigh " perfect. There is a good deal of Simple Simon about Romney Leigh, the " Christian Socialist." There is a good deal of the impossible about Marian Earle, that " daughter of the people." The best character in the book is Aurora Leigh ; and the success of this character no doubt lies in the fact, that, in accordance with her own dictum, in which she expresses her conception of the essence of the poetical art, Mrs. Browning " wrote as she looked into her own heart."

No doubt George Eliot could have managed the characters better than Mrs. Browning has handled them in " Aurora Leigh," and yet George Eliot could not come near the devoutness and wisdom which abound in this poem.

Amongst other things, Mrs. Browning would have us learn from this poem that Environment (one of the catch-words of Evolution) has not that effect upon character with which it is so often credited. One of the most detestable characters in the book, perhaps we ought to say the most detestable, is Lady Waldemar, who, although moving in the highest society, has the spirit of one of the devils, that would pull angels out of heaven. One of the most lovable characters is Marian Earle, who, although she was born in the lowest stratum of society and of the lowest of low people has in her much that is pure, noble, and self-sacrificing. It is quite true that Marian Earle passes through a dreadful experience in Paris; and yet Mrs. Browning takes care to let us know that that was Marian's misfortune and not her fault—"She was murdered, not seduced."

And then, Mrs. Browning would have us learn that Socialism, at least of the kind typified in Romney Leigh, is a distinct failure as a cure for the evils of our time.

Poor Romney Leigh, beginning with the best intentions as a reformer of the age, had to acknowledge, in the end, that he had clearly failed—"slipping the ends of life." He had failed to bridge the gulf between the rich and the poor, —failed even to get the return of gratitude for all his lifelong efforts. At last the people whom he had tried to help burned Leigh Hall to the ground, calling it "Leigh Hell." The fire left standing a stone staircase, typical of Romney's own life, which had led up to nothing at all.

And still another lesson is, that whilst Art is much, Love is more. A great part of "Aurora Leigh" is concerned with magnifying the office of the Poet, as against that of the "Carpet-duster," or of the "Social Reformer." And yet great as is the office of the Poet in bearing witness to the soul and God—to all, indeed, "behind this show," Love is more. Gifted as Aurora Leigh was as a Poetess, she was only satisfied when deep answered to deep—in her love to Romney Leigh, and Romney Leigh's love to her. Elsewhere Mrs. Browning writes—

> "Let us love, let us live,
> For the acts correspond."

III

In characterising Mrs. Browning from a literary point of view, reference might be made to the wide range of her poetical power. She has attempted and adorned every form of Poetical Literature—the Drama, as in " The Drama of Exile "; the Ballad, as in " Little Ellie "; the Lyric, as in the " Best Thing in the World "; and the Epic, as in her " Aurora Leigh." As a writer of Sonnets, Mrs. Browning takes rank beside Shakespeare himself.

To be convinced of her great and accurate scholarship, we have only to read her " Wine of Cyprus," or her " Vision of the Poets "—

> " Oh, our Aeschylus, the thunderous—
>   How he drove the bolted breath."

> " Oh, our Sophocles, the royal—
>   Who was born to monarch's place."

> " Our Euripides, the human,
>   With his droppings of warm tears,
> And his touching of things common
>   Till they rose to touch the spheres.
> Our Theocritus, our Bion,
>   And our Pindar's shining goals,—
> These were cupbearers undying
>   Of the wine that's meant for souls."

> " And my Plato, the divine one."

It has been said that, compared with man, a woman has one nerve more in her heart, and a cell less in her brain. Such an Aphorism does not, however, hold good with regard to Mrs. Browning, for she has more than the ordinary share of nerves in the woman's heart, and clearly more than the ordinary share of cells in the brain of either man or woman. Her intellectualism is much in evidence all through her writings.

As might have been expected, her Poetry abounds in womanliness—woman's best jewel. There are, certainly, passages in her husband's Poetry which Mrs. Browning could not have written : they are so profound and intense ; but it is also true, that there are many passages in Mrs. Browning's Poetry which her husband could not have written—touches, at once simple and naïve, which bespeak the woman's heart and hand.

We must not enter on this inviting theme, but we may give this from the " Drama of Exile," as indicating a woman's sphere and work in the world—

> " Henceforward, arise, aspire
> To all the calms, and magnanimities,
> The lofty uses, and the noble ends,
> The sanctified devotion, and full work,
> To which thou art elect for ever more—
> First woman, wife, and mother.
>
> .   .   .   .
>
> Rise, woman, rise,
> To thy peculiar and best altitudes
> Of doing good, and of enduring ill.
>
> .   .   .   .
>
> But go to ! thy love
> Shall chant itself its own beatitudes
> After its own life working. A child's kiss,
> Set on thy sighing lips, shall make thee glad ;
> A poor man served by thee, shall make thee rich ;
> A sick man helped by thee, shall make thee strong ;
> Thou shall be served thyself, by every sense
> Of service which thou renderest. Such a crown
> I set upon thy head."

There is, perhaps, not a more touching poem in the English language, and certainly not, so far as we know, one more comforting to a mother bereaved of her babe than " Isobel's Child."

At the outset the mother is tortured at the thought, that the first who should teach her the form of shrouds and of funerals should be her own firstborn, and so she prays, and prays so earnestly, that her babe should be spared. But against the prayer of the mother rises the cry of her little child, that the mother would lose her prayer, with its most loving cruelty—a prayer holding back the child from the Better Land.

The prayer of the little child prevails, and by and by the mother is seen, " at once God-satisfied and earth-undone "—

> " Oh you,
> Earth's tender and impassioned few,
> Take courage to entrust your love
> To Him so named, who guards above
> Its ends, and shall fulfil !
> Breaking the narrow prayers that may
> Befit your narrow hearts, away,
> In His broad, loving will."

Perhaps none of Mrs. Browning's poems has been more quoted than " The Cry of the Children "—a poem which proved of great service in bringing about better times for the children who had to work in factories and coal pits—

> " Do you hear the children weeping, Oh my brothers !
> Ere the sorrow comes with years ?
> They are leaning their young heads against their mothers,
> And *that* cannot stop their tears.

The young lambs are bleating in the meadows,
　　The young birds are chirping in the nest,
The young fawns are playing with the shadows,
　　The young flowers are blowing toward the west ;—
But the young, young children, Oh my brothers !
　　They are weeping bitterly,
They are weeping in the playtime of the others,
　　In the country of the free."

It goes without gainsaying, that only a woman
could have written as Mrs. Browning has done in
" Aurora Leigh,"—" Women know the way to rear
up children, to be just "—

　" They know a simple, merry, tender knack
　　Of tying sashes, fitting baby shoes ;
　And stringing pretty words that make no sense,
　And kissing full sense, into empty words."
　　　.　　.　　.　　.　　.　　.　　.
　　　.　.　.　.　" Fathers love as well,—
Mine did, I know,—but still with heavier brains."

And we have this as a description of Marian
Earle's baby, as seen by Aurora in that sad tene-
ment in the outskirts of Paris—

　　　　" There he lay upon his back,
The yearling creature, warm and moist with life
To the bottom of his dimples—to the ends
Of the lovely tumbled curls about his face.
　　　　Both his cheeks
Were hot and scarlet as the first live rose
The shepherd's heart-blood ebbed away into
The faster for his love.　And love was here
As instant ; in the pretty baby-mouth,
Shut close as if for dreaming that it sucked,
The little naked feet, drawn up the way
Of nestled birdlings ; everything so soft
And tender,—to the tiny hold-fast hands,
Which, closing on a finger into sleep,
Had kept the mould of 't."

IV

There are very few who excel Mrs. Browning as a
Literary Artist. In artistic excellence she is perhaps
next to Tennyson, and certainly superior to her
illustrious husband. Tennyson remarks of Robert
Browning, that whilst he had music in him he could
not get it out. It was otherwise with Mrs. Browning, for she had both the rhythmic thought and the
rhythmic expression. Although Tennyson would
" kick the geese out of the boat," referring to the
trick of introducing in Poetry too much of the letter
" S," there is one line of Mrs. Browning's that is
effective in the highest degree. It is that line
where, in describing subdued speech in the church,
amongst the company who had gathered for Romney
Leigh's marriage, she writes of " A spray of English
S's, soft as a silent hush."

The English language was plastic to her will,
answering perfectly every mood of thought and
shade of feeling. Now she writes verses, soft as the
zephyr, sweet as the sweetest lullaby that ever
mother sang to the child upon her knee ; and now
she writes verses that have in them the lightning's
flash, and all the force and rush of the torrent.

And, as Mrs. Browning is careful to teach, the
best way to secure good literary form is to let the
form take care of itself, once the soul is on fire.
Her watchword is, " Inward, ever more to Outward,"
—" Trust the Spirit, as sovran Nature does, to
make the form "—

" Keep up the fire,
And leave the generous flames to shape themselves."

This is what she says about rich people who
have been made rich out of the sufferings of little
children—

> "They look up with their pale and sunken faces,
>   And their look is dread to see,
> For they mind you of their angels, in high places,
>   With eyes turned on Deity."

And they say—

> "Our blood splashes upward, Oh gold-heaper!
>   And your purple shows your path;
> But the child's sob, in the silence, curses deeper
>   Than the strong man in his wrath."

She hurls a terrible curse on the selfish nation
which, after becoming itself free and prosperous,
yet utters no thought, and puts forth no effort, to
help other nations that are struggling after like
blessings—

> "Ye shall watch while kings conspire,
> Round the people's smouldering fire;
>   And warm for your part,
> Shall never dare,—Oh shame!
> To utter the thought into flame
> Which burns at your heart.
>   This is the curse.   Write.
>
> Ye shall watch while nations strive
> With the bloodhounds, die, or survive,
>   Drop faint from their jaws,
> Or throttle them backward to death;
> And only under your breath
> Shall favour the cause.
>   This is the curse.   Write."

For perfect simplicity there is not much to match
the Romance of "The Swan's Nest," or that *morceau*,
"The Best Thing in the World"—

" What's the best thing in the world ?
June-rose by May dew impearled ;
Sweet South-Wind, that means no rain ;—
Truth, not cruel to a friend ;
Pleasure, not in haste to end ;
Beauty, not self-decked and curled
Till its pride is over-plain ;
Light, that never makes you wink ;
Memory, that gives no pain ;
Love, when, *so*, you're loved again.
What's the best thing in the world ?—
Something out of it, I think."

Mrs. Browning describes with rare power, not only the scenery of the South of England, but also people she has met with in Society. Her pen-portraits of the most illustrious of the " Prophets of the Beautiful " are given with strokes few but fit.

She writes of Wordsworth's " solemn-thoughted idyll "; of Tennyson's " enchanted reverie "; of Browning, " as some pomegranate which, if cut deep down the middle, shows a heart within, blood-tinctured of a veined humanity."

Here is a verse or two from her " Vision of Poets "—

" Here Homer, with the broad suspense.
Of thunderous brows, and lips intense,
Of garrulous God innocence.

There Shakespeare, on whose forehead climb
The crowns o' the world ! Oh eyes sublime
With tears and laughters for all time.

.   .   .   .   .   .

And Burns with pungent passionings.
.   .   .   .   .   .

And Shelley in his white ideal,
All statue-blind.

.   .   .   .   .   .

> And poor, proud Byron, sad as grave,
> And salt as life, forlornly brave,
> And quivering with the dart he drave.
>
> .   .   .   .   .
>
> And visionary Coleridge."

This is how she hits off Lady Waldemar as a type of the brilliant stuff of which Society is made, the lady of the salon—whose crinkling silks were so impressive, who " took no thought of her garments falling off," so different from those who keep their bosom wholly to their babes—

> " The woman looked immortal. How they told
> Those alabaster shoulders and bare breasts ;
> On which the pearls drowned out of sight, in milk
> Were lost, excepting for the ruby clasp !
> They split the amaranth velvet-boddice down
> To the waist, or nearly, with the audacious press
> Of full-breathed beauty. If the heart within
> Were half as white !—but, if it were, perhaps
> The breast were closer covered, and the sight
> Less aspectable by half, too."

V

A touching and prevailing note of Mrs. Browning's Poetry is the note of sadness. The element of sorrow in human experience is not only fully recognised, but actually welcomed. Here, without any doubt, she writes after looking into her own heart. She could neither call her life nor her song happy. She speaks of having wept all day and night, of her sweet, sad, melancholy years, and of her " sad perplexed minors."

It was, indeed, a firm element in her creed that

no true Poet could avoid being sorrowful. "The
Poets on the tripod writhe." The vision comes only
when the head is on the stone. When she gathers
all the great Poets of the world into the Cathedral,
she has a verse startingly descriptive of the fact,
that each and all of them have been stricken with
sorrow—

> "But where the heart of each should beat,
> There seemed a wound instead of it,
> From whence the blood dropped to their feet,
>
> Drop after drop—dropped heavily.
> As century follows century
> Into the deep eternity."

We do not, of course, mean to say that there is
neither brightness nor happiness in Mrs. Browning's
poems, for there is much of both, and yet the prevailing note is the note of sadness. Ruskin speaks
of her as "weeping." It may be that the prevailing sadness may be accounted for, to a certain
extent, by the fact that she was at no time of
robust health, that for long she was a confirmed
invalid, and also by the circumstances of estrange-
ment from the old home. But the real cause lies
deeper.

Mrs. Browning knew well enough that her books
were not lively; indeed, she purposely avoided
writing lively books, preferring the yew to the ash,
for the yew, as she said, "is green longer, and alone
found worthy of the holy Christmas time."

Her sorrow was a sorrow of heart, the sign of
her sympathy with an age low, selfish, covetous, and
materialistic—an age in which people were eating

clay by handfuls, like men of the West; eating clay by lumps, until they were filled up to the throat with clay, and grew the grimy colour of the ground on which they were feeding; an age in which there were many even whose names are written in the Christian Church to no dishonour, "who diet still on mud, and splash the altars with it"—

> " The plague of gold strikes far and near,
>   And deep and strong it enters;
> This purple chimar which we wear
>   Makes madder than the Centaur's:
> Our thoughts grow blank, our words grow strange,
>   We cheer the pale gold-diggers,
> Each soul is worth so much on 'Change,
>   And marked, like sheep, with figures.
>   Be pitiful, O God!"

Although there is an undertone of sadness in her poems, yet they are not pessimistic. There may be loss in the world; there is no perdition. In " The Drama of Exile " the last word is, " Exiled, but not lost."

Her most welcome message is that purification, not pain, is the fruit of pain—that "saddest sighs swell sweetest sounds." Tears may be plentiful, yet they clear the vision. The drink may be bitter, but it is wholesome. One of her prayers is that God would bless our losses—our losses, not our gains. And so she concludes the whole matter by praising God for the "anguish which has tried, and the beauty which has satisfied "—

> " I know—is all the mourner saith,
> Knowledge by suffering entereth,
> And life is perfected by death.

.   .   .   .   .

'Glory to God—to God!' he saith:
    'KNOWLEDGE BY SUFFERING ENTERETH,
    AND LIFE IS PERFECTED BY DEATH.'"

VI

It is of great value to discover what a gifted woman like Mrs. Browning has to say on those problems which perpetually haunt the human mind.

Regarding Nature, she is an Idealist. She would remind us that the crucial heresy is the heresy of isolation, understanding our natural world too insularly, as if no spiritual counterpart completed it. She would teach as a cardinal truth, that there is nothing single or alone, that the Great Below is clenched by the Great Above, the body proving spirit as the effect the cause. She teaches as a doctrine, amounting almost to a revelation, that a "*twofold world must go to a perfect cosmos.*" It is impossible, without recognising this quality—the twofold cosmos understood by a twofold creature, to understand aright either Nature or Man. To go wrong here is to go wrong in everything—in Art, Morals, and Life.

It is a great mistake to separate the natural from the spiritual, or the spiritual from the natural. Without the spiritual the natural is impossible, and without the natural the spiritual is impotent. If we remember aright, this is what Carlyle means when he says that "matter exists spiritually." In this direction also lies Tennyson's assurance that he knows spirit better than he knows matter.

As Mrs. Browning says, the whole temporal show

is "related royally," and has "eterne significance."
Perhaps her finest passage is that which illustrates
this great truth, that spiritual significance burns
through the hieroglyphic of material show—

> "Nothing's small !
> No lily-muffled hum of a summer bee
> But finds some coupling with the spinning stars ;
> No pebble at your foot, but proves a sphere ;
> No chaffinch, but implies the cherubim ;
>
> . . . . . .
>
> Earth's crammed with heaven ;
> And every common bush afire with God ;
> But only he who sees, takes off his shoes."—

So far as Art is concerned, Mrs. Browning sends
home the important lesson that truth is beauty—
"the truest truth the fairest beauty." In her
estimation, only those Artists are great who are true
to Nature without, as sacramental, because witnessing to "what is behind the show," and who are also
true to Nature within. So far as Poets are concerned,
with the qualifying word that Art is selection, those
Poets are the greatest who are truest to themselves.

Mrs. Browning has an unqualified admiration for
the old saying, "Look into thine own heart and
write," adding, where "Nature is," God is. Art is
not the mere imitation of Nature, it is rather the
interpretation of Nature, getting at the significance
through the symbol, past models to Nature, and
past Nature to God Himself. Hence also this
saying of hers—"Where Poetry is, God is."

It is because Shakespeare is so true to himself,
and it is because Wordsworth threw himself, not at
Nature's feet, but on Nature's bosom, that they take

rank as the greatest of Poets. There is no Poet so individualistic as Shakespeare, and yet there is none so universal, simply because he lays bare his own heart, and so is kin to the whole world, for whom he thus speaks.

Mrs. Browning preaches the gospel of Work with as much intensity as Carlyle himself. She says, in one of her Sonnets, that God has anointed us with His odorous oil " to wrestle, not to reign." Get work, she writes, 'tis better than what you work to get. " Whoso fears God, fears to sit at ease." " After Adam, work was curse; but after Christ, work has turned to privilege."

It is evident from the whole trend of her writings that she has a deep reverence for man as man. She quotes with true insight this word from the Book of Revelation, " The measure of a man, that is, of the angel." There are, she thinks, infidels to Adam, as well as infidels to God. There is more real interest in any beggar boy than in all the streams or stars of the world.

Sure that man is not easily satisfied, she reminds us, in one of her Sonnets, that the secret of his torture lies in the " straitness of his place." There are those who think that they will find relief from the burden of unrest by travelling from place to place, from country to country. Not so, writes the Poetess. Relief is not to be found by travelling from the town to the country, nor from the country to the town, but only by travelling upward to the Throne of God, the soul's true rest.

Without doubt, Mrs. Browning is much of a

Democrat. She looks favourably on Democracy, as she thinks all true Poets do, being not disloyal to the high, but loyal to the low.

She is passionate for Liberty—" O Bella Liberta —O Bella," as she makes the little girl sing in the streets of Florence, in her " Casa Guidi Windows." Gazing on the procession as the people passed waving their flag, having for its motto, " Il popolo, Il popolo," she writes: "That word means dukedom, empire, majesty ; and kings in such an hour might read it so."

She cannot away with the mockery of the assumption of lordship and privilege, when we must come back to this at last, " that all's plain dirt "—" the first gravedigger proved it with his spade."

As might have been expected, full justice is done by her to the Passion of Love. Than Love, according to her teaching, there is nothing better in the world. Where, in all Literature, is there anything equal to her " Sonnets from the Portuguese," in " Tolling Love's silver Iterance " ?—

> "How do I love thee ! Let me count the ways—
>   I love thee to the depth, and breadth, and height,
>   My soul can reach, when feeling out of sight
> For the ends of Being, and ideal Grace.
> I love thee to the level of every day's
>   Most quiet need, by sun, and candle light.
>   I love thee freely, as men strive for Right ;
>   I love thee purely, as they turn from Praise ;
>   I love thee with the passion put to use,
> In my old griefs, and with my childhood's faith.
>   I love thee with a love I seem to lose
> With my lost saints,—I love thee with the breath,
>   Smiles, tears, of all my life ! and, if Good choose,
> I shall but love thee better after death."

Here is how she sings of the truth, that true Love means the union of hearts—

I

"Oh, wilt thou have my hand, Dear, to lie alone in thine?
As a little stone in a running stream, it seems to lie and
    pine.
Now drop the poor, pale hand, Dear, unfit to plight with
    thine.

II

Oh, wilt thou have my cheek, Dear, drawn closer to thine
    own?
My cheek is white, my cheek is worn, by many a tear run
    down.
Now leave a little space, Dear, lest it should wet thine own.

III

Oh, must thou have my soul, Dear, commingled with thy
    soul?
Red grows the cheek, and warm the hand; the part is in
    the whole;
Nor hands nor cheeks keep separate, when soul is joined to
    soul."

Although Mrs. Browning is far from being an advocate of peace at any price, she is distinctly a lover and a singer of peace. In her estimation, the method of settling quarrels by means of war is unadvanced and unchristian, witnessing to the Savagery, rather than the Civilisation, of mankind.

She says that children use the fist until they are of age to use the brain. And she longs for the time when people will fill the breach with olive branches, quench a lie with truth, and smite a foe upon the cheek with "Christ's most conquering kiss,"—" when drums and battlecries will go out in the music of the morning star," and thinkers take the place of fighters.

And yet, as has just been said, she will not have peace at any price, for there are circumstances when war is not only necessary, but an imperious necessity. She loves peace ; would write that word on Trees,—on Trees, but not on Gibbets, nor on Dungeons, nor on Chain-bolts, nor on starving Homes. Rather than have such a peace, a peace which is not fellowship, and includes not mercy, she would have—

> "The raking of the guns across
> The world, and shrieks against Heaven's architrave ;
> Rather the struggle in the slippery fosse,
> Of dying men, and horses, and the wave
> Blood-bubbling."

Mrs. Browning has much to say on the problem called "Social," a problem which has been called the problem of the age. Her best, and her last, work, "Aurora Leigh," is full of this problem. Romney Leigh, who figures there so largely, who is elbow-deep in social problems, is the type of a Christian Socialist. After doing his very best to solve the problem, Romney has to acknowledge utter failure. The people whom he sought to raise by his social methods turned upon him and rent him, burning, as has been already said, Leigh Hall, calling it "Leigh Hell."

One of the secrets of the worth of "Aurora Leigh," as a poem, is the light which it casts on the failure of Socialism to renovate Society.

For one thing, Socialism is too materialistic in

its methods to satisfy human nature. Romney Leigh looked upon the world as "a great carnivorous mouth," and to get worms to satisfy this mouth he tore up the violets, but found that all the worms he could supply could never satisfy that mouth.

Mrs. Browning, dealing with this theme of Socialism, has one sentence worthy of being written in letters of gold,—"The Soul's the way." No amount of barley feeding, or of material ease, will ever save or satisfy a human being: for a starved man is superior to a fed beast.

If a human being is to be saved or satisfied, it is only in Christ's way, and that is by "taking the soul," and so possessing the whole man, body and soul. "Not even Christ Himself can save man, else than as he hold's man's soul "—

> "It takes a soul
> To move a body,—it takes a high-souled man
> To move the masses, even to a cleaner stye.
> It takes the ideal, to blow an inch inside
> The dust of the actual; and your Fouriers fail,
> Because not Poets enough to understand
> That life develops from within."

And then Socialism, in Mrs. Browning's estimate, is too abstract; there being too much talking by aggregates, and thinking by systems, and facing evil in statistics. After all, if Society is to be changed, it must be changed by changing the units of which it is composed. If you want a grove of oaks, you must plant acorns. And if Society is to be changed, it can only be changed by changing individual hearts and lives; for what is Society but the expression of "men's single lives"—the loud sum of silent units.

And then, she does not fail to warn all who would seek to refine and elevate the people, to avoid going by any "pattern on their fingernails," instead of going by the pattern on the Mount. It is wise to leave room for God, and to work with Him in all social work. And so the conclusion of the whole matter is summed up thus—

> . . . . "Work humanly,
> And raise men's bodies still, by raising souls
> As God did first."
>
> .   .   .   .   .   .
>
> "Fourier's void,
> And Comte absurd,—and Cabet puerile.
> Subsist no rules of life, outside of life,
> No perfect manners, without Christian souls;
> The Christ Himself had been no Lawgiver
> Unless He had given the life, too, with the law."

VII

Mrs. Browning is to be hailed as a powerful ally of all those who have the cause of true Religion at heart. Neither atheistic nor sceptical, she is heartily and devoutly Christian, and a helper of many.

She knows too much of Church History, and of her Bible, to have any sympathy with the Roman Catholic Church, as a Church. An Apostolical Succession, filtering through the hands of Popes like Joan and Borgia—"a harlot and a devil"—"savours of the unclean." The Infallibility of a

Pope is as nothing compared with a better Infallibility still—the Infallibility of those who speak
the truth.

Since the whole tribe of Levi has been dis-
possessed, there is now no special priestly caste.
There is but one Temple, and but one Priest, and
that is the great High Priest—" He, He alone, He
alone for ever."

All Ritualism, juggling with the sleight of
surplice, candlestick, and altar-pall, is an ana-
chronism—the revival of what has long since
served its day. It is "the old temple wall over-
looking the churches of Christ."

Like her illustrious husband, she was very sure
of God, and that not by way of proofs, not by
scaling painfully the logic ladder step by step, but
" by way of sight which goes faster."

Her highest conception of God was a God of
Love, His Crown Name, more than which can
never be. She believed in the articulated Gospels
which showed " Christ crucified on the Tree." To
her the dearest name of Christ was the " Saving
One."

She believed in the Immortality of the soul for
one great reason, that the soul, different from the
body, held its youth. The body falls from the
chariot in the race, both weak and cold. Not so
the soul; and so she cries out rapturously, " On,
chariot! on, soul!"—

> " On the heaven-heights of truth,
> Oh, the soul keeps its youth,
> But the body faints sore." . . .

Prayer was very precious to her, because it fastened the soul on high; and as for the Church, she considered that its chief function was to awe "the times down from their sins." She loved all who loved the truth.

Mrs. Browning longed to see on the Literature of the age the Hand of Christ, a Hand whose touch she herself had felt, and whose touch brings blessing.

Like every Christian, her hands are lifted towards the East. Her last word is a word of hope. The work of God shall be done in the world. If by us, good and well, yet whether by us or not, that work shall be done. If God cannot work by us, He will work over us, and work towards the dawning of the new and dear day, and the coming of the "Perfect Noon." She closes her great work, "Aurora Leigh," with these words—

> —"Jasper first, I said;
> And second, sapphire; third, chalcedony;
> The rest in order: last, an amethyst."

The one word which Mrs. Browning uttered, as she breathed her last in her husband's arms in the old home at Casa Guidi, was the word "Beautiful"—fit word at once to close and designate her own life.

Let us say of her as she said of Savonarola—

> "Bring violets rather.—
> And having strewn the violets, reap the corn;
> And having reaped and garnered, bring the plough,
> And draw new furrows 'neath the healthy morn,
> And plant the great Hereafter, in this Now."

ROBERT BROWNING

"Why, he at least believed in Soul, was very sure of God."

BROWNING, "La Saisiaz."

"Aspire, break bounds! I say,
Endeavour to be good, and better still,
And best! Success is nought, endeavour's all."

BROWNING,
"Red Cotton Night-Cap Country."

"The year's at the spring
And day's at the morn;
Morning's at seven;
The hill-side's dew-pearled;
The lark's on the Wing;
The snail's on the thorn:
God's in His heaven—
All's right with the world!"

BROWNING, "Pippa Passes."

ROBERT BROWNING

I

BROWNING'S life was not an eventful one, in the usual sense of the word. It was rather a still, studious life, the main facts of which are easily recorded. He was born at Camberwell, London, in 1812; died at Asolo, Venice, on December 12th, 1889, and was buried on the last day of that year in the "Poet's Corner" in Westminster Abbey.

We gather one or two interesting facts about Browning from a volume recently published by Mrs. Sutherland Orr, a book for which we are upon the whole thankful, although it has been very severely and justly condemned for much of its spirit.

We learn from this source that his father was a bank clerk, and that his mother had Scotch blood in her veins. Carlyle calls Browning's mother "a divine woman," and Browning revered her deeply to the day of his death. Whatever Browning had of evangelical Christianity, he got from his mother; and to her, it has been said, he owed the metaphysical cast of his mind. The Brownings were Dissenters, although Mrs. Orr seeks to qualify this fact by remarking that they "were not bigoted ones,"—a very doubtful compliment.

We are told that Logic and Mathematics had no place in Robert Browning's education, and perhaps this may account, to a certain extent, for that tangledness which is so often laid to his charge. There is, unfortunately, some foundation for this charge; at the same time, it has to be said that the unintelligibility of his writings has been exaggerated.

Browning was evidently born a Poet. He could make verses when his head was no higher than a table, and was actually the Author of a volume of verse at the age of twelve. From his youth onwards he was an omnivorous reader, and came very early under the influence of Byron, Shelley, and Keats,—notably under the influence of Shelley, whom, in his first great poem, "Pauline," he calls "Sun-treader."

For a time he was both a Vegetarian and an Atheist.

To qualify himself for the vocation of Poet, Mrs. Orr, without any indication of poking fun at Browning, says that he read and digested the whole of Johnson's *Dictionary*. His way to popularity and fame was long and hard. For twenty years he had to suffer public neglect, owing, it has been hinted, to a critic characterising his Poetry as "balderdash."

It has been said that the most important thing that Browning ever did was to marry Miss Elizabeth Barrett—perhaps the very greatest of women-poets. There is much that is romantic about the courtship, the marriage, and the flight.

It was a case of love at first sight. Marriage seemed an utter impossibility, from the state of Miss Barrett's health, and at the same time her father's face was set like a flint against his daughter marrying Robert Browning, or any other person. Having refused his consent to allow his daughter to spend the coming winter in the South, there was before Miss Barrett but one course, and that was to break with the old home, and travel South as Mr. Browning's wife.

Browning's poems have been published in a series of seventeen volumes, and it must be confessed that they form very hard reading. As the Poet himself has said, "He brews stiff drink." They are not all of equal merit. There are whole poems and many passages which we must confess we do not understand; and we make this confession all the more readily, that Browning himself acknowledged his own inability to understand some of his own passages.

One or two of his tragedies must be pronounced dreary to a degree. Of all his works, we admire most "Pauline," the "Ring and the Book" (and more particularly, in the "Ring and the Book," the Pope's Summary); "Rabbi Ben Ezra," "La Saisiaz," and the "Death in the Desert."

The "Ring and the Book" is deservedly regarded as his masterpiece. It is the story of a Roman murder case, told ten times over from different points of view. It is a marvel of scholarship, of intellectual discrimination of character, and of poetic expression.

Browning excels in his delineation of " Pompilia,"
perfect in whiteness—" My flower, My rose I gather
—for the breast of God," as the old Pope says.
One of the most interesting characters is the Pope
himself, and one of the most suggestive portions of
the book is the old Pope's Philosophy of Life, well
worthy of being pondered by everyone, Pope or
peasant, Catholic or Protestant.

Browning's style varies very much.   Now it is
sweet and simple as a bird-note, and now of the
most painful and tortuous description—subjects
divorced from predicates; prepositions awanting;
all sorts of involutions, parentheses, and qualifying phrases; the structure of the passage often
compelling the reader, crablike, to go sideways,
and even to go backwards to get the meaning.
He takes, at times, remarkable liberties with
the English language, and with the rules of
grammar.

We understand that, after the publication of
" Pauline," someone very foolishly complained of
his verbiage; and it has been said that the young
Poet was so much stung by the criticism, that he
resolved that henceforward nobody would blame
him for being verbose.   Hence, say some, the condensed, and obscure character of his style.

II

Browning has been called the " Poet of the
Soul"; and when he is named thus he is, we
think, rightly named.   It is not too much to say

that there is some great Soul-idea at the foundation
of all his greatest poems.

He closes "La Saisiaz," with these words:
"Why, he at least believed in Soul, was very
sure of God." In his preface to "Sordello," a
great mystery to many, he says that it contains
incidents in the "development of the Soul," and
declares that little else is worth study. In that
remarkable poem, "A Death in the Desert," in
a deep metaphysical mood he writes of three
Souls in every person—What does, what knows,
what is. He looks upon the last Soul, What is,
as man's self. "The Soul holds God, and is upheld
by God."

When we designate Browning the "Poet of the
Soul," we mean that he has taken, as his sphere,
man's passion and man's mind. "Mine," he writes,
"be man's thoughts, and loves, and hates." In
"Ferishtah's Fancies," one of his latest poems, his
words are, "God is Soul—Souls I and Thou; with
Souls should Souls have place."

This Soul-passion accounts for many of the characteristics of his Poetry.

Here lies the secret of its pervading Individualism. He does not write upon man, but
upon men; not upon woman, but upon women.
He is very concrete, making his studies for the
most part studies of individual character. In
his works we come across all sorts of men and
women, good and bad, and neither good nor
bad, just as they are to be met with in History
and in everyday life. In "Pauline," where we

may trace Browning's spiritual autobiography, occur
these striking words—

> "I am singled out by God,
> No sin must touch me."

Elsewhere he writes—

> "Thou, and God exist."

Probably we may find in the fact that Browning
concerns himself so much with man's Soul, which,
as compared with man's body, is under lock and
key, the secret of the innerness and obscurity which
are notes of his Poetry.

In a humorous *jeu d'esprit* he takes the edge off
any unreasonable demand for lucidity in the discussion of mental and spiritual states, at the same
time counselling carefulness in coming to conclusions—

> "You are sick, that's sure—they say:
> Sick of what? they disagree—
> ''Tis the brain,'—thinks Doctor A.;
> ''Tis the heart,'—holds Doctor B.—
> 'The liver'—my life I'd lay!—
> 'The lungs!'—'The lights.'
>   Ah me!
> So ignorant of man's whole
> Of bodily organs, plain to see;—
> So sage and certain, frank and free,
> About what's under lock and key—
> Man's soul!"

It is this Soul-passion that gives to Browning's
Poetry its prevailing humanness. Unlike Scott or
Wordsworth, he cannot be called a Poet of Nature.
His song is not about the dark blue sea,—not, indeed,

about Nature at all, in the ordinary acceptation of
the word.   He goes straight for his theme to the
inmost chamber of the human heart—"Love, hope,
fear, faith; these make humanity.   These are its
signs, and note, and character."

We are of opinion that it is this master-passion
that likewise holds the secret of that seriousness
which characterises all his writings.   It would be
wrong to think that there is no humour in Browning, for there are true touches of humour here
and there; and yet it can scarcely be said of
him, as can be said of Burns and of Carlyle, that
humour is one of his notes.   There is humour in
" Fra Lippo Lippi," and in " The Pied Piper of Hamelin."   There is humour, and good sound moral
counsel as well, in a tripping little piece called " The
Twins "—Date and Dabitur.   " The Pied Piper of
Hamelin " concludes humorously, with a moral far
superior to the verse in which it is written—

" So Willy, let me and you be wipers
    Of scores out, with all men—especially pipers !
    And, whether they pipe us fróm rats, or fróm mice,
    If we've promised them aught, let us keep our promise ! "

And yet it is evident that Browning as a Poet
takes life seriously, although neither ascetic nor
sour.   Full of intensest life, he is so concerned with
such great problems as God, Freedom, and Immortality, that he has neither the desire nor the time
to give full play to the humorous mood.

And then, we are inclined to think that it is
because Browning has made the Soul the sphere of
his art that he is so universal in his sympathies.

With the exception of Shakespeare, there is no Poet so many-sided as Browning. He offers food to satisfy the hunger of every part of human nature. He has literally made the earth his vineyard.

Hence we find him delineating all kinds of life —ancient and modern, eastern and western, simple and profound. "Saul," "Rabbi Ben Ezra," and "The Death in the Desert," speak to his sympathy with Hebrew life. There are pictures of life purely Eastern in "The Muléykeh" and in "Ferishtah's Fancies." The throbbings of Greek life find faithful expression in "Balaustion's Adventure" and "Aristophanes' Apology." Italian life finds expression in many a poem, but notably in his Opus Magnum, "The Ring and the Book." We have Parisian life in "Red Cotton Night-cap Country," and Russian life in "Iván Ivànovitch." We have, of course, English life in abundance. Justice is done to scholarly life, in "The Grammarian"; to Artistic life, in "The Pictures at Florence"; to Musical life, as in "Abt Vogler"; to Soldier life, in "Clive"; to Sailor life, in "Hervé Riel"; to Commercial life, in "The Shop"; and to Ecclesiastical life, as in "Bishop Blougram's Apology."

A very distinctive note of Browning's Poetry, due to his intense interest in the Soul, is its religious tendency. He is, of course, too robust and earnest in spirit to indulge in any cheap sentiment in this sacred sphere.

When we speak of the Religiousness of Browning's Poetry, we do not simply mean that his Poetry is as a well which is undefiled, although it has to

be said to his praise that his Poetry is as pure as
the Alpine snows.   There is not, in all his writings,
a thought or word which the purest could wish
unuttered.   In this jasper quality of pureness he
makes for himself a place of honour side by side
with Wordsworth and Tennyson, neither of whom
" uttered anything base."

The Religiousness of Browning's Poetry manifests
itself in the fact that it gives a supreme place to
the two great realities, the Soul and God, and that
these are for each other,—the Soul needing, seeking,
and finding God,—the Soul loving and being beloved
by God.

The present writer cannot put into words what
he owes to Browning for strengthening him in the
Christian Faith, and encouraging him in the Christian life.   Just as Browning himself says, that
neither frost nor fire will ever freeze or burn out
of him his thankfulness to God in Christ for truth
thus received, so the present writer desires to put
it on record that neither frost nor fire will ever
freeze or burn out of him thankfulness to Browning
for the help which he has given.

Browning thinks but little of the Ritualisms of
the Church, speaks, indeed, of the elaborate Cere-
monial in St. Peter's, Rome, as the " Raree Show of
St. Peter's Successors," and has ill-concealed disgust
for what he calls " To-day's Buffoonery of Posturings
and Petticoatings."   He believes that the best return
that one can make to God, and to His true Church,
for blessings received—that " the best gifts where-
with to gift the Church," is to live a pure life.   In

"Red Cotton Night-Cap Country" he tells of a guilty pair, M. Léonce Miranda and Clara, who sought to make amends for a guilty life by giving to the Church a magnificent jewel, and by presenting to the Virgin some rich lace.   Says Browning—

> "Your jewel, brother, is a blotch;
> Sister, your lace trails ordure.   Leave your sins,
> And so best gift with Crown, and grace with Robe."

If we mistake not, Browning traces for us in "Pauline" the development of his own Soul to greater power.   He there acknowledges the influence upon him of the Poet Shelley, "Sun-treader," and likewise the influences of Greek Literature and Philosophy, more particularly the Philosophy of Plato and the Poetry of Euripides.   The land of Greece had then a great fascination for him, with its "dim clustered isles in the blue sea."

In "Pauline" he tells what may be called the story of his conversion.   In a crisis of his life, with all his powers full upon him, he was tempted to accept worship rather than render it.   His Soul was like a temple; "only God was gone."   Shadows, troops of shadows, came kneeling to him, proffering to him their worship.   Suddenly this searching question rushed into his mind, "Should my heart not worship too?"   In this crisis he was able, happily, to answer affirmatively.   Yes, his heart would worship too—and worship God.   What was he hungering for but God?—

> "My God, my God,—even from myself
> I need Thee,
> And I feel Thee, and I love Thee."

And then follows one of the most beautiful apos-
trophes to the Lord Jesus Christ that has ever been
penned, beginning with, " O thou pale form."—In
the course of it he says—

> "Let me die
> Ages, so I see Thee ;—
>
> .   .   .   .   .   .
>
> A mortal, sin's familiar friend, doth here
> Avow, that he will give all earth's reward
> But to believe, and humbly teach, the faith
> In suffering, and poverty, and shame,
> Only believing, he is not unloved."

As all readers of Browning will remember, the
Poet confesses more than once that he has " touched
the hem of His garment."   And in his " Christmas-
Eve, and Easter-Day " he thus describes his relationship to the Son of God—

> "I have looked to Thee from the beginning,—
> Straight up to Thee—through all the world."

We cannot say that he has made any discovery
in the spiritual world.   He says nothing that has
not been said before by writers like his gifted wife,
by Tennyson, and Ruskin, and Carlyle ; nevertheless,
he says what he has got to say with an originality,
a depth, and an intensity that endow truth with a
new worth.

III

We regard Browning as essentially a religious
man, and a religious writer.   Neither unchristian
nor antichristian, he is at once a defender and a
strengthener of the Faith.

If he be otherwise, we must confess that, after

a careful study, we are entirely unaware of it. There is not a single Christian Doctrine or position assailed by him,—nay, the very opposite is the case, for it is not too much to say that there is not a single Christian position or Doctrine which is not made stronger by his writings.

His creed is not only very definite, but, if we compare "Pauline" with "Asolando," his first volume and his last, with an interval of half a century between them, it will be found that he has not varied essentially in his religious views. This may be taken as the summary of both these volumes,— "I believe in God, in truth, and love." He concludes "La Saisiaz," one of the greatest and least dramatic of his poems, with the confession, that he at least "believed in Soul, and was very sure of God."

He was no Atheist, for God to him was the great reality. He was no Materialist, for he believed in Soul, believed, indeed, that matter was here for the sake of Soul, and that man was only man in so far as Soul obtained its right pre-eminence. In "Sordello" he teaches that Joy comes when so much of "Soul is wreaked in Time on Matter, and that Sorrow comes by subliming Matter beyond the scheme." In "Rabbi Ben Ezra" he asks—

> "What is he but a brute
> Whose flesh has soul to suit—
> Whose spirit works, lest arms and legs want play?
> To man propose this test,—
> Thy body at its best,
> How far can that project thy soul on its lone way?"

Browning was intensely earnest, too, with his

beliefs. "Strive" is one of his favourite words,
" Strive and thrive " being the very last words which
he uttered. It is the devil, that old stager, who
leads downwards, "fiddling all the way." His
words in " Rabbi Ben Ezra " are well known—

> "Then welcome each rebuff
>   That turns earth's smoothness rough,
> Each sting, that bids nor sit, nor stand, but go !
>   Be our joys three parts pain !
>   Strive, and hold cheap the strain ;
> Learn, nor account the pang ;—dare, never grudge the throe."

As all readers of his " Paracelsus " will remember,
he is no worshipper of " poor intellect."

His Biographer, Mrs. Sutherland Orr, to whom
we have referred, comes, reluctantly it is true, yet
comes to the conclusion that Robert Browning was
a " Christian *in his own way*." Well, the great
matter, as will be readily admitted, is that he was
a Christian at all, and by any way. So be it that
Browning got to the City, the way he took is
neither here nor there. It is said that he became
religious by "reading his own Soul." If so, this
testifies, surely, to the clearness of the writing in the
volume which is within. We recall one of his most
striking words,—words of the Pope in the "Ring and
the Book,"—" Correct the portrait by the living face,
man's God with God's God in the mind of man."

Here we would only ask, which is the portrait
and which is the living face ? Browning may consider, as we rather think he does, that the portrait
is in the Book, and that the living face is in the Soul,
and another may consider that the living face is in

the Book, or, better still, in the Christ, and that the portrait is in the Soul; but surely it is wise to allow liberty.

It is said that Browning did not believe in Dogma, which we take to mean that he did not believe in Christian Doctrine, precisely or scientifically expressed. It may be granted, that he had no sympathy with discussions about the names of God, when there was so much more important work to do; and it may also be granted, that he would have had difficulty in accepting the Thirty-Nine Articles; and yet it is well to remember, that if Browning did not compress his religious beliefs into the mould of the understanding, he most assuredly passed them all through the furnace of his heart, trying them there as gold is tried in the fire.

So far as we can make out, he believed in a Personal God, in a Personal Christ, in His Divinity and Incarnation, and in the Immortality of man, quite a precious bundle of Christian Doctrines, any one of which, sincerely believed, is revolutionary in its power.

It is clear that Browning believed in the transcendent importance of Christ. To him Christ was the Crux of the whole world, spiritual, intellectual, moral, and social. We believe that he was speaking for himself, as well as for the Apostle John, when he put on record these words, in "A Death in the Desert,"—"I say, the acknowledgment of God in Christ, accepted by thy reason, solves for thee all questions in the earth, or out of it." We also recall how he closes this remarkable poem—"Call Christ, then, the illimitable God, or lost." And in that striking poem, "An Epistle," which contains

the strange medical experiences of Karshish, The
Arab Physician, he concludes—

> " The very God !
> Think Abib; dost thou think !
> So the All-great, were the All-Loving too,—
> So, through the thunder, comes a human voice,
> Saying, 'O heart, I made, a heart beats here !
> Face, my hands fashioned, see it in Myself !
> Thou hast no power, nor may'st conceive of mine,
> But love, I gave thee, with myself to love,
> And thou must love me, who have died for thee.' "

Browning has sufficient insight to see somewhat
into the mystery of the Cross.   To him the Crown
of Thorns, as a sign of divine love, suffering for those
who are loved, is more resplendent than all the
jewelled crowns of earth,—" the topmost, ineffablest,
uttermost crown."

He believes, too, in Christ as beyond all Moralities.
With the look of genius he sees that it is one thing
to tell people what to do, and quite another thing
to get people to do it.   And so he says with great
wisdom, that the real God-function—a function
which God in Christ is always performing, is " to
furnish a motive, and an injunction for practising
what we know already."

With equal wisdom, Browning sees that the
glory of Christianity—a glory which lifts it clean
above all schemes of Morality, ancient and modern—
lies in the fact that Christianity shifts faith from
the region of the abstract to the region of the
personal.   What is the point, asks the Poet, on
which Christ Himself lays stress ?   His words do
not run—" Believe in good, in justice, and in truth ";

but His words are—" Believe in Me, who lived and died, yet essentially am Lord of life."

Referring to Christ's claim to Divinity, he calls it " an important stumble which none other in the world ever seriously made." And so we venture to remark that this element in Christianity, which centres all things in the Person of Christ, *is an important stumble*,—a stumble which differentiates it, ethically considered, from all the moral schemes of the world.

As all readers of Browning's works know, one of the truths which shines through his pages with the intensity of an Arctic sun, is the truth that " *God is love.*" Whether Browning got this Doctrine by reading his own Soul, or in any other way, the fact remains that he got hold of this truth, and that he would not let it go. He believes that God is Love, and that a loveless God is an impossibility—

> " God is good, and the rest is breath,—
> .   .   .   .   .   .
> His love, the nobler dower.
> For the loving worm, within its clod,
> Were diviner than a loveless God
> Amid His worlds "—

Believing in those great verities, we are not surprised that Browning also holds that the essential feature in any man's Religion is the heart's response to this Divine Love of God in Christ,—love answering to love as deep calleth to deep. To him Love is at once the truth of Life and of Religion—

> " Whole centuries of folly, noise, and sin !
> Shut them in ;
> With their triumphs, and their glories, and the rest !
> Love is best."

Next to his insistence on the central Doctrine that God is Love, is his hope in the Immortality of man. We do not say that in this hope Browning is abreast of the Gospel, for he is not. We welcome, however, his great poem on this subject —"La Saisiaz," as a preparation for the Gospel.

We are not of those who think that in this poem Browning culpably overlooks the teaching of the Bible on the all-important theme of Man's Immortality. It is the honest effort of an earnest soul to solve this question for himself, and from himself.

The circumstances in which it was written are at once interesting and pathetic. Just as we owe Tennyson's great poem, "In Memoriam," to the loss of a great friend, so we owe Browning's great poem, "La Saisiaz" to a similar cause. He had arranged to climb with a lady friend to the platform of Salève, and thence survey "Mont Blanc together." When the morning came, Browning was ready and waiting for his companion, but no companion appeared at the appointed hour. "For once from no far mound, waved salute a tall white figure." "All awaits us, ranged and ready, yet she violates the bond, neither leans, nor looks, nor listens,—why is this?"

The answer to the question was to be found in the sad fact of the startlingly sudden death of his lady friend. She was gone, and never again on earth would he see that earnest face. Paying piteous duty, Browning buried his friend, or rather what seemed his friend, in a quiet spot at the foot

of Salève, where "low walls stopped the vine's
approach." Five days after this sad event he
made the ascent all alone, to "Salève's own platform, facing a glory which strikes greatness
small."

It was when he was on the platform of Salève
that the idea of this poem, "La Saisiaz," came
into his mind. It was there, and during his
descent in the sunset, that he found and forged
this chain, finding afterwards that a something in
him would not rest until he had unravelled every
tangle, link by link. In this poem Browning, like
Tennyson, fights with death, and, we are pleased to
add, gets and claims the victory.

These are some of the forms in which he puts
the question, to which in his poem he sets himself
to give an answer—"Does the soul survive the
body?—is there God's self, no or yes?" "Was
ending, ending once, and always, when you died?"—

> " Did the face, the form I lifted, as it lay, reveal the loss,
>   Not alone of life, but soul? A tribute to yon flowers and
>   moss,
>   What of you remains beside."

Or again—

> " We who, darkling, timed the day's birth,—struggling
>   testified to peace,—
>   Earned, by dint of failure, triumph,—we, creative thought,
>   must cease!"

There is perhaps nothing in Literature to equal
the straightforwardness and the earnestness of this
questioning, unless it be that earnest cry of his

brother-poet Tennyson after the loss of his dear
friend, Arthur Hallam—

> " And saying; 'Comes he thus, my friend?
>   Is this the end of all my care?'
>   And circle moaning in the air:
> Is this the end ? Is this the end ?"

Browning knows well that his answer will
be the answer of weakness, and yet he says that
weakness need not be falseness. He is going to
tell out to others what has been the " whisper of
his Soul " to him. He neither professes to utter
what the Bible contains nor what the Church
teaches on this great question; but he does profess
to utter what has been the whisper which his Soul
has whispered to him. It is true that, after all,
the solution does not come to much, ending only in
the hope of Man's Immortality—

> "So, I hope,—no more than hope, but hope,—no less than
>   hope."

Yet the moral worth of this poem rests on the
fact, that the revelation of the Book of the human
Soul, as interpreted by the Poet, is in perfect
harmony with the revelation of the Bible. The
response of man's Soul, however, is inadequate and
feeble compared to the response of God—

> " Well, and wherefore, shall it daunt me, when 'tis I myself
>   am tasked,
>   When, by weakness, weakness questioned, weakly answers,
>   —weakly asked?
>   Weakness never needs be falseness; truth is truth in each
>   degree,
>   Thunder-pealed by God to Nature, whispered by my soul,
>   to me;

> Nay, the weakness turns to strength, and triumphs in a
> truth beyond,
> Mine is but man's truest answer,—how were it, did God
> respond ? "

The very fact that Browning draws such a contrast between the response of his Soul and the response of God, opens not only a door for a Divine Revelation, but makes for that revelation a large and a wealthy place. Instead of being hostile to Revelation, it is a true *preparatio evangelica.* " La Saisiaz " prepares the way for a revelation from God, because of its strenuous expression of the Soul's longing and crying for a fuller light than that which it possesses in itself.

" La Saisiaz " is the twilight, whilst Divine Revelation is the noontide. It is the whisper, whilst Revelation is the sphere song. It is the clod, whilst Revelation is the avalanche. Browning has asked, " How were it, did God respond ? " and we can answer the question,—It is well; for God has responded through the Lord Jesus Christ, Who has abolished death, and brought Life and Immortality to light through His Gospel.

Browning's problem was to solve, on a natural basis, the certainty of man's personal Immortality. But the Poet confesses that he has failed to reach this certainty on such a basis. He cannot thus attain to certainty; nay, he is very bold, for he declares that such certainty is undesirable, and would be indeed disastrous.

But whilst he confesses to a conclusion of uncertainty as to Immortality, so far as he can interpret the Soul of man, he at the same time confesses to a Hope,—a constant, arrowy Hope of Man's Immortality. A large part of the poem is taken up with the reasons why he cannot attain to certainty, and how, nevertheless, he not only hopes, but justifies his Hope of Immortality—a Hope which is to him, to use the well-known words of Wordsworth, "A Presence which is not to be put by."

Browning reminds us that the so-called "Proofs" fail to bring about in him a certainty of Immortality. He passes them in review very rapidly, and as rapidly dismisses them as incapable of producing assurance.

There are those who argue for the assurance of Immortality, because *God seems good and wise.* In dealing with this argument, he says that this is just what he is not sure about on natural grounds. Another argument is, that *God seems potent.* Browning replies, that if God be potent, why, then, are right and wrong at strife? Well, then, say others, in dealing with this great question of Immortality, *we want it anyhow.* Alas! the Poet writes of many wants and many hopes which in this life never have complete fulfilment.

Others say, again, *that the soul is not the body.* True, answers the Poet—

> " And the breath is not the flute ;
>   Both together make the music :
>   Either marred, and all is mute."

Last of all, there are many who say, when giving the ground of their assurance in Immortality, " *we believe.*" But even here the Poet will not allow a foundation for assurance. Why he does not, we must confess we do not understand ; but the fact remains, that he does not. Slow, sorrowful, yet decided, Browning overturns this proffered cup of comfort.

Although he has upon his side the support of many able philosophical thinkers in dealing thus with the proofs of Immortality, yet we would venture to make these two observations.

It seems that Browning has neither enumerated all the arguments in favour of Immortality on the natural basis, nor has he given the best of them. He ought to have given a more prominent place to the Maker of man,—to the universal and quenchless aspiration of man after Immortality,—to the Justice of God,—or, as Emerson has put it, to the fact that "The Creator will keep His word with us." Neither has he given, as he ought to have done, a place to the fact of human Personality, nor to the fact of human Freedom, carrying along with it moral Responsibility.

And then Browning evidently has forgotten that whilst each argument, taken singly, may fail to produce certainty, yet when argument is added to argument certainty almost invariably arises from their accumulation. As Newman has pointed out in his *Apologia*, it is in this way—through the assemblage of probabilities, that certitude arises.

In justifying his Hope of Immortality, which is the only conclusion that Browning declares he can come to on a natural basis, he falls back on experience, and on his own experience. Nay, he falls back on only one datum of experience, and that is the fact of his own existence—" The midway point," " I am."

Of this he is sure. This fact is the foundation of all knowledge, and the rest is but surmise. It is, then, on this one fact that he bases his hope of Immortality, not on Nature above him, nor around him, nor beneath him ; not in his " deepest sentient Self, not in Aspiration, Reminiscence, plausibilities of Trust," but on this one fact, *that he is*—" caused and a cause."

This fact of existence of which he is so sure compels him to make certain presuppositions or assumptions. It has been said, that in making those assumptions Browning places himself at issue with scientific thought. To this we cannot agree, for Science is compelled to make assumption after assumption before it can proceed a single step.

Browning assumes two facts to begin with—" God there is, and Soul there is." These he declares to be facts, and to be, indeed, for him the only facts. Should anyone call upon the Poet first of all to prove his facts, then he replies, as if dowered with the scorn of scorn—

> " Prove them facts ? that they o'erpass my power of proving, proves them such :
> Fact it is, I know, I know not something which is fact as much."

Browning also assumed that this earth is but a pupil's place ; and life and time, with all their " chances, changes, just probation-space." He lays

12

very great stress on this last fact, making it, indeed, his sheet-anchor. He writes of Life as being—

> " My whole sole chance to prove,—although at man's apparent cost,—
> What is beauteous, and what ugly, right to strive for, right to shun ;
> Fit to help, and fit to hinder,—prove my forces every one ;
> Good and evil,—learn life's lesson, hate of evil, love of good ;
> As 'tis set me, understand so much as may be understood."

If we deny to the Poet this assumption, and if we also deny to him the fact that the very conception of this life points to the realisation of a higher and a better, then he declares that there gathers around his Soul a darkness that may be felt, and a sorrow that breaks out in an exceeding bitter cry, forcing upon him the conviction that in this world " sorrow has it over joy," and God is dethroned. Browning gives expression to his feelings on this matter in a passage of marvellous force and vehemence—

> " If the harsh throes of the prelude die not off into the swell
> Of that perfect piece they sting me to become a-strain for,—if
> Roughness of the long rock-clamber lead not to the last of cliff, etc.
>
> .   .   .   .
>
> I must say—or choke in silence—'Howsoever came my fate,
> Sorrow did and joy did nowise,—life well weighed,—preponderate.'
> By necessity ordained thus ? I shall bear as best I can ;
> By a cause all-good, all-wise, all-potent ? No, as I am man ! "

The conclusion, then, of the whole matter, so far

as the Poet's experience is concerned, is just this, that the granting of the Second Life will not only put him at perfect peace with this one, will not only enable him to see in this present life a wonderful meaning and power, but will likewise lead him actually to glory, not only in this life, but in all its misfortunes, its defeats, its sorrows, and its trials—

> " Only grant my soul may carry high, through death, this
> life unspilled ;
> Brimming though it be with knowledge, life's loss, drop by
> drop, distilled ;
> I shall boast it mine,—the balsam,—bless each kindly
> wrench, that wrung
> From life's tree its inmost virtue tapped the root, whence
> pleasures sprung,
> Barked the bole, and broke the bough, and bruised the
> berry, left all grace,
> Ashes in death's stern alembic, loosed elixir in its place ! "

It is surely very significant, as showing the attitude of Browning to this great theme of Immortality, to remember that his very last words to those who loved him, as recorded in his last Book of Poems, *Asolando*, are—

> " One who never turned his back but marched breast forward,
> Never doubted clouds would break ;
> Never dreamed, though right were worsted, wrong would
> triumph,
> Held we fall to rise, are baffled to fight better,
> Sleep to wake,
>
> No, at noonday in the bustle of man's work-time
> Greet the unseen with a cheer !
> Bid him forward, breast and back as either should be,
> ' Strive and thrive ! ' cry, ' Speed,—fight on, fare ever,'
> There as here ! "

IV

It is instructive to note what a thinker and scholar, what a Humanist and Poet like Browning has to say on those subjects which lie close to the hearts of all.

He has much to say on the part which Doubting plays in man's beliefs. It might have been expected that one who felt so fully the pressure of the age would give a considerable space to this matter of Doubting,—this "malady of thought," as someone has called it, so characteristic of our time. And in this we are not disappointed, for Browning, like Tennyson, looked the subject full in the face and got the victory; getting and giving peace.

To him Doubting is simply inevitable in the history of the development of every earnest and thoughtful Soul. He has nothing but scorn for the finished finite clods, "untroubled by a spark." We are not, indeed, sure if Browning would not go as far as to say, that it is impossible to have Faith without having Doubt as well. Although we cannot altogether agree with this, we are quite ready to recognise that no one can have the joy of Faith who has not also had the pain of Doubt.

It is, however, a clear element in Browning's creed that Doubting is a stepping-stone to that higher mood which we call Faith, and that Doubting is always more or less with us.

In the poem called " Rephan," where "all's at most," where there is "no want,—no growth,—no beginning,—no ending,—no distaste,—no blessing, —no curse,—no springs,—no hope,—no fear"— where there is a "standstill throughout eternity," all happy—all serene—there life grows a-tremble to turn to our human life, with all its hopes, and fears, and loves, and hates.

The dweller there longs to exchange his residence in the star Rephan, for a residence in this earth of ours, with all its unrest—

"So wouldst thou strive, not rest?

. . . .

Burn, and not smoulder, win by worth;
Not rest content with a wealth, that's dearth?
Thou art past Rephan, thy place be Earth."

So, too, is it that in "Rabbi Ben Ezra" he declares, "I prize the doubt."

In "Bishop Blougram's Apology," a poem almost entirely devoted to reasoning on this matter, the conclusion is, that the great difference between the believer and the unbeliever may be thus expressed: "The unbeliever lives a life of Doubt, diversified by Faith; whilst the believer lives a life of Faith, diversified by Doubt." In that same poem there is a fine passage, in which the writer shows the great difficulty which the unbeliever has got in guarding his unbelief, just when he thinks he is safest—

"There's a sunset touch,
A fancy from a flower-bell, someone's death;
A chorus-ending from Euripides."

And ere the unbeliever is aware, fifty hopes and

fears not only enter into the Soul, but dance there round that ancient idol—The Grand Perhaps!—

Browning would seem to urge contentment upon all who are able to say, that whilst Doubt is great, Faith is greater still. With me, says the Bishop, Faith means "perpetual unbelief kept quiet, like the snake 'neath Michael's foot, who stands calm just because he feels it writhe."

Of this, however, he is sure, that there can be no comparison between the blessings and the peace which come of Faith, and the unrest and barrenness which go along with unbelief. Positive belief brings out the best of a man, and bears fruit in power, peace, pleasantness, and length of days. "Positive belief does this, and unbelief no whit of this."

Browning has very worthy conceptions of man; he is not Byronic,—to him man is neither a brute nor an angel, but a "God in germ."

One of his fundamental beliefs, making him a writer essentially optimistic, is that man has been placed in this world, not to be miserable, but to be joyful. He has, of course, to acknowledge that there is much in life that is not only black, but very black; but then, he is also sure that there is much in life that is not only white, but very white. In his optimism, not only does the white predominate, but he is very sure that it will do so as time goes on. This is the first and last of his Philosophy—"Blacks blur thy white? not mine."

He holds that joy is the end of life—that where-ever enjoyment is, there God is; that joy is gain, and gain is gain, however small—

> "I find earth, not grey but rosy,
>   Heaven not grim, but fair of hue.
>   Do I stoop? I pluck a posy.
>   Do I stand and stare? All's blue."

We have a similar note in that exquisite little song which Pippa sings as she passes the villa on New Year's morning—

> "The year's at the spring
>   And day's at the morn;
>   Morning's at seven;
>   The hill-side's dew-pearled;
>   The lark's on the wing;
>   The snail's on the thorn;
>   God's in His heaven,—
>   All's right with the world."

We are not sure but that we may accept the last two lines of Pippa's song, "*God's in His heaven, All's right with the world,*" as the shortest expression of Browning's views regarding the course of Divine Providence as directing human life and history.

Although he writes so distinctly about joy being the end of life, he does not regard life as full of sugarplums. Instead, he acknowledges to the full the earnest, stern, probationary side of existence. He knows well, and expresses forcibly the truth, that life is pregnant with responsibility, disappointment, temptation, and sins.

He knows right well that there is much wickedness in life, and gives ample utterance to the great law of Retribution. He furnishes a terrible illustration of this law in the poem just referred to, "Pippa

Passes," where he delineates the wicked loves of
Ottima and Sebald,—Ottima, magnificent in sin,
and the horrible, awful ending of it all.   These
are Sebald's words to Ottima, his guilty paramour,
" I'm proud to feel such torments; I've done the
deed and pay its price.   I hate, hate, curse you.
God's in His heaven."

Browning also gives expression to this same law
of Retribution in that intensely interesting Tragedy,
" A Blot in the 'Scutcheon."   It is poor, erring,
wicked Lady Mildred who says—

> "Sin has surprised us.   So will punishment.
>
> •   •   •   •   •   •   •   •
>
> ^   All our woeful story,—
> The love, the shame, and the despair,—with them
> Round me, aghast, as round some cursed fount
> That should spirt water, and spouts blood."

Lady Mildred speaks of the " brief madness and
the long despair "—

> " I was so young, I loved him so ; I had
> No mother, God forgot me, and I fell."

And the outcome is of the saddest, ending in her
own death, the death of her young lover, and the
suicide of her brother—

> " A froth is oozing through his clenched teeth,
> Both lips, where they're not bitten through, are black."

These are her brother's dying words—

> .   .   .   " You see how blood
> Must wash one blot away : the first blot came,
> And the first blood came."

There is a clear sterling ring about Browning
when he comes to the motives which ought to govern

the life of man. Belonging to the school of Wordsworth, Carlyle, and Kant, he would have us " do our
duty, for duty's sake." " He looked beyond the world
for truth and beauty, sought, found, and did his duty."

Yes, Browning would have us look beyond the
world for the supply of motive forces, for he would
have us look up to God Himself. This is the
great theme of " Rabbi Ben Ezra," in which, in
harmony with the metaphor which he there adopts
of the Wheel and the Potter, he reminds us that
the great end of the cup—that is, the great end
of life—is to " slake the Thirst of God." This is
another way of answering the great question,
" What is Man's chief end ? " and it is just answering it in the familiar but deep words, " Man's
chief end is to glorify God, and to enjoy Him
for ever "—

> "Look not thou down, but up
> To uses of a cup."

Browning faces, and faces successfully, the problem
of Pain and Suffering. Although there are those who
affect to be terribly shocked because there is in life
so much pain and suffering, he is not at all amazed.
There is, he is sure, not only a purpose in it all, but
the purpose of a Mind both wise and good ; the
" blessed evil," as it has been called, being capable
of evolving in man the highest moral qualities, those
that lead to sympathy, love, and help, and to being
loved as well. But for pain and suffering, what
room would there be " for thanks to God or man " ?

He is no Utilitarian ; does not keep his eye
constantly fixed on the matter of happiness. He

would, indeed, be sorry for any human being who had no care, no doubt, no aspiration, no pain and no struggle.   Such a state reduces man to the level of the bird, with its crop full, and of the " maw-crammed beast."   Birds whose crops are full, and beasts whose maws are crammed, have no cares, and no doubts ; they are satisfied,—but with a low, sordid, animal satisfaction.

Such a satisfaction for man fills Browning with loathing.   He is sure that man is here not to " feast on joy—to solely seek, and find, and feast." He does not think that getting, simply getting, and always getting, satisfies man's true nature, and so he rejoices when a " spark disturbs our clod."   Man holds, he believes, " nearer to God who gives, than of His tribes who take."

He enters a strong protest against measuring the worth of any man by the " vulgar mass called work," by those things that take the eye and have their price.   He would rather measure a man's worth by all the world's coarse thumb and finger failed to plumb—

> " All instincts immature,
> All purposes unsure,
> That weighed not as his work, yet swelled the man's amount.
>
> Thoughts hardly to be packed
> Into a narrow act,
> Fancies that broke through language and escaped,
> All I could never be,
> All men ignored in me,
> This I was worth to God, whose wheel the pitcher shaped.
>
> •   •   •   •   •   •   •   •
>
> Was I aspired to be
> And was not comforts me."

And so we find that Browning's look is onward and forward. All things, and more particularly Man, are moving towards perfection. " Progress is indeed man's distinctive mark,—man's, and not the beast's." There is a movement in Nature up to Man, and there is in Man himself a movement, ever higher and higher, to the ideal of completeness. And then, when man is at his best, there is a movement higher still, and that is " *a tendency to God* "—

> " In completed man begins anew
> A tendency to God.
>
> .   .   .   .   .   .
>
> Prognostics told man's near approach—
> . . . So in man's self arise
> August anticipations, symbols, types
> Of a dim splendour ever on before,
> In that Eternal Circle life pursues."

MATTHEW ARNOLD

" We shall in general, in reading the Bible, get the surest hold on the word 'God,' by giving it the sense of *the Eternal Power, not ourselves, which makes for Righteousness.*"

.   .   .   .

" Religion is the solidest of realities, and Christianity the greatest and happiest stroke ever yet made for human perfection."—ARNOLD, *Literature and Dogma.*

"The two noblest of things, *sweetness and light.*"
                    ARNOLD, *Culture and Anarchy.*

MATTHEW ARNOLD

I

MATTHEW ARNOLD is well named the Apostle of
Culture. Whilst it can hardly be said that he has
deeply influenced modern thought, being more an
echo than a voice, yet there can be no doubt that
he has succeeded in making familiar many a word
and phrase. The word "Culture" is one of his
favourites—"I am," he says, "above all a believer
in Culture."

To Arnold we owe the currency of such phrases
as "Sweetness and Light" (a couplet borrowed
from Swift), "Sweet Reasonableness," "the Dissi-
dence of Dissent," "Conduct, as three-fourths of
life," and, "the Eternal, not ourselves, that makes for
Righteousness."

By Culture, Arnold means the study of perfection
and the love of it, the harmonious expansion of all
our powers, the acquainting ourselves with the
best that has been known or said in the world.
A cultured person is a person like Goethe, one
of his heroes, or perhaps a person like Arnold
himself; that is to say, a person who is neither
narrow nor provincial,—not a Philistine, nor a Protestant, nor a Puritan, nor a Dissenter—especially

not a Dissenter, for a Dissenter is Arnold's *bête noire.*

It may be said of Arnold's face, to judge by the portrait given in one of the best editions of his poetical works, as was said of Dante's, that it is one of the saddest and mournfullest that has ever been painted; so sad and mournful is it that we feel inclined to say, "Why, look ye, that man has been in Hell."

There is an undertone of sadness in his prose writings, but this becomes an upper tone in his poetical works, for these are, without exception, the saddest of verses. In his poems he tells us that his mood is that of melancholy, and distinctly claims his right to tears.

The more one gets to know what Arnold thought and felt, the less can there be surprise at his marr'd aspect. To him this world was dead, and Christ was also dead—

> "Now he is dead! Far hence he lies
> In the lorn Syrian town;
> And on his grave, with shining eyes,
> The Syrian stars looked down."

Poor Arnold had not where to cast his anchor: he had not where to rest his head. To him God was no loving God and Father, but a pitiless Power. The Bible was to him no sure guide-book; it was honeycombed with legends. The Future was to him no bright Hereafter, but "a Perhaps,"— at best an absorption into the Eternal order. And life was to him no time of joy, but a hard, helpless, hopeless struggle. It was, to use his own figure, a long steep journey through sunk gorges, over mountains in snow, where on the heights "comes the storm, and, at last, at nightfall the lonely inn mid the rocks."

Surely with beliefs, or, as we should rather say, with unbeliefs like those, there need be no surprise, that he is the " last of the race of them that grieve."

Were we asked to say what gospel Arnold has got to preach, or what message he has got to give to the world, it would be hard to give an answer. Good comes to the moral and spiritual side of our nature from writers like Tennyson and Browning, and there is moral stimulus to be had from writers like Carlyle and Emerson. " There is a ray of real Heaven in Ruskin"; but what can be said of Arnold ?

It must not be said that there is no good to be got from him, for there is some. There is, of course, the charm of his lucid style. But there is something better about Arnold than even his style; there is his intense devotion to Righteousness. Just as Emerson is said to have glorified Virtue, so it may be said that Arnold has "glorified" Righteousness, for this word is written on his heart. And if Arnold has done nothing else, he has at least done something to guard people against a one-sided and propositional Religion, and to direct attention, almost to irritation, to Conduct as being the main thing, the one thing necessary.

Although there is much that is morally worthy in Arnold's writings, yet the balance of their influence is towards negation and unsettlement, sadness and despair. In his " Rugby Chapel," he tells how it was the glory of his father to save many as

well as himself, but Matthew Arnold, the son, issues
at last from the struggle all alone :—

> " Friends, Companions, and train
> The Avalanche swept from our side."

He has been called an " elegant Jeremiah." We
think he might also be called a Daniel come to
judgment, and a very dogmatic one as well. To
quote a line from his " Bacchanalia," we may say,
" And a famous critic judges all."

Matthew Arnold has passed in review almost
everything under the sun, and there is nothing, or
almost next to nothing, on which he has not passed
a sweeping sentence of condemnation.

There may be a good deal of sweetness and light
in his creed, but there is more vitriol than honey in
his criticisms.

He has nothing to say against Wordsworth or
Goethe, and it is noteworthy that he is reverential
towards the Founder of the Christian Faith. It is
true that in one place he just ventures to suggest
that, perhaps, there is over much Hebraising in the
Christian system, yet, with this single stricture, he
is reverential to, almost worshipful of, the Founder
of the Christian Faith. To him Christ is an
" Absolute "; you can't get above Him, nor beyond
Him. With these exceptions everything else and
everybody else is in a bad way.

As for the Age, it is a " hopeless tangle," with a
ground tone of human agony. The crowd to-day
who bluster and cringe make life " hideous, and arid,
and vile." " The complaining millions of men darken

in labour and pain." One world is dead; the other is powerless to be born.

The Bible—it is full of errors and legends. As a man of Culture, Arnold can so depend upon this accomplishment for interpreting Scripture, that he is sure that Jesus never uttered the words, "God so loved the world," etc.

The Apostles do not escape his criticism: Paul, he declares, is given to word-splitting like a pedantic Rabbi, and John saddles Christ with Metaphysics.

The Creeds, all of them,—the Apostle's Creed, the Nicene Creed, the Athanasian Creed, are founded on a blunder.

As for Doctrines, not only must they go, but they are already all gone. Predestination, Original Sin, Imputed Righteousness, Justification by Faith, Conversion, Sanctification, Witness of Spirit,—they are all gone.

As for Theologians, there is not one of them to be trusted—from Augustine down to the Bishop of Gloucester; whether they be Trinitarian or Unitarian, they are all alike worthless.

He makes short work of favourite evangelical Hymns, for he cavalierly dismisses them as doggerel.

The Classes and the Masses of the people are likewise all in a bad way. The Aristocrats are Barbarians; the Middle Classes are Philistines; and the Working Classes are the Populace.

In one of Carlyle's works we read of a person having the wildest notions about the world and all in it and on it. The notions of this man were, however, quite discounted when it was discovered that the secret of their extravagance and stupidity lay in the fact that the man was standing on his head, instead of standing on his feet. We are inclined to think that it is not otherwise with Matthew Arnold, and feel sure that there is something seriously wrong with *his point of view.*

It is always satisfactory when one is able to find the key to a man's character and writings, and there can be little doubt that the key to Matthew Arnold and his writings is to be found in his "*conception of God.*"

It was because Arnold went wrong here that he went wrong all along the line. His conception of God is Pantheistic. He is frantic with those who think or speak of God as a Person; this, he declares, is no blessed truth, but an egregious blunder. God is not a Person, but, as Arnold tells us times without number, He is the "Eternal, not ourselves, that makes for Righteousness."

It would seem as if Arnold's own sad history is a notable illustration of the importance of Dogma; and would almost lead one to reverse his famous dictum about "Conduct being three-fourths of life," and to put the word "Dogma" in the place of the word "Conduct."

Arnold's conception of God as impersonal is the hinge on which all his other views turn.

This explains his pronounced Anti-supernaturalism,—his tilting against miracles,—his girding at such Doctrines as Election and Conversion and Justification by Faith,—his silence about Forgiveness of Sins and about Prayer.

In dealing, therefore, with Arnold as a thinker

and writer, the main thing is to concentrate attention on his conception of God.

Is God personal or impersonal? that seems to be
the great question at stake.   If God be impersonal,
then we could accept a great many of Arnold's conclusions.   If, however, God be a Personal God,—a
Being who thinks and loves,—the Moral Governor
of the Universe, then Arnold himself is frank enough
to declare that he could accept the Bible, with all
that is said about its infallibility and inspiration,
its Doctrines of Predestination, Conversion, and all
the rest.   All would then be to him legitimate,
scriptural, and reasonable.

Here, then, is the crux of the whole.   Arnold maintains with a vehement pertinacity, that whatever else
God is, God is not a Person, and that we only think
rightly about God when we think of Him as the
"Eternal, not ourselves, that makes for Righteousness."

One of the grounds on which he objects to the
Personality of God is that such a conception is
Anthropomorphic, that is to say, a conception of
God in accordance with which we make Him after
our own image.

Without entering at any length upon the examination of this objection, it is well to remember that
there is a poor Anthropomorphism and a rich Anthropomorphism, and, as it happens, Arnold has
gone in for the poor kind.   In the matter of
Anthropomorphism, there is really no choice, for
after this fashion we must think of God.   The man
of Science is as much Anthropomorphic as the Poet
or the Theologian.   Arnold tries to poke fun at the

Theologian, who has a conception of God which amounts to nothing else than a conception of Him as " a magnified and non-natural man." Without considering whether Arnold is dealing as fairly by the Theologian as he ought to do, it is surely better to think of God as a " magnified and non-natural Man " than to think of Him as a magnified natural Force, or Power, or Tendency, or something or another in that line. It is surely better to think of God as " He," than to think of God as " It."

As there is nothing in the whole Universe so wonderful as our own personality, with its characteristics of unity, identity, and universality, with its functions of thought, desire, and will, so it is no degradation to think of God as having, in the highest degree, those characteristics which we possess, and as exercising perfectly those functions which we exercise but feebly. As Lotze has remarked, " Our personality is but a faint copy of the perfect Personality of God." We may indeed think of God in another way ; but the conclusion is hard to resist, that we cannot think of Him in a better way.

It is unfortunate that Arnold went wrong in his conception of God, for, as he said of Clifford we may say of himself, it has put him " all abroad in Religion." As our own life might teach us " that we can never die," so our own personality should teach us to hold firmly fast by the Personality of God. Writing of Goethe, Arnold says—

> " For he pursued a lonely road,
>   His eyes on Nature's plan ;—
> Neither made man, too much a God,
>   Nor God, too much a man."

Our grievance with Arnold is that he makes God too little a Man,—that he makes God, indeed, so much less than man, for man is more than a mere force, or power; he is a person who thinks, and loves, and wills.

One reason why Arnold objects to the Personality of God is that such a view is Anthropomorphic; but this is not his chief ground of objection. His chief ground of objection is that this view of God is one which cannot be verified. And he boldly declares that he will neither have a God, nor a Doctrine, nor a Religion that cannot be verified. He wants a Religion of which he is sure,—as sure as that fire burns, or that two and two make four. Arnold advances this element of assurance or certainty as one of the excellent features of his own conception of the Supreme—the " Eternal, not ourselves, that makes for Righteousness," as against the idea of a Personal God, which he avers is an idea that cannot be verified.

Without entering fully into the consideration of his demand for proofs, it may be sufficient to observe, that one is rather surprised to find him insisting so much on proofs when he himself seems to look upon Religion as an Intuition. He writes often of that Intuition of God which Israel possessed, and of Christianity as the restoration of the Intuition.

Of course, it is as unnecessary to prove an intuition as to prove that the sun is shining in the sky, when we see it doing so. If Arnold only means that there is room for experience in Religion, then no one will dispute his position. Experience has undoubtedly a large place in assisting to the assurance of the Personality of God, just as large a place, indeed, as Arnold claims for the certainty which he has of the "Power, not ourselves, that makes for Righteousness."

As Illingworth has pointed out in his Bampton Lecture, the belief in a Personal God is *an instinctive judgment*, and all proofs or arguments are just the process by means of which this instinctive judgment is intellectually justified.

Over against Arnold's demand for proofs in Religion we might set the saying of Tennyson, that "nothing worthy can be proved"; or these words of Robert Browning in "La Saisiaz," with this remark, that whether as Poet or Metaphysician, Browning will be found quite a match for Arnold—

> " Call this—God, then, call that—soul, and both—the only facts for me.
> Prove them facts? that they o'erpass my power of proving, proves them such.
> Fact it is. I know I know not something which is fact as much."

II

Having glanced at Arnold's cardinal position, which we consider to lie in his conception of God, it may be well to notice some other aspects of his life and writings.

It need scarcely be said that we have Arnold in his best literary form in his Essays and Poetry, and that there it is of the purest, as might have been expected of one who filled for many years, with distinction, the Chair of Poetry in Oxford University.

And yet, apart from the excellence of the form, reminding one constantly of the wise reserve of Grecian Art, there is not much either of light or leading.

In his Essays, Arnold passes in review most of the best known names in Literature, — Burns, Milton, Goethe, Shelley, Amiel, Spinoza, etc., and yet he says nothing about any one of them that is either peculiarly penetrative or abiding. He finds fault with Robert Burns, because, forsooth, he was not "hearty enough in his Bacchanalian Songs!"

We are greatly impressed with much of his Poetry, particularly with some of his Sonnets, and with such narrative poems as his "Balder" and "St. Brandan." His "Rugby Chapel" is, we think, the best of all, setting forth Arnold's strong point —excellence in description.

In attempting to read his "Sohrab and Rustum," we were reminded of what Ruskin says regarding his attempt to read Shelley's "Revolt of Islam,"— that for the life of him he could not make out who revolted, against whom or what.

All through Arnold's Poetry there runs that upper tone of sadness to which we have already referred,—a feature which puts him to great disadvantage as a Poet when compared with his contemporaries Browning and Tennyson, with their cheery optimism.

III

Were we to offer any criticism on Arnold's special theme of " Culture," we would be inclined to say that the distinction which he draws between Hebraism and Hellenism is not so thoroughgoing as he seems to think.　The impression left upon the mind by his writings is that one must go outside of the Bible, and the Christian Faith, to obtain sanction for Culture and impulse to Hellenism.

We do not think that this is the case.　Accepting at once the statement that we have an intellectual side and a moral side, we observe that Arnold calls the Culture of the former, Hellenism, and the culture of the latter, Hebraism.　A little reflection, however, will make it plain that the Hebraism of the Bible includes all the Hellenism that Arnold pleads for, and a great deal more.　It is interesting to note that the motto which he himself has selected for his Volume on *Culture and Anarchy*, " Estote, ergo vos perfecti," is a text from the New Testament Scriptures.

It is only fair, of course, to state that, with all his love of Culture, he has a warm side to the Hebraism of the Bible, with its stern discipline. He believes that a Baptism unto death works better things in the world than the Cult of the Alma Venus, and leads to something infinitely purer than gazing, as devotees did in Greece as part of their worship, on a handsome Courtesan stepping naked into the sea.　He quotes, as significant of much in the way of Morality, the saying of Carlyle, that Socrates was "terribly at ease in Zion," meaning by that, that this noted Greek teacher, the wisest man amongst them all, cared little about his own sins, and less about the sins of other people.

Arnold clings somehow to the fancy that Culture is a sort of "Morrison's Pill" for the maladies of the age. He considers, for one thing, that Culture is necessary to interpret aright the Word of God. He also thinks that if our country cared less for coal, and iron, and steam, and electricity,—less for money making, and more for "Sweet Reasonableness," for beauty and intelligence, for "Sweetness and Light," the nation would be both greater and happier. He quotes, with scorn, what the mother of one who afterwards became a Knight, Sir Daniel Gooch, was in the habit of saying, every morning to her boy, "Ever remember, my dear Dan, that you should look forward to being some day manager of the concern!"

Arnold also believes that Politicians may find in Culture the key that will open the door to the right seat of authority in the State, for he thinks that this is to be found neither in the classes, nor in the masses, but in the exercise of right reason, and in the discovery of our best self.

Alas! however, for Arnold's "Pill" of Culture as a regenerator of mankind by itself. It has been weighed in the balances, and has been found wanting. He himself has passed sentence of condemnation on poor Heine, who did so much to revive Hellenism, and it is the opinion of many that Goethe, with all his culture, was far from being a paragon of moral excellence.

As indicating how far the Pagan world succeeded, with all its culture, we quote those words of Froude the Historian. Writing of the Greeks, he says: " With a few rare exceptions, pollution, too detestable to be even named amongst ourselves, was of familiar and daily occurrence amongst their greatest men." As for the Romans, he writes: "The Rome of the Cæsars presents, in its later ages, a picture of enormous sensuality, of the coarsest animal desire, with means unlimited to gratify it." And perhaps there are no lines of Arnold's better known than these—

> " On that hard Pagan world, disgust
>   And secret loathing fell;
> Deep weariness, and sated lust,
>   Made human life a hell."

Our only remark would be, that the tree of Culture, like all other trees, is known by its fruits.

We must not say that Arnold has been of no service to Religion, a theme which so absorbed the closing period of his life, and yet we have to say that his service has been more of a negative than of a positive kind.

We think that Arnold has been of service, amongst other things, in uttering such a vigorous protest against a too great devotion to the systematising of religious truths. It may be granted that Metaphysics have played too great a part in Religion, without saying, as he does, that Metaphysics " have nothing to do with Religion "; and it may also be granted, that systematising religious truths has been overdone, without ad-

mitting with him that Dogma or Theology is alien
altogether to Religion.   It must never be forgotten
that Athanasius defined because Arius shuffled, and
that if we are to have a Theology at all, it is well
to have it of the best sort.

If Arnold has been of some service to Religion
from a negative point of view, we fear it has to be
said that positively he has been very injurious to
the Sacred cause, and that chiefly because he is so
far wrong in his conception of what Religion really
is.   To him Religion is " Morality," " Conduct,"
" Righteousness,"—this, and this alone.

He is here very bold, and claims, indeed, to have
the Bible on his side.   He declares that the master-
word of the Bible is " Righteousness "; that this is
the master-word of the Old Testament, and the
master-word of the New Testament as well.   More
than once he defines Religion as that which " binds
to Righteousness."   He persistently maintains that
Religion is a something which is practical and
ethical,—" morality lit up with feeling," " morality
plus emotion."

We are compelled to join issue with Arnold, inasmuch as we consider that such a conception of
Religion is not only defective, but seriously so.
We do not, of course, deny that Religion is practical
and ethical, but we take leave to say that this is
the second intention of Religion, and not the first.
The first intention of Religion is always upwards
towards God.   As Joubert says, of whom Arnold
has written so well, Religion involves " an indissoluble engagement with God."   So far as we

understand Religion, its leading injunctions are not, " Cease to do evil, and learn to do well," but they are injunctions such as those, " Fear—Love, and Obey God."

It is a remarkable fact that Arnold, designedly or otherwise, is at once silent and blind towards this side of Religion. This defect, equal to leaving Hamlet out of the play, proves fatal to any claim which he puts forward, either as a Teacher or Reformer, in this all-important sphere.

This very serious limitation on the part of Arnold explains much in his writings regarding his attitude to Miracles,—his dislike to Theology,—his severe strictures against Calvinism,—his repugnance to the Doctrines of Grace, as associated, for example, with the name of Wesley.

Wesley, Arnold says, attaches so much importance not to what man brings, but to what God gives. This, it has to be acknowledged, holds true as a tenet both of Calvinism and of Wesleyanism; and this, of course, must seem all moonshine to a person like Arnold, who leaves a living, loving God out of count altogether. As well leave the keystone out of the arch, or the sun out of the heavens.

This defective conception of Religion also explains a terrible falling away on Arnold's part, so far as the great fact of personal Immortality is concerned. Not only did he not believe in personal Immortality, but we do not see how he could have done so, seeing he did not believe in a Personal God, for these two beliefs are riveted together by indissoluble links. Arnold believed in an " Eternal order which never dies,"—in absorption at death into this "Eternal order,"—a belief, alas! not one grade above Buddhism, and altogether in line with the rankest Materialism.

IV

As might have been expected, Arnold holds very peculiar views about the Bible, views so peculiar that the wonder is that he does not, once for all, give it up, or only refer to it as he would to a book of Fairy Tales. He does not, of course, believe in any such thing as a Revelation from God. He holds that the antithesis between natural and revealed is a false antithesis,—revealed truth being, as he puts it, only natural truth received and acted upon with earnestness. The Bible, in his view, is full of errors, and teeming with Legends.

And yet, and this is the remarkable thing, he declares that there is no Book in the world to be compared with it. Here is a passage, for example, from his *Literature and Dogma*: "As long as the world lasts, all who want to make progress in Righteousness will come to Israel for inspiration, as to the people who have had the sense for Righteousness most glowing and strongest. . . . As well imagine a man with a sense for Sculpture not cultivating it by the help of the remains of Greek Art, or a man with a sense for Poetry not culti-vating it by the help of Homer and Shakespeare, as a man with a sense for Conduct not cultivating it by the help of the Bible."

He is quite sure that the race will always return to the Bible, and for this very good reason, that they cannot do without it. It is, he says, " such a grand book," not only a National Book, but " the Book of the Nations."

He is very sorry that the working classes are getting detached from it. This he considers a pitiful business, for, in his opinion, a course of the Bible is ever so much better for them than a course of Herbert Spencer, or Universal Suffrage, and so on.

Arnold therefore comes forward as a Reformer, proposing to recast the Bible and give to the people a right view of it, putting aside all its errors and Fairy Tales. Unfortunately, however, in his reforming he takes away so much of the Bible that we do not know what he has left, or what he would leave behind.

" He wants the people to enjoy the Bible,"—but we venture to ask, with all humility, what bit of it would he allow them to enjoy? If anyone takes out of the Bible, as he does, all that is Supernatural, what, then, is left behind? And to this question the answer must be returned, that not much is left behind, — neither Genesis, nor Exodus, nor the Psalms, nor the Prophets, nor the Gospels, nor the Epistles ;—not, we should think, one single page of the Bible, except perhaps a text like this, so congruous to Arnold's own mood, " Vanity of vanities, all is vanity." Arnold might, in his pruning, leave a text here and a text there, but we are convinced that even these would soon pass away with the rest, leaving as residuum, simply nothing worthy of being named the Word of God.

Before passing from this matter, we take the liberty of directing attention, by way of specimen, to the arbitrary manner in which Arnold ventures to handle the Divine Word. According to him, the Churches are all wrong in the meaning which they attach to the Sacrament of the Lord's Supper, inasmuch as they associate this Sacrament with the "Forgiveness of sins." Now, Arnold tells us that, in his opinion,—an opinion which he sets against the view of the Churches,—the real meaning of the Sacrament consists in what he calls the "consecration of absolute individualism." In support of his view, he quotes from the New Covenant, as written in the Book of the Prophet Jeremiah, in which it is said that "God will write His law in the hearts of the people."

This Covenant, quoted likewise in the New Testament Scriptures, was, in all likelihood, in the Saviour's mind at the Institution of the Ordinance, and yet, and this is the point to which attention is directed, whilst Arnold quotes one sentence of the New Covenant, to which reference has been made, —the sentence about God writing His Law in the hearts of the people,—he deliberately refrains from quoting another sentence which gives the essential part of the Covenant, that part which reveals the Grace of God in His promise to "forgive the sins of His people."

The terms of the New Covenant, as given by the Prophet Jeremiah, to whom Arnold refers, closes

14

thus : " For I will forgive their iniquity, and I will remember their sin no more."

V

Arnold has no hesitation whatever in stating his position regarding the Miracles of the Bible. At the touch of Ithuriel's spear, Miracles have dissolved. With a bold brevity he says that they simply *don't happen*; and even if they did happen, they would not possess any evidential worth in his eyes. Arnold does not take upon him to say, like Spinoza and Mill, that a Miracle, being a contradiction of the Laws of Nature, is simply impossible, and cannot therefore be established by any amount of evidence. He would grant the possibility of Miracles—nay, Arnold would believe in them, if only he could believe in a Personal God.

He declares that the reporters of the Miracles were mistaken ; that they were liable to err, and did err. Arnold, classing Church-Miracles and Bible-Miracles together, says, that as we now in this enlightened age have got to understand the former, so we have also got to understand the latter.

Without attempting to enter fully upon this *quæstio vexata*, we may be allowed to remark, that it is more than bold for anyone to declare that all the reporters of Miracles of all the Bible ages are entirely mistaken.

It is, we think, quite easy to draw a sharp distinction between what are called Bible-Miracles and what are called Church-Miracles. We do not believe that Saint Patrick kindled a fire with icicles; although we believe that Christ fed miraculously five thousand people with bread. We believe the latter, and disbelieve the former, because Saint Patrick was Saint Patrick, and Christ was Christ.

In a well-known passage Arnold says: "Suppose I could change the pen with which I write this into a penwiper, I should not make what I wrote any the truer or more convincing." This, no doubt, is perfectly correct; and yet it has to be observed, that it is mere supposition,—that he is not able to do what he supposes—that if he did so, it would savour much of the showman—and that we do not expect a mere man, like him, to do anything of the kind.

We do not expect Arnold to turn his pen into a penwiper, but we do expect One, who is the Eternal Son of God, to speak and act like the Eternal Son of God. The Miracles of Christ are not at all supernatural to Him; they are only supernatural to us. This is the Bible view of Miracles, and one, surely, reasonable in the highest degree. Miracles are called there by the simplest of names —*the works* of Christ. It was as easy for Christ to walk on the sea, as it is for us to walk on dry land.

VI

When Arnold touches on Nonconformity or Dissent, which he does very frequently, then he seems to lose all his "sweetness," and almost all his

" light." Nonconformists or Dissenters are his pet aversion.

Fortunately, they are, in his estimation, not altogether without a redeeming good quality : they have cultivated the art of preaching, and of free prayer. They have a kind of Righteousness, an Old Testament kind, not the best kind certainly, yet a kind of Righteousness, that of smiting the Lord's enemies under the fifth rib. Otherwise Dissenters are very bad.

Occasionally Arnold is simply outrageous in his diatribes against them. He goes so far as to say that their temper hinders Christianity, as much as loose living, drunkenness, and beer shops. The services of Nonconformists correspond to their own crude culture. Dissenters, he says, are fond of this way of it, inasmuch as their tastes are gratified by such condescension, and their sense of self-importance is thereby fostered. Their Religion, if Religion it can be called, is a hole-and-corner sort of thing. They have a fetish of separation. Like the wild ass, they like to be alone, and are full of strife and bitterness. They are animated by jealousy of the Establishment, by disputes, tea-meetings, openings of chapels, and sermons.

One can easily understand why Dissenters are charged with jealousy of the Establishment, although the charge is a most uncharitable one ; but one fails to see why Dissenters should be singled out for opprobrium for the very innocent dissipation of tea-drinking in a social capacity ; or for opening a chapel, once it is built ; or for preaching sermons, so be it the sermons are worthy of that function.

He launches out against what he calls the "un-blessed mixture" amongst Dissenters of Politics and Religion, because of which both Politics and Religion are spoiled. Now, whilst we believe that Politics, at times, get along well enough without Religion, we as certainly believe that Religion is bound to concern itself with Politics in the best sense of the word. We are surprised that a writer like Arnold, who makes so much of "Righteousness," seems to have forgotten that there are departments of it called civic and national. Surely no section of Christians, Dissenters or otherwise, deserve to be scourged for laying to heart the interests of the community, municipal or national, of which they form a part, or for endeavouring by word and deed to advance in the nation the sacred and saving cause of Righteousness. Instead of censure, praise would be wiser.

Arnold is clearly on the side of the Church of England as by Law established. Connection with this Church leads into what he calls the "national current of life," although what that means exactly we do not quite understand. This, however, seems clear, that if "the national current of life" be so "hideous and vile" as he has declared it to be, the more one keeps clear of it the better, unless for the high purpose of changing it.

He lifts up his voice against the "Disestablishment Crusade" by crying out, and this is almost all that he has to say, that the *Church is there*— and that the clergyman, poor soul, cannot help being the Parson of the parish. This argument, however, proves too much, for once upon a time as much could have been said on behalf of Feudalism and Slavery, and as much could be said now of Popery and of the Wicked One himself. It is not sufficient to justify anything, simply to say that the thing is there; we must also be able to say that it is there in harmony with the demands of right and justice.

One of Arnold's pleas on behalf of the Establishment of the Church is, that such an arrangement on the part of the State produces men who contribute the best works in Literature and Art. We neither can nor care to dispute the fact that there have been and are great names in Literature and Art associated with the Church Established by the State, neither can we dispute the fact that the names of great men have been more numerous in connection with the Establishment than with Nonconformity. Black-faced sheep eat more than white-faced ones, simply because there are more of them.

At the same time, it is undeniable that since Nonconformity has had time to grow and consolidate, the names associated with Nonconformity, in the spheres of Literature, Scholarship, Theology, and Mission enterprise, can at least hold their own with honoured names in the Church Established by Law. Arnold has been good enough to mention Hooker and Butler. We take the liberty of referring to the names of Milton and Bunyan in years gone by; and to such names in modern times as Carlyle, Emerson, and the Brownings.

VII

We conclude with a reference to Arnold's attitude to Christianity. We have already said that he is reverential to the Founder of the Christian Faith, and we have now to say that he is loud in the praises of what he calls the "natural truths of Christianity." We do not know what the "natural truths" of Christianity really are, but we know that to Arnold they mean Christianity cleared of all that is miraculous or supernatural.

The world, he says, cannot do with Christianity as it is, and yet the world cannot do without it; it is the "greatest and happiest stroke" ever made for the advancement of mankind. Christianity has a future which is unknown, and a possible development which is immense. It has taught the world the pre-eminence of "Righteousness," and has engaged for the conduct of men the mightiest of forces, the forces of love, reverence, gratitude, hope, pity, and awe.

He writes of the *Infinite* of the Religion of Jesus. Readers of Arnold's works get familiar with the words, "the Secret of Jesus" and "the Method of Jesus." The Secret of Jesus is said to be "dying to live," or self-renouncement; and the Method of Jesus, the "Method of inwardness," or self-examination.

Our chief objection to Arnold's attitude to Christianity is that it comes so far short of what it might be. When we read his answers to some of the fundamental questions of the Christian Faith, we are sure that the writer of them has entirely missed the great and open secret. Arnold has surely grossly misread the Christian Faith when he says that " Easter " means that Jesus was victorious over death by dying ; that " the kingdom of God " means the " Ideal Society of the Future," and that Immortality means to " live in the Eternal order, which never dies."

Without saying a single word against his contentions for self - renouncement, self - examination, and righteousness—each and all praiseworthy in their own place, we take leave to say that the " Arrow is beyond him "—that he has failed utterly either to mark or comprehend the " Infinite," as he calls it, of the Religion of Jesus.

To complete his sketch of the Christian Faith, much more than he attempted or accomplished remains to be done. He must add Upwardness to his inwardness, and self-changement to his self-renouncement. The Master said much, it is true, of dying to live,—but He said more of receiving Divine Life through the Spirit of God, thus making the tree good. The Method of Jesus is simplicity itself ; it is contained in these two words, " Follow Me." We must look for the Secret of Jesus, not in any rule, however good, but in Himself,—very man of very man, and very God of very God, in Whom are hid all the treasures of wisdom and knowledge. " Thou art the King of Glory, O Christ."

HERBERT SPENCER

"Evolution is an integration of matter and concomitant dissipation of motion; during which the matter passes from an indefinite, incoherent homogeneity, to a definite, coherent heterogeneity; and during which the retained motion undergoes a parallel transformation."—SPENCER, *First Principles.*

"Pure egoism, and pure altruism, are both illegitimate. If the maxim—'Live for self' is wrong, so also is the maxim—'Live for others.'"

.   .   .   .

"General happiness is to be achieved mainly through the adequate pursuit of their own happinesses by individuals; while reciprocally, the happinesses of individuals are to be achieved in part by their pursuit of the general happiness."—SPENCER, *The Data of Ethics.*

HERBERT SPENCER

I

HERBERT SPENCER—a name familiar to all interested in Science and Philosophy—may well be called
the Apostle of Agnosticism, and of Evolution.

Although the term " Agnosticism " is the invention of Huxley, yet the theory is not only closely
identified with Spencer, but forms a very large
part of his philosophical system. Spencer's name,
closely identified with Agnosticism, is even more
closely identified with Evolution, for Spencer was
an Evolutionist before Darwin, and commits himself
to this theory in a way that leaves Darwin far
behind.

Not only has our era been called the era of
Evolution, but it has been said that this theory is
the great contribution of Science and Philosophy
to the thought of the age. Undoubtedly Evolution
is largely in evidence; we hear about the Evolution
of this, and the Evolution of that,— the Evolution of
the heavens, and of the earth; of plants, animals,
man, mind, morals, religion, society, language,
science, art; the Evolution of things inorganic,
organic, and superorganic. Evolution is in the air;

and of all Evolutionists, Herbert Spencer is the most thoroughgoing.

Although the present writer is neither an Agnostic nor an Evolutionist, yet, in accordance with Spencer's own saying, that there is " a soul of truth lying in error," he believes that there is a measure of truth in both theories.

Without concluding, as Spencer does, that the riddle of the world is not only unsolved, but also insoluble, it may be frankly acknowledged, that there is much mystery both within and without us; much mystery about mind, matter, life, religion, and God. And yet, granting mystery, it is surely going too far to pronounce that the solution of the problem is hid forever in a realm of impenetrable darkness. It seems unscientific to declare so dogmatically regarding the impossible.

It is bad enough to say that we have meanwhile no key to open the door, but it is unwarrantable to declare so oracularly that no key can be found to open it.

It may be true that there is great darkness around many things,—more particularly about their origin; yet there is that within us which creates and fosters the hope, that more light will break. The pressure of the problem has to be frankly conceded; still, the courage to face, and the hope to solve it, are immortal in the human soul.

What, indeed, is every discovery in Science, but a gain to the realm of light over the realm of darkness? As the old couplet puts it—

"Nature and Nature's laws lay hid in night,
God said, 'Let Newton be,'—and all was light."

Now, although it cannot be said that all is light since Newton's day, yet it must be admitted that since his great discovery there has been more light. In Astronomy, for example, the system of Ptolemy was an advance on the poetical conception that the Sun was a chariot drawn by horses. The system of Ptolemy was an advance on the old poetical conception, and the system of Copernicus is a great advance on the system of Ptolemy. And if we are to believe Spencer himself, we must come to the conclusion that he has brought to light in his Law of Evolution, a principle that explains ever so many things, in heaven and on earth, in the mind and history of man.

All that we plead for is, that it is well to be careful in pronouncing the enigma of the Universe insoluble. An old Puritan said there was " more light to break from the Word of God," and so we venture to say, there is more light to break on ever so many things, as the ages roll on. The Science of the Nineteenth Century has made discoveries altogether unknown to those who lived before this age, and it is likely that those who come after will make discoveries of which we do not now even dream—

> "The Veil
> Is rending, and the Voices of the day,
> Are heard across the Voices of the dark."

There is, we may be sure, a grain of truth in Agnosticism—" the sea is so great, and our boat is so little "; and there is also, we are convinced, something in Evolution.

Although we are unable to accept the theory of Darwin, or the more thoroughgoing theory of Spencer on Evolution, yet it has to be said that the discussions in connection with this theory have accentuated the fact that there are, to use Emerson's phrase, "*stairs in the world*"—and that we are on one of them.   Although it has yet to be proved that the stair above has grown out of the stair below, the fact has been made clear that there are grades of being in the world; and that whether or no there has been any progress in the subhuman spheres, there has been much, and continued progress in the human sphere.

Spencer himself acknowledges that there are no traces of development, so far as the ken of man has gone, in the present flora and fauna of the world. The foxglove of to-day is the same as the foxglove of yesterday, and of past ages; and the bee of to-day is the same as the bee of yesterday, and of past ages.

Neither ought it to be forgotten, that much as has been said and written about the Origin of Species, no new species has ever been known to have originated.   Dr. Hutchison Stirling concludes his volume on "Darwinianism" with these words: "In the whole of Darwin's *Origin of Species* there is not a single word of origin.   The very species which is to originate, never originates.   Nay, as no breeder ever yet made a new species, so the Darwins confess, 'we cannot prove that a single species has changed.'"

The only progress that comes within the ken of

history and of experience, is the progress of man himself—

"Progress is Man's distinctive mark alone ;
Not God's and not the beast's. God is, they are,
Man partly is, and wholly hopes to be."

But whatever may be the opinion of the present writer, there can be no doubt that Herbert Spencer is an Agnostic and Evolutionist of the most thorough-going type; and that through his writings he has greatly influenced the thought of the age.

II

A few facts about Herbert Spencer may not be uninteresting. He was born at Derby, 1820, where his father was a teacher, and is still, fortunately, with us busy thinking and writing. His father and mother were Nonconformist, one a Methodist and the other a Quaker. It was expected that Spencer would have followed his father's occupation, but instead, after being engaged for a little while as a Civil Engineer in the construction of a new railway, for want of employment he drifted to London, at the age of twenty-two. Eventually he became sub-editor of the *Economist* newspaper, and indicated his literary and philosophical ability by contributing some splendid Essays to *The Westminster Review.*

Gradually he settled down to Literary Life, choosing as his sphere of thought subjects connected with Science and Philosophy. The year 1860 is memorable in Spencer's history, for it was in that year, in great weakness of bodily health, that he issued the plan of his "Synthetic Philosophy," a plan which involved the publication of some ten volumes, demanding at least twenty years of thought and effort, if not, as it then seemed, an entire lifetime.

It is to the imperishable honour of Spencer that he grappled heroically with the great scheme which he had set before him, and he is to be sincerely congratulated on the fact that he has been able to finish the work which he so bravely set himself to do.

However one may disagree with the conclusions of his philosophical system, it is only right to acknowledge the nobility of spirit which led to such an undertaking,—a notable instance of knowledge loved for its own sake, and truth sought for in the same pure mood. And our tribute of praise for such a noble effort ought to be given more readily when it is remembered, that after twenty-four years of Herculean labour the profits from his books were exactly nothing.

It cannot be said that Spencer's books form easy reading, or that they are ever likely to become popular, demanding, as they do, the closest study.

His chief works are—*First Principles, Principles of Biology, Principles of Psychology, Principles of Sociology, Data of Ethics, Essays,* and his *Study of Sociology.*

Although we consider that his favourite and famous analogy between the individual and the social organism is more fanciful than real, yet we

think that Spencer has done much service in pointing out that the character of Society depends on
the character of its units, inasmuch as Society is just
what those who compose it are.

People, says Spencer, stand too much in awe of
a State agency, made up of " a cluster of men,—a few
clever ; many, ordinary ; and some, decidedly stupid."

One of his maxims is that the less the State
interferes with its citizens, the better; and we
certainly agree with him, when he points out that
Culture does not make people good, inasmuch as
there is no vital connection between knowledge and
good behaviour.

As is well known, Spencer condemns Gambling,
because the benefit received does not imply effort
put forth, and because the happiness of the winner
is the misery of the loser.

It may be well to observe, that although Spencer
has been called an Atheist, he neither likes to be
called so, nor does he deserve to be so called. Of
course, he does not believe in God as all true
Christians do; and yet he believes in What is to
him as God—an " Infinite and Eternal energy,
Unknown, and Unknowable, from Which all things
proceed."

Neither is he a Materialist, although he under-
takes to explain all things in the world and in man
in terms of Matter, Motion, and Force.

He is not a Materialist, because he is not pre-
pared to speak of Matter, Motion, and Force, as
purely material agencies, but rather as symbols of

that inscrutable, unknown Reality which is behind them. He does not call them material, neither does he call them spiritual. Although Spencer may not be called a Materialist, yet he comes perilously near Materialism, when he writes of Thought as due to nervous shocks, and of the physical face of moral phenomena. Spencer frankly declares that Thought is contingent upon the size of the mental apparatus, upon phosphorus, and upon the blood that goes to the brain.

Every one, of course, acknowledges that mind uses the brain as an instrument; but if Spencer's way of it be true, it would not be at all difficult to manufacture, easily and abundantly, any quantity of geniuses, and of thinkers like Spencer himself. If he has discovered the secret of Thought, then instead of sending young men and women to colleges, or to the study of books, for the development of mind, the wise thing would be to send them to the Druggist's shop; to Indian Clubs; or to the Golf Course.

Without saying a word against the Druggist's shop, as the store where Phosphorus is sold; or against physical exercise of any kind,—as all might know, Spencer himself did not come by his mental superiority in this way; and neither does any other person. Mayhap the very reverse of Spencer's way of accounting for the origin of Thought is the truth; that instead of mental life being due to organisation, or to the transmutation of physical force, it is all the other way; organisation being due to mental life, and physical force due to that which is intellectual and spiritual.

Spencer casts ridicule upon what he calls the " Insanities of Idealism." Now, whilst no one can defend the " Insanities of Idealism," or of anything else, the question has still to be asked, whether Idealism does not stand for the source of all reality, and of all knowledge ? Even Spencer himself is indebted to Idealism for his own philosophical system ; for where had that system origin except in his own fertile mind ? In the last box we find Thought, Idea, God ; and so, with Carlyle, we fall back on the priority of Intellect, and of Soul.

If the question be asked, since Spencer is neither Atheist, nor Materialist, nor Deist, nor Christian, what then is he ? Perhaps the best answer to return to this question is to say that Spencer is a Philosopher—a Philosopher first and last. He is a great thinker, a great thinker about the Universe,—certainly a great enough subject for Thought. He will have the Universe to yield up to him its secret ; he longs to get hold of some one principle,—some one Law that lies behind, and will explain everything— the heavens, the earth, plants, animals, man, mind, morals, and society. To use his own words, he seeks to "*unify knowledge*," and that not only partially, as the Sciences do, but completely, as it is the work of Philosophers and Philosophy to do.

Spencer claims that his efforts in this quest have been crowned with success ; he is sure that he has come to the one principle behind all things, and to the one Law which explains them all.

That one Principle is the " Infinite or Eternal energy, from which all things proceed — an Inscrutable and Persistent Force, absolute, unknown, and unknowable." This is the one Principle,—and the one Law is what he has formulated and submitted as the Law of Evolution.

It is necessary to look a little more closely into the outcome of Spencer's philosophical system, represented by this Principle and this Law.

III

Some one has said that another name for an Agnostic is an "Ignoramus"; but it must go without gainsaying, that such a name cannot be applied to a thinker and writer like Herbert Spencer; for, whatever else he is, he is no "Ignoramus." He has intermeddled with all knowledge, is at home in the most difficult mathematical calculations, and has made himself masterfully conversant with every Science.

Spencer is not only an Agnostic, he is one on principle; for he has assured himself that the Ultimates in Science, Philosophy, and Religion are not only not known, but that they defy all powers of knowledge to know them.

The "Absolute," says Spencer, cannot be known; nay, the very simplest fact is incomprehensible. He is especially emphatic in declaring, that the Power, or Force, behind all things, is utterly inscrutable, being Unknown and Unknowable.. So too is it with ever so many things. He sweeps them one after another into the realms of darkness, and of the "*unthinkable*," to use one of his favourite words.   Space, motion, matter, mind, sensation, self-cognition,—each and all of them, according to Spencer, are " unthinkable," and therefore unknown.

Remarking on such a thoroughgoing Agnosticism as this, we take leave to express astonishment that a writer who espouses so completely the side of uncertainty, and ignorance, is so very sure of so much.

It is somewhat strange that one who knows nothing, and can know nothing, about the " Absolute," is so sure about our absolute ignorance,—the absolute mystery,—and the absolute Unknown. One would imagine that a mind that is so certain on the negative side, has power in it to make headway on the positive side of things.

When Spencer writes about the " Incomprehensibility of the simplest fact," we do not know what he would like to be at ; for surely if the " fact be the simplest," we have got as far back in the realm of facts as there is any need to go.

Amongst other things, we are surprised that Spencer dismisses, as "unthinkable," the fundamental psychological fact known as " self-consciousness," or the cognition of self. Instead of self-consciousness being " unthinkable," it is rather, we should say, the very secret and hinge of all thinking ; the one thing that we do know, and are sure about. " We are," and we know that we are.   There is no other fact so clear, or so sure, as this.   If we are not sure,— absolutely sure, of this, we ask where do we get, and where does Spencer himself get, that idea of

Force, and of the Persistence of Force, of which he makes so much, and on which he builds his whole philosophical system ?

We are of the opinion that Spencer shows more of the Scholastic in his Philosophy than would have been expected. One is astonished to find such a powerful thinker defining the Absolute as a "possible existence, independent of all relations," and yet reminding us that we have a " vague consciousness " of it. Is not this equivalent to saying that the Absolute is in consciousness, and yet out of it,—in relation to consciousness, and yet not in relation to consciousness ?

We somehow think that the root of Spencer's perplexity, as of the perplexity of many, with " The Absolute," is in thinking of it as if it were a substantive, whilst it is really not a substantive, but an adjective. We have been struck, at any-rate, with the frequency with which Spencer himself uses the word " absolute " as an adjective. He speaks of an " Absolute Mystery," of " Absolute Ethics," and himself defines the word as meaning —" total," " complete," or " perfect."

And then, we also think that Spencer has put himself too much under the bondage of the well-known definition of Thought given by Hamilton and Mansell. According to these writers, and so according to Spencer, all Thought is " Limitation "; or, to use their favourite philosophical phrase, " *To think is to condition.*"

Coming to the concrete, in the discussion of this crucial principle, we ask, is this so ? Take, for example, Spencer's great Law of Evolution, thought out by him with such immense labour and erudition. Looking to it, we ask, has Thinking been " Limitation " here ? Surely the answer to be returned is, that instead of Thinking being " Limitation," it has been the very reverse. As the outcome of Spencer's thought, we have submitted a something termed " Law "—a something unlimited in its sweep, and unconditioned in its character. Spencer is as sure of this Law, the product of his thought, as he is that two and two make four.

IV

Regarding his application of the principle of Agnosticism to Religion, he says that in Religion, as in Science and Philosophy, the ultimate brings face to face with mystery,—with a mystery so impenetrable, that all that can be said about the Reality behind all things is that that Reality—that Power or Force that manifests itself to us, is absolutely Unknown, and Unknowable.

He is of the opinion, that it is in this recognition of Absolute mystery that Science and Religion are reconciled. They shake hands, in so far as they acknowledge defeat, once we get back far enough.

We cannot, however, accept Spencer's views on the all-important matter of Religion. We are pleased to think that he frankly acknowledges the necessity of Religion for the well-being of Society, and yet we are surprised at some of the things that he has written on this all-important subject.

We are disappointed that one who has so much
of the scientific spirit should be so unfair when he
comes to write of Religion, as it is ordinarily understood by the vast religious community of our own
and other lands.

We do not, as we dare not, judge Spencer from
a religious point of view, and yet we venture to say
that he does not represent fairly the tenets of the
Christian Religion, when he writes as if the Christian Religion committed itself, or is to be identified
with, the " Carpenter theory of Creation "—as if the
Christian Religion taught as a leading characteristic
that punishment is a Divine Vengeance,—that
Divine Vengeance is eternal, and that the motive
of the Christian Faith is Other-worldliness.

Every one who knows the Christian Religion must
recognise at once, that in Spencer's representation
of it essentials have been left out, and much has
been put in that ought not to be there.

The Bible Doctrine of Creation does not warrant
any Carpenter theory. It is more akin, in its
sublime simplicity and Idealism, to a Poetical
theory of Creation—certainly the highest possible
conception.

And then, Punishment, in the Christian scheme,
is always represented as the sure outcome of impenitent wickedness, and as a penalty lasting as
long as impenitent wickedness lasts.

Surely the charge of Other-worldliness, as the
supreme motive of the Christian Faith, disappears
at once in the light of the Sermon on the Mount;
or under the guidance of that text, said to be the

" finest summary of all Religion,"—" What, O man, doth the Lord require of thee but to do justly, and to love mercy, and to walk humbly with thy God ? "

In regard to Spencer's statement, that Science and Religion are reconciled in the acceptance by each of Absolute Mystery as the ultimate, all that we care to remark is, that before Spencer made a statement like this, it would have been well to have assured himself that Science and Religion were at variance, and that he was speaking about Religion as revealed and understood in the right and highest quarter.

It is, we take the liberty of saying, not at all so clear that Science and Religion are at variance ; or at anyrate, at such variance as they are and have been declared to be. Science and Religion are not antithetic ; the opposite of Science is Nescience, or Ignorance, and the opposite of Religion is Irreligion.

Quite possibly, Religion of a sort flourishes best in the soil of ignorance, giving sanction to the old saying, that " Ignorance is the mother of devotion," yet it is simple truth, that Religion also lives and flourishes where the purest Science holds sway. " The heaviest heads bend."

We venture the assertion, that Spencer is, to say the least of it, peculiar, if not entirely wrong, in his conception of Religion.

It may be difficult to state what Religion really is, but we are convinced that they alone are on right lines who associate Religion with the Upward look,—with an " indissoluble engagement to God," to use the words of Joubert,—with a personal relationship to the Supreme. It may be difficult to point out what Religion really is, but it is not difficult to show, that whatever it is, it is not what Spencer makes it out to be.

To Spencer, Religion is only a " Theory of Causation,"—it has to do with solving in some way or another the problem of the Universe; its ultimate is mystery—the realm of the Unknown and Unknowable. Religion is to him a something academic, philosophical, scientific.

Here, then, we venture to join issue with Spencer, and ask this plain question—What Religion corresponds to such a conception as this? If we take the highest Religion that the world has ever witnessed,—the Religion called " Absolute,"—the Christian Religion, we ask, does the Christian Religion correspond to the definition just given, that Religion is a " Theory of Causation"? Does the Christian Religion land ultimately those who accept it, in unpenetrated and impenetrable darkness?

We have only to ask this question to get an answer. The Christian Religion is no " Theory of Causation," whatever else it is. The Christian Religion reveals one God, named by the highest and best of names, even by the name of " Father." This Religion emphasises sin, and makes known the way of salvation from sin, through faith in the Saviour-Christ. The Christian Religion unfolds duty, declaring love to God and to man as its summary. The Christian Religion offers Eternal Life, and reveals the great Hereafter as a Hereafter of unutterable splendours and terrors.

Instead of the Christian Religion landing those who accept it in impenetrable darkness, it claims and proclaims as a distinctive note, the power to translate out of darkness into a great and marvellous Light,—a Light which grows stronger, purer, and more lasting.

We do not, of course, here refer to the Christian Religion as the true Religion, although we most assuredly believe that it is so, but simply for the purpose of indicating, however inadequately, that Spencer's definition of Religion does not square with the facts of the case when confronted with a Religion which has been, and deserves to be, recognised as the highest and best.

He is very severe on what is known as Anthropomorphism in Religion ; that is, as he puts it, "making the objects of worship like ourselves." According to Spencer, this is what they do who think of God as Personal, living, good, just, and true. He declares that this is making God like themselves, bigger perhaps, yet just like themselves.

He wants to make people give over thinking of God after this fashion. Condescending to an illustration, he writes, that in thinking thus about God, people are simply doing what a watch would do if it could think about the watchmaker. Were the watch to think about the watchmaker, it would think of him as made up of springs, and escapes, like itself.

Spencer's illustration, however, proves a little too much, for it brings the Scientist and the Philosopher into a like condemnation with the man of Religion and the Theologian. When the man of Science speaks of Law; when a Philosopher, like Spencer, speaks of a "Persistent and Inscrutable Force," what can the man of Science and the Philosopher be compared to, but just the watch thinking about the watchmaker? There is, however, this great difference, that whilst the watch, in the person of the man of Religion, makes use of the ideas of personality, life, and goodness, the same watch, in the person of the man of Science, makes use of the ideas of law and force,—only, the ideas of the man of Religion are infinitely higher than the ideas of the man of Science and Philosophy.

Surely, if the watch is going to think at all, it is well that it should think in the best way.

What we want to make clear is this, that man, in his thinking about the Universe or about God, can no more help being Anthropomorphic than he can jump off his own shadow.

Although Spencer does not seem to see it, yet it is obvious that he is as much Anthropomorphic in his thinking about the Universe as Theologians are in their thinking about God. The only difference is that Spencer uses one set of ideas, and Theologians use another, and a higher set.

The only other remark which we make on Spencer's position as an Agnostic, is to observe once again, what has often been remarked, that although Spencer commits himself to a Philosophy of the Unknown and the Unknowable, yet it is more than surprising to note how much he claims to know about the so-called " Unknown and Unknowable Reality behind all Phenomena."

He knows that it is a Power, Force, or " Energy from which all things proceed,"—that it is " Infinite, Eternal, and Persistent,"—that it is Unknown and Unknowable,—that it manifests itself,—and that it manifests itself to us in the Universe.

Here there is not only knowledge, but a knowledge which is at once precise, extensive, and spermatic. Almost unbidden, the question arises,—if so much can be known about this Reality which is behind all phenomena, why not more and more ? We cannot resist the conclusion, that were Spencer to develop further on his own lines, then, like Saul among the Prophets, he would blossom into the most orthodox of Theologians, and the most honoured of Christian Teachers.

V

He is very thoroughgoing in his Agnosticism, and he is as much so as an Evolutionist. Like Aaron's rod, Spencer's swallows up all other Evolutionary rods. He sees no reason for not thinking that as an individual grows in twenty years, to what he becomes, out of a single cell ; so the whole human race, in millions of years, may have grown to what it has become, also out of a single cell.

It has to be noted, that Spencer is an Evolutionist on purely philosophical grounds. We do not know that he has ever been called a Monist, but Monist he clearly is in his endeavour to comprehend the whole Universe under one Principle and one Law. Such an effort is not only intellectually praiseworthy, but also permissible, as being in harmony with rational ideas, and yet it is more than doubtful if it can be crowned with success.

Instead of being Monistic, it is nearer the truth to say that the Universe is Dualistic, for whenever we are forced back upon Ultimates we are necessitated to think of self and non-self, mind and matter, soul and body, God and the world, persons and things.

We are inclined to think that Spencer's radical mistake here is his search after a Unity, which can never be found. He has failed to show that the various forces in the world—physical, vital, mental, moral, and social—can be transmuted into each other, and has also failed to show that these are governed by one and the same Law. These forces are acknowledged by scientific thinkers, as able as Spencer himself, to be essentially different; and, as a matter of course, forces which are essentially different must act in accordance with essentially different laws.

As an Evolutionist, Spencer does not object to the Doctrine of Primal Creation, although he has on this subject little to affirm or deny, because the mystery is so great. What he does object to is the Doctrine of Special Creations, or " special divine interferences " (as it has been called) with the world process, or processes. Like some other Evolutionists, he objects to gaps, or interferences; is fond of growth and rhythm.

If we mistake not, one reason given by him to sustain his objection against " Special Creations," is that thereby so much more work is laid upon the Creator ; but surely the idea of additional work is altogether out of place when it is remembered that the Creator, even according to Spencer himself, is in possession of an Energy at once " Infinite and Eternal."

The present writer has no difficulty in accepting the Doctrine of " Special Creations," for he considers that everything is granted once the Doctrine of Creation is granted. If there be one " divine interference," why not thousands upon thousands,—as may seem good to that Omnipotent, Omnipresent, and Omniscient Power behind all things ?

Regarding Spencer's attitude towards Evolution, it may be noted that this attitude was, and still is, only a theoretical one, a fact often overlooked by many. He begins with what he calls, after Kant and La Place, the Nebular Hypothesis ; the theory which supposes that once upon a time the world existed as a diffused vapour,—that this diffused vapour, somehow or another, began to rotate, concentrate, and so originate stars, planets, and their satellites.

Spencer was inclined to think that there is still in the world masses of this primitive nebulous matter, out of which worlds are being made, although he got undeceived somewhat on finding, by means of Lord Ross's Telescope, that what was supposed to be nebulous matter was really groups of stars.

Spencer over-boldly considers it an insult to ask any educated man to accept the Mosaic account of

Creation given in the Bible. We refrain from characterising the theory associated with the names of Spencer and others, which educated men are expected to accept in place of the account recorded in the Scriptures.

In all fairness, it ought to be remembered that Spencer himself only advances in Evolution that which is to him a " working hypothesis." He found and left Evolution a theory. Virchow has voiced the exact state of matters when he said regarding the Evolution of man : " We cannot designate it as a revelation of Science, that man descends from the ape, or from any other animal."

Neither ought it to be forgotten that Evolutionists, instead of agreeing amongst themselves, are arrayed in hostile camps. We find Wallace attacking the fundamental principles of Darwin, inasmuch as Wallace maintains that there are " new departures in Nature, at the introduction of life, consciousness, and man ; and that therefore there is need of some new power or cause, from an Unseen Universe." We find Wallace attacking the fundamental principles of Darwin ; and we find Weismann attacking Spencer ; and Spencer, in defending himself from Weismann, declaring, that if there be no transmission of acquired characters, then " Evolution is a dream." We find Romanes and Wallace at loggerheads about mental development. We find Mr. Kidd and Professor Drummond at sixes-and-sevens as to whether there is a natural basis for the altruistic feeling. And then we find Professor Drummond taking up the cudgels against Darwin, Spencer, and all the rest, for maintaining, as he thinks they do, a one-sided view of Nature.

Spencer's supposed great discovery is that Law of Evolution which he considered capable of explaining everything in the Universe, inorganic, organic, and superorganic; from the movement and rotation of the primal mist, to the making of man in body, mind, and conscience, with all his language, art, society, etc. Here is Spencer's own statement of this great Law of Evolution:—"Evolution is an integration of matter and concomitant dissipation of motion; during which the matter passes from an indefinite, incoherent homogeneity, to a definite, coherent heterogeneity; and during which the retained motion undergoes a parallel transformation."

Someone has well said that the Universe heaved a sigh of relief after the above Law was uttered. Without doubt, such a ponderous Law, in its crude and undigested state, must have lain upon it as a weary weight.

Remarking on this Law of Evolution, we take leave to say, that one of the most serious objections against it is that Spencer, in his strong desire for unity, has been led to apply to spheres and forces, which are essentially different, a Law or Principle which is applicable to only one of them.

Spencer's magic word is Evolution, and his favourite idea, concentration or consolidation;—the sun's substance gravitating to the sun's centre, and the earth's substance gravitating to the earth's centre.

There is, of course, no doubt that concentration holds true in the material sphere, but we must not say that what holds true of matter holds true of mind, morals, and society.

Coming to vital forces, we find that there is not only a new idea—that of vitality, but that there is likewise a new principle or law, better expressed by the term " expansion " than by the term " concentration."

When mental forces come in, there is not only a new idea—that of consciousness, but there is likewise a new principle or law, better expressed by " comprehension," gathering " the many into one," than by " concentration."

So also is it with moral forces. There is not only a new idea here—the idea expressed by the word " ought," but there is likewise a new principle or law, best expressed by the term " self-determination."

Not only is Spencer's Law not equal to covering the whole field under consideration, but we are convinced that there is no one Law able to explain movements which are so essentially different. Spencer's success would have been greater had he divided more.

And then, we question whether it be the case that, in accordance with the leading principle of Spencer's Law, there is a universal movement from a state of homogeneity to heterogeneity, or from simplicity to complexity. Is, for example, Spencer's " primal mist " so very simple as it seems to appear, seeing that in that mist there was in germ the entire Universe, with its suns and systems,—earth, with its plants and animals ;—man, with his Science,

Art, and Religion ; even Spencer himself, and all his Philosophy ?

Although Spencer has no love for Carlyle, yet Carlyle seems to have hit the nail on the head when he declared, that before there can be " Evolution " there must have been " Involution."

If so much comes out of that " primal mist," how much must have been in it, to begin with ?

It is not otherwise with the original cell, which, to Spencer, is so simple and structureless. The more, however, one considers the " primal mist," or the " original cell," the stronger is the conviction sent home, that whatever else they may be they are far enough from being simple.

، We have been struck with the way in which the transition is made in Spencer's Philosophy from the physical to the vital forces. " We owe," he writes, " plant life to the light and heat of the sun." Here he tries to cross the Rubicon so quietly, that one almost fails to note that he has tried to cross it.

The Rubicon, however, between the physical and vital forces is not crossed quite so easily. If we remember aright, Spencer's illustration of this important transition lies in the fact that we require heat to hatch an egg ; and so, according to his teaching, all life comes from the light and heat of the sun.

A moment's thought is enough to show, that whilst it is true that heat is required to hatch an egg, it is also true that we require the egg to begin with, plus all the mystery of its composition. Were anyone to put a round stone, instead of an egg, under the hen, all the heat of the hen, and all the heat of the sun, would never get a chicken out of that stone.

What we are contending for is, that instead of the " primal mist " and the " original cell " being, as Spencer's Law requires them to be, simple, indefinite, and incoherent, they are instead complex, definite, and coherent.

Although atoms may be very small, they are the very reverse of simple. As an eminent Scientist has said : " An atom of pure iron is probably a vastly more complicated system than that of the planets and their satellites."

There is a bit of unconscious humour in Spencer's illustration of the movement from homogeneity to heterogeneity, so far as the development of man is concerned, inasmuch as he quotes the case of the Papuan, with his short legs, and the European, with his longer legs, to illustrate such a movement. It is clear, however, that to support the principle laid down by Spencer, the European would require to have either something different from legs altogether, and to have more than two, for legs are legs all the world over.

Spencer has only failed, where success was impossible, in the attempt to bridge the chasms ; to get life out of no-life, consciousness out of non-consciousness, mind and morals from a source where they do not exist.

We need not quote the oft-quoted words of Tyndall regarding the unthinkableness of the " passage from the physics of the brain to the corresponding facts of consciousness." It is impossible, says Martineau, to establish that which " shall link mind and matter into a single line."

VI

We conclude with a reference to Spencer's ethical system, to which he attaches great importance, regarding it, indeed, as the building, of which the rest has been but the scaffolding.

He purposes, in his ethical investigations, to discover a "scientific basis for Conduct." After strenuous efforts he comes to the conclusion that " the good is the pleasurable, and that the evil is the painful." Although an advanced Utilitarian, he is yet Utilitarian enough to hold that, in the matter of morals, Pleasure must come in somewhere. As Aristotle defined Happiness in terms of Virtue, so Spencer defines " Virtue in terms of Happiness."

Although he writhes under Carlyle's comparison of Utilitarianism to a Pig's philosophy of the Universe, yet apparently his bitterness of spirit is due to a suspicion that there is so much truth in the comparison.

He retorts, with great unfairness upon Carlyle, by calling him the " Apostle of Brute Force," insinuating that Carlyle favours the power of might more than the principle of right. It may be, of course, that Carlyle, like all other emotional writers, is chargeable with occasional inconsistencies and extravagances, and yet, it is only just to acknowledge, that the weight of his teaching is clearly on the side of the invincible power of a strength, neither that of the brute, nor the purse, nor the army, nor even of intellect, but a strength which is moral—the strength that lies in the consciousness of being on the right side, and doing the right thing. These are Carlyle's own words :—" No son of Adam is more contemptuous than I am, of Might, except when it rests on the origin of Right, —its eternal Symbol."

Whilst there is much that is suggestive in Spencer's ethical system, we miss as elements and motive powers in morality, the great ideas of conscience, duty, obedience, struggle, aspiration, and God. It may be something to condemn pure Egoism, and pure Altruism, and it may be something to come to this as the conclusion of the whole matter in morals, " Seek your own happiness, and seek also the happiness of others "; and yet we are sure that this is neither the best conclusion, nor the last word, on the great theme of Ethics.

With a brave, logical consistency, Spencer does not hesitate to apply to Ethics his own Law of Evolution, maintaining that in Ethics, as in all else, there is development from the indefinite, the incoherent, and the simple, to that which is definite, coherent, and complex.

Were we to test this Evolutionary Law in Ethics, by coming to the concrete, we suppose that Spencer would grant that there was no developed morality, in say, a determined villain; and yet it will be found that the conduct of this grossly immoral person cannot be characterised as either indefinite, or incoherent, or simple. The very opposite, indeed, is true of this bad man's conduct, clearly indicative of the fact, that conduct must be judged of by some other Law than the Law of Evolution. In other words, the important matter in all conduct is, not what is, but what " ought " to be.

There is one noteworthy statement in Spencer's Ethics which contains a germ in Morals out of which he himself might have developed a truer system than that with which he has identified himself. The statement we refer to is, " that Happiness ought to be made the supreme aim, because it is the concomitant of the highest life." We are not aware that he has uttered a wiser or truer word than this, that " Happiness is the concomitant of the highest life." Accepting this conclusion, surely the all-important question comes to be, what is the highest life ? and as surely the all-important duty comes to be, to make for that highest life with all one's heart, and soul, and strength, and mind. Well did Carlyle say, " leave Happiness on its own basis." Worthy also of being written in Letters of gold is his Everlasting Yea—" Love not pleasure, love God."

" Altruism " is not the highest word in Ethics. There is a greater word still, that grand word " Ought,"—a word which grasps within its divine embrace, not only "altruism," but ever so much else in the sphere of Ethics. Morality thrives best, not in the atmosphere of instinct, but in the atmosphere of freedom, spirit, intelligence, law, and intention.

" There is nothing good in the world, except a good will,"—so writes Kant.

" Stern daughter of the voice of God, O Duty," writes Wordsworth.

Spencer's system of Ethics is good enough, so far as it goes; but we miss in it the grandeur of a system like that of Kant, where the bare sense of duty plays such an important part, and we also miss the simple grandeur and the compelling warmth of a Scheme of Morals infinitely superior to both, and that is the Scheme associated with the Name and Spirit of the Founder of the Christian Faith.

JOHN RUSKIN

"My work is amongst Stones and Clouds and Flowers."—
RUSKIN, *Political Economy*.

"You can't paint or sing yourselves into good men ; you must
be good men before you can either paint or sing."—RUSKIN,
" Inaugural Lecture at Oxford."

" 'Whatsoever He saith unto you, do it,'—these words are the
sum of all that I have been permitted to speak in God's Name,
now, these seven years."—RUSKIN, *Fors Clavigera*.

JOHN RUSKIN

I

WHEN Ruskin's name is mentioned, as it often and deservedly is in the present day, he is referred to as a beautiful writer of the English language, as a celebrated Art-critic, or, it may be, as holding peculiar views in Social and Political Economy.

Such notes of Ruskin are justifiable—he is a beautiful writer of the English language—none more so; he is an Art-critic of commanding influence, and he does hold peculiar views in Social and Political economy; and yet, when Ruskin names himself, he chooses significantly the name of "Prophet."

This self-chosen name of Prophet does justice to what is perhaps the most important side of his nature—the moral and religious side.

John Ruskin had "visions of the heart," and these he has uttered faithfully and fearlessly: he is intensely earnest about moral and spiritual verities. His whole nature has its roots deeply set in Religion and God.

Comparing himself to John the Baptist, he delivers as his own message to the age the old message of the Baptist,—" And now also the axe is laid unto the root of the trees : therefore every tree which bringeth not forth good fruit is hewn down, and cast into the fire."

When Carlyle, gifted beyond most with intuition into character, wrote of Ruskin, it was as a "Prophet" that he wrote of him. "Of all men now alive," says Carlyle, "Ruskin has the best talent for preaching,"—and again, "There is in Ruskin a ray of real heaven."

In these two sentences the Master hits off admirably the essential characteristics of John Ruskin, who was pleased to consider himself one of Carlyle's pupils. There is, indeed, a ray of real heaven in Ruskin; nay, we may go further and say of him, as was said of Spinoza, that he is a "God-intoxicated man." He is essentially a preacher— a preacher of Righteousness; his books are his sermons.

It is impossible to enter into fellowship with him through his writings without receiving impulses—towards things that are true, things that are lovely, and things that are good.

As is well known, Ruskin holds many peculiar notions. He is, for example, dead against Railroads, Machinery, and Usury. He does not think that the people of our day are either healthier, wiser, or happier, because they are dragged from place to place "behind a kettle," even at a mile a minute. He is a strong believer in people using their limbs to walk with, and their hands and arms to work with; and in such natural forces as wind and water.

Ruskin gets wild about Usury, increasing Capital by lending it; declaring that Usury is God-forbidden guilt; that it is worse than theft—obtained either by deceiving people, or by distressing them, —generally by both. According to his teaching, all Usury is increase to one person, by decrease to another; "increment to the rich, and decrement to the poor,—the labourer's deficit, and the capitalist's efficit."

In response to one who inquired, how it came to pass that, holding such strong opinions about Usury, he himself took rent from his houses, and interest on his money lying in the Bank; Ruskin requested that this correspondent and others would meantime suspend their judgment regarding him on this matter. And in response to one who inquired, why he himself used the Railway, whilst pouring out upon it the vials of his indignation, he replied, that he would "use the Devil himself, as a local black, if he were available."

The secret of Ruskin's severe denunciations of railways, factories, and so on, is not far to seek; it arises in a great measure from his intense love of Nature, and his laudable desire that people should get face to face with Nature as much as possible. "He wants to keep the cheeks of England red, and her fields green." He wants to keep the air pure, and the rivers clean.

He is well aware that there are many sinners against the light, beauty, and purity of Nature, both in England and in Scotland. The "Water of Leith" is—"well, one can't say in civilised com-

pany," writes Ruskin, "what it is." "At Lin-
lithgow," he writes, "of all the palaces so fair,
built for royal dwellings, the oil floating on the
streams can be ignited; burning with a large
flame." "Talk about the beauties of Nature, with
the Teviot as 'black as ink.'" "I saw," he goes on
to say, "the putrid carcase of a sheep lying in the
dry channel of the Jed, under Jedburgh Abbey—
the stream being taken away to supply a single mill."

Peculiar in many things, he is also peculiar in
his notions of how houses should be built, and
towns constructed. He has a beautiful and pregnant passage, to the effect that we ought not to
forget that God dwells in our cottages, as well as
in our churches; sending home the lesson, that we
should see to it that God is as well housed in the
one as in the other. This passage is fairly well
known: "I should like to destroy most of the Railroads in England, and all the Railroads in Wales.
I would destroy, and rebuild, the houses of Parliament, the National Gallery, and the East end of
London. I would destroy, without rebuilding, the
New Town of Edinburgh, the North Suburbs of
Geneva, and the City of New York."

Ruskin, it may be observed, is no party man in
Politics. He confesses that he has a sincere love
of Kings, and that his chief desire is to see them,
although he holds strange ideas of what they really
ought to be.

He is neither a Liberal nor a Tory;—never voted
in his life for a Member of Parliament, and never
means to do so. Sometimes he calls himself a

Tory—a Tory, that is to say, of "the old school,"
—the school of Walter Scott, and of Homer.
And sometimes he calls himself a Communist—a
"reddest of the red." "We Communists," he
writes, "of the old school, think that our property
belongs to everybody, and that everybody's property
belongs to us."

As in Politics, so in Religion; Ruskin belongs
to no Sect, or Church. He is neither Presbyterian,
nor Episcopalian, — neither a Protestant, nor a
Roman Catholic. He calls himself a "Catholic of
the Catholics."

There are two texts in the Bible, very dear to
him, which express best his religious beliefs. There
is that word of the Hebrew Prophet, Micah, in the
Old Testament—"What doth the Lord require of
thee, O man, but to do justly, and to love mercy,
and to walk humbly with thy God?" And there
is that word of Mary in the New Testament,
"Whatsoever He saith unto you, do it."

He writes of what he calls that miserable question
—the Schism between Catholic and Protestant;—
a "miserable question, in view of the Eternal
schism, cloven by the very sword of Michael, between him that serveth God, and him that serveth
Him not."

Ruskin is peculiar also in the titles of his books;
in the way in which he would have them pur-
chased, and in the price which he sets on them.
Many of his books have strange titles; such as
Fors Clavigera, Sesame and Lilies, The Eagle's Nest,
Ethics of the Dust, " *Unto this Last,*" *Construction of*

Sheepfolds, and so on. There is an amusing story told of the misleading character of the title of the last book referred to, *The Construction of Sheepfolds*. It is said that a farmer, having purchased this book, in the hope of finding therein information that might be useful to him in his ordinary employment, was greatly disappointed on discovering that, instead of dealing with Sheepfolds for ordinary sheep, this book was full of Letters on the "Lord's Prayer"—addressed to the "Clergy of the Church of England."

In answer to a correspondent, who wrote to him about the cost of his books, drawing his attention to the fact that his *Modern Painters* had been sold for £38, Ruskin replied, that he knew that his Books were dear; that he made nothing by them; that he will not consent to advertising; that he sees to it that everything about them—paper, printing, and illustrations is the best possible; and that he thinks that each of his Books is worth at least a Doctor's fee.

We cannot but think that it is in many respects unfortunate that Ruskin's Books are so costly; a fact particularly conspicuous in those days, when Classics in Literature, ancient and modern, are, to use a current phrase, marvels of cheapness, and, begging Ruskin's pardon—"cheap without being nasty." What a great boon Ruskin would confer on the millions of readers of the present day were he to see his way to issue cheap editions of his Books, than which none are more worthy of being read and pondered.

II

Ruskin has told the story of his life, partly in
Fors Clavigera, and more fully in his *Præterita*.
He was born in London in 1819. He was the
only child of his parents, and does not hesitate to
say that he was rather spoiled, inasmuch as his
upbringing was too luxurious, and he himself too
much indulged.

His father, a wine merchant in Billiter Street,
London, sold, so his son tells us, the "finest Sherry
in the world." The father must have been a suc-
cessful merchant, for he left his son a fortune of
over a hundred and fifty thousand pounds. Ruskin
is loud in praise of his father's integrity; and
mentions it as a peculiar fact, that his father
selected his clerks more for their incapacity than
for their capacity, inasmuch as he could not bear
to be excelled in anything.

In course of time Ruskin took up with what he
calls his "Turner insanities," much to the disappointment of his father, who meant him for the
Church, and who was sure that he would become
a Bishop by and by.

Like almost all great men, Ruskin was blest
with a good mother. Like Hannah of old, she
dedicated him to the Lord before he was born.
It was her earnest desire that he should become
an evangelical Clergyman; and it may be added,
that although both his father and mother were
disappointed in the particular form in which
Ruskin manifested his Religiousness, their desires,

if not fulfilled in the letter, have certainly been
fulfilled in the spirit.

There is not much more interesting reading in
the delightful Autobiography, with which Ruskin
has favoured us, than the account of the efforts of
his mother to train up her son in the " nurture
and admonition of the Lord." Up till the time
that he went to Oxford, every morning, first thing
after breakfast, mother and son read the Bible
together, going through the whole Bible, from
Genesis to Revelation, hard names and all. Every
morning young Ruskin learned a few verses by
heart; learning in course of time, as he tells us,
the whole body of the fine old Scotch Paraphrases
— characterised by him as " good, melodious,
forceful verse."

It is worthy of note, that Ruskin himself
attaches immense importance, every way, to these
Bible exercises with his mother, from morning to
morning, in the earlier years of his life. This determined, as he says, " the best part of his taste
in Literature," and formed the " most precious,
and indeed the essential part of his education."
He is sure that no one will write superficial
English who knows by heart the 32nd chapter of
Deuteronomy, the 119th Psalm, the 15th chapter
of 1 Corinthians, the " Sermon on the Mount,"
and the " Apocalypse."

Amongst the portions of the Bible for which
he has a special fondness, he singles out the
119th Psalm. Although it cost him so much to
learn this Psalm, and although, because of that it

was almost repulsive, yet it became to him the most precious of all, in its overflowing and glowing passion of love for the Law of God. He tells how he and his mother had a struggle for three weeks over accenting the " of " in the lines, " Shall any following spring revive the ashes of the urn "; the mother wanting the accent to be upon the " ashes," and young Ruskin putting it on the " of."

As a boy, he was given to preaching sermons, in imitation of the Rev. Mr. Howell, over the red sofa cushion, " eleven words long," and of the purest gospel, beginning with the words, " People, be good." Here the child was, indeed, father of the man.

Ruskin takes us into confidence over a little love affair with Adèle Clôtilde, daughter of Mr. Domeq, his father's partner, and of French connections, in which he considers himself to have behaved rather foolishly.

Her usual name was Clôtilde, but Ruskin called her Adèle, because this rhymed best with " shell," " spell," and " knell." He wrote her a French letter seven quarto pages long—at the French of which Clôtilde laughed immensely. He also wrote her a Story about Naples, and the bandit Leoni. It was all, however, without success ; Clôtilde received it with rippling " ecstasies of derision."

About this time he came under the influence of Byron and Shelley. He admired the veracity of Byron, but got harm from Shelley, in attempting, in imitation of him, to write lines like " prickly, and pulpous, and blistering, and blue." He went perseveringly through Shelley's " Revolt of Islam," to find out who revolted—against whom, or what. This, he says, he did not find out, and does not know till this day.

It may be observed, by the way, that the literary judgments of Ruskin are at once decisive and valuable. To him, Scott is of the world, worldly; Burns, is of the flesh, fleshly; and Byron, is of the devil, damnable. Wordsworth, says Ruskin, seems to think that Nature could not get on without him, and that, being a Philosopher, he " must say something."

When Ruskin entered as a Gentleman-Commoner at Christ's Church, Oxford, the expectations about him, more especially those of his father, were of the highest order. His father hoped, so the son tells us, that at College " he would enter into the best society,—take all the prizes every year, and a Double First to finish with,—marry Lady Clara Vere de Vere,—write Poetry as good as Byron's, only purer, —preach sermons as good as Bossuet's, only Protestant,—be made at forty, Bishop of Winchester, and at fifty, Primate of all England."

This is how Ruskin humorously describes himself at this period: " There was not the slightest fear of my gambling, for I had never touched a card, and looked upon dice as people now do on dynamite. There was no fear of my being tempted by the strange woman, for was I not in love? and besides, never allowed to be out after half-past nine. There was no fear of my running into debt, for there were no " Turners " to be had at Oxford, and I cared for nothing else in the world as material possession. There was no fear of my breaking my neck out hunting, for I could not have ridden a hack down High Street. There was no fear of my ruining myself at a race, for I never had been at a race in my life, and had not the least wish to win anybody else's money."

At College he once committed the terrible mistake of writing, like a vulgar student, an Essay of some length, and with some meaning in it; forgetful of the fact, that it was the law amongst Gentlemen - Commoners, that an Essay should never contain "more than twelve lines with four words in each." Student Ruskin was reminded, that if ever he did such a thing again, "Coventry" wasn't the word for the place he would be sent to.

By and by Ruskin took his Degree, although he confesses, that had it not been for excellency in other subjects,—Philosophy, Divinity, and Mathematics,—he would have been ploughed for his shortcomings in Classics ; he says he never could distinguish between First and Second Futures, nor tell where the " Pelasgi " lived.

III

Very interesting it is to learn the crises which determined Ruskin's history.

One day, on the road to Norwood, he noticed a bit of ivy round a thorn-stem, which seemed to him not ill composed. He drew it, and liked it all the more, the more he drew.

One day he drew a small aspen tree against the blue sky. More and more beautiful the lines appeared. Thus the thought came into his mind, that God had made everything "beautiful in His time,"—that the trees of the wood were more beautiful than all Gothic tracery, than all "Greek Vase" Imagery, than all the daintiest embroideries of the East.

Simple as all this may seem, it yet reveals the secret of Ruskin's determination to Pre-Raphaelitism, —his resolution to keep close, absolutely close, to Nature, in all that concerned Art. This determination furnishes the key to his manifold Art-critiques, and is the source of his great artistic influence.

Another, and very important, crisis in Ruskin's history took place on his receiving from Mr. Telford, one of his father's partners, the present of a copy of Rogers' *Italy*, with illustrations by Turner. This formed his first introduction to Turner,—a name which must be for all time closely linked with his own, for whose works of Art he had, and has, literally a passion.

Ruskin wrote his greatest work, *Modern Painters*, —a work which occupied seventeen of the best years of his life, necessitating the hardest study, for the very purpose of defending the name and fame of Turner, and of expounding his Artistic merits. He says that Turner is "the greatest landscape painter that the world has ever witnessed," and does not hesitate to associate him with Shakespeare and Verulam,—the "greatest men of genius in all history."

Whether he has succeeded in showing that Turner is "the greatest landscape painter in the world," worthy of ranking with the greatest men of genius in all history, we do not take upon us to say, but this has to be said, that the praise-worthy attempt to do so led him into the most searching studies both of Nature and Art. Finding here his life-work, he has permanently enriched the Literature of our country, and of the world. "My work," he writes, "is amongst stones, and clouds, and flowers." He has studied Nature closely, originally, and reverently, in every aspect of cloud, mountain, river, forest, earth, sea, and man. He has studied Art, as represented in every school and age; and in all its varied forms of Painting, Sculpture, and Architecture.

Another crisis of Ruskin's life, which, fortunately, did not prove too serious, took place on his hearing, one Sunday morning, at Turin, in a Waldensian Chapel, a little squeaking idiot preach to seventeen old women and three louts, that they were "the only children of God in Turin"; and that all the people in Turin "outside the Chapel, and that all the people in the world out of sight of Monte Viso," would be damned. Ruskin says, that he came out of that Chapel an "unconverted man," and bade farewell, for a time, to his mother-law of Protestantism.

As all readers of Ruskin's works know, the Alps

became one of the passions of his life. It is impressive to read his account of his first sight of these mountains. He first saw them from the garden terrace at Schaffhausen, one summer evening, and this sight of the Alps formed still another crisis of his life. "The Alps were infinitely beyond all that had ever been thought or dreamed. The seen walls of lost Eden could not have been more beautiful, nor more awful round Heaven the walls of Sacred Death." He went down that evening from the garden terrace of Schaffhausen with his destiny fixed, in all of it that was to be sacred and useful. "Venice and Chamouni became his two bournes of earth."

A fact or two about his Books, from his own pen, may not be uninteresting. He wrote his *Modern Painters* at twenty years of age; the *Stones of Venice* at thirty; "*Unto this Last*" at forty; the *Inaugural Lectures at Oxford* at fifty; the *Fors Clavigera* at sixty.

His best works are *Modern Painters* and *Stones of Venice*. Written with utmost care, they show marvellous patience, wonderful accuracy, and profound scholarship. Of all his works, *Fors Clavigera* is the most readable. This work appeared in the form of Letters, some ninety-six altogether, addressed to the "Labourers and workmen of Great Britain." In these Letters Ruskin writes frankly, in the mood in which he chances to be, and on subjects which may turn up, nailing down many a truth which he longs to send home, and exposing many follies which he wishes people to avoid. These Letters are of the most varied contents,—from Goosepies, to Glaciers; from the works of Sir Walter Scott, to the founding of St. George's Company; from Lectures on the 19th Psalm, to Lecturings on Love and Courtship.

IV

All readers of Ruskin's writings acknowledge the charm of his Style. Although never dull, he is occasionally prolix, taking a long time to tell his story; but then, he has a story to tell, and tells it in a charming way. One of his natural gifts—a certain capacity for " rhythmic cadence "—he has made one of his conspicuous graces. He reminds us that he wrote his *Modern Painters* after the style of Hooker's *Ecclesiastical Polity*; but whoever or whatever was his model, it is not too much to say, that he stands unapproached for the exquisiteness of his Literary Style.

Although everybody confesses the charm of his fine writing, it is instructive to note, that Ruskin himself is getting somewhat tired of it. It is like to drive him mad, to hear people, who pay no heed to what he actually says, talk about his " fine writing." There is a marked difference between the style of *Modern Painters* and that of *Fors Clavigera*, and of late his writings contain more of the pungent than of the fine. " I used," says Ruskin, " to be called a good writer— not so now. If anybody's house is on fire, I now simply say, ' Sir, your house is on fire,' but I used to say, 'Sir, the abode in which you probably passed the delightful days of your youth is in a state of inflammation.'"

Ruskin lacks that vein of humour so characteristic of his master, Carlyle, and has a tendency to the serious fault of exaggeration, being apt to overdo in praise and censure. Whatever be the cause,—unbelief, steam, railways, or factories, things are certainly bad enough, socially, amongst us, but no good comes from making things worse than they really are.

Our social condition is bad enough, but surely the picture is overdrawn when Ruskin writes that the greater part of the labour of England is spent unproductively,—" Spent on iron plates, and iron guns, and on gunpowder ; on infernal machines— infernal fortresses, standing still; infernal fortresses, floating about ; infernal means of mischievous locomotion ; infernal law-suits ; infernal parliamentary elections ; infernal beer ; infernal gazettes, and statues and pictures."

Things are bad enough, but surely Ruskin goes far over the score when he says that our cities are " a wilderness of spinning-wheels, instead of palaces, yet the people have no clothes. We have blackened every leaf of English green wood with ashes, and the people die of cold ; our harbours are a forest of merchant-ships, and the people die of hunger."

Although there is not much in his writings of the nature of humour, there are amusing incidents here and there. He speaks very highly of an old servant of the family, called Ann; and says that he never knew of Ann doing harm to anybody, excepting that of saving some two hundred pounds, and odd money, and leaving it to her relations; in consequence of which, some of them, after her funeral, did not speak to the rest for several months.

He has another story about this same Ann, showing that she had a will of her own. It was the desire of Ruskin's mother to have a certain cup placed at her right hand every morning, at the breakfast table; but Ann, although told about this from time to time, persistently placed the cup on the other side. And Ruskin says that his mother used to declare, as regularly as Ann did this contumacious thing, that if ever there was a woman possessed with the devil, that woman was Ann.

Ruskin puts on record a remark made to him by his Cousin Jessie, when, as a boy, he spent a holiday at Perth. It seems that Jessie and John, more boisterous on the Lord's Day than they ought to have been, had to be rebuked by his Aunt for jumping on, and jumping off, certain boxes in the room. To comfort John, his Cousin Jessie said: "Never mind, John, when we are married we'll jump off boxes all day long, if we like."

Ruskin's writings abound with a charming opinionativeness. He has opinions, and most decided ones too, on all sorts of persons and things— kings, bishops, capitalists, workers, artists, authors;

on pictures, cathedrals, churches, etc.; and he is not afraid to utter them.

Well aware that he is dogmatic in his judgments, he justifies his manner by declaring that he never writes a word about anything of which he is not fully cognisant. As a rule, he finds that all other people are wrong, and considers it his vocation and burden to set them right. He had this opinion-ativeness when a youth; if anything, he is more decided now.

When he was a youth, everybody told him to look at the roof of the Sistine Chapel; and he looked at it, and liked it. Everybody also told him to look at Raphael's Transfiguration, and Domenichino's Saint Jerome. He did as he was bid, and without the smallest hesitation pronounced Domenichino's a bad picture, and Raphael's an ugly one; and thenceforth paid no more attention to what anybody said on the subject of Painting.

In his St. George's Schools he would teach children, not the three R's, but the elements of Music, Astronomy, Botany, and Geology. Someone having written to him, that by doing so he would get into conflict with H.M. Inspectors of Schools, he replied: "That although ten millions of In-spectors of Schools were collected together at Cader Idris, they should not make him teach in his Schools a single thing he did not choose to teach."

Here are some of the Epigrams which shine in his writings like stars in the heavens:—

"The most beautiful things in the world, are the most useless—peacocks and lilies, for instance."

"There is material enough, in a single flower, for the ornamenting of a score of cathedrals."

"To be baptized with fire, or to be cast into it, is the choice set before all men."

"I believe that stars, and boughs, and leaves, and bright colours, are everlastingly lovely."

"I do not wonder at what men suffer, but I wonder at what they lose."

"Nothing must come between Nature and the artist's sight."

"Nothing must come between God and the artist's soul."

"To paint water, is like trying to paint a soul."

"To live is nothing, unless to live be to know Him by whom we live."

"No royal road to anywhere worth going to."

"To see clearly, is Poetry, Prophecy, and Religion."

"The sky is not blue colour only; it is blue fire, and cannot be painted."

"When you have got too much to do, don't do it."

"Women and clergy are in the habit of using pretty words, without understanding them."

"If you can paint a leaf, you can paint the world."

"Anybody who makes Religion a second object, makes Religion no object."

"He who offers God a second place, offers Him no place."

V

Before touching on the Message, or Messages, which Ruskin delivers to our age, it may be well to refer briefly to the three great principles—Nature, the Bible, and God, which form the rock-foundation.

Ruskin's love of Nature is at the root of his Pre-Raphaelitism in Painting, and also determines his sympathies in Architecture. As all readers of his books know, he is a passionate admirer of Gothic Architecture, and he is so because convinced that Gothic Architecture is the Architecture of Nature. "No leaves," he said, "are square-headed—they have all the pointed arch."

From his *Modern Painters* we learn that Ruskin has never varied in this, as his main aim and principle, to " declare the perfectness, and eternal beauty of the work of God."

He would test all works of man by their concurrence with, or subjection to, the work of God; and would submit as a criterion for all works of art, this question—" Has the artist been true to what is most perfect in Nature?"

Another of his fundamental principles is loyalty to the Bible, carrying along with it faith in Christ. There is, perhaps, no other great writer of the present day who confesses Christ all through his works as Ruskin does. Atheism is far away, and cannot but be far away, from one who sees, like him, into the inner soul of things. Like Carlyle, he has an open contempt for Materialism and Darwinianism. He is surprised to hear people shrieking because attacks are made upon their Bibles, and their Christ; and says, with great wisdom, that " if People would obey their Bibles, and their Christ, they would not care who attacked them."

These words of Mary, the mother of Jesus, " Whatsoever He saith unto you, do it," sum up, as he reminds us, all that he has been permitted to speak in God's name for many years. He writes as a Christian to Christians, in the hope of a literal, personal, perpetual life, with a "literal, personal, perpetual God."

It may be remarked, that Ruskin has but a poor opinion of the age to which he delivers his message. He thinks that a worse age than the present could not be,—and that in every sense, religious, artistic, moral, and social. This, he thinks, is the real age of darkness. We are living " in the most perfectly miscreant crowd that ever blasphemed creation, and that, not with the old snapfinger blasphemy of the wantonly profane, but with the deliberate blasphemy of Adam Smith—'Thou shalt hate the Lord thy God; damn His laws, and covet thy neighbour's goods.' "

This is how he sketches the civilised nations of modern Europe—"A mass of half-taught, discontented, mostly penniless populace, calling itself The People;—a thing which is called a ' Government,' that is, an apparatus for collecting and spending money,—a number of Capitalists, many of them rogues, and most of them stupid, having no other idea of existence than money-making, gambling, and champagne-bibbing; Literary men, saying anything they can get paid for; Clergymen, saying anything they have been taught to say; Natural Philosophers, saying anything that comes into their heads; and Nobility, saying nothing at all."

Ruskin maintains that the profoundest reason of all this sadness and darkness of soul, in this age of ennui, jaded intellect, and uncomfortableness in soul and body, lies in the fact that it is an age having " no hope, and without God in the world." A red

Indian or an Otaheitian savage, he maintains, has a
surer sense of a Divine existence round him, and
a God over him, than the plurality of refined
Londoners and Parisians.

Nearly all our powerful men, he notes, are
unbelievers; the best, in doubt and misery; and
the others, in reckless despair. Our best Poets and
Thinkers are doubtful and indignant; one or two
anchored, but anxious and weeping. In Politics, he
considers that Religion is now a name; in Art, an
hypocrisy, or affectation. There are but two classes
who believe—the Romanist and the Puritan.

Ruskin declares that whilst the Classical age was
an age of Pagan faith, and the Middle age an age
of confessing Christ, the Modern age is an age of
denying Him, going on to say that this last
characteristic, that of " denying Christ," is intensely
and peculiarly modern.

To this age, dark and sad because of its unbelief,
he delivers his message,—does so with fidelity,
and earnestness, and happily not without hope.
" I," he says, " a man clothed in soft raiment,—I, a
reed shaken with the wind, have yet this message
to all men, entrusted to me, ' Behold the axe is laid
to the root of the tree; whatsoever tree, therefore,
bringeth not forth good fruit, is hewn down, and
cast into the fire.' "

VI

Ruskin has a message to all engaged in Art.
This is the burden of that message—" Be yourselves

good, if you would have good Art; be yourselves
noble, if you would have noble Art." He is absolutely sure that no supreme power in Art can be
attained by impious men, and would have this truth
written in letters of fire. He is anxious to im-
press upon all Artists the fact, that the end of Art
is not to amuse, but to interpret divine things.
He expresses himself finally thus in his " Oxford
Lectures": 'You cannot paint or sing yourselves
into good men,—you must be good men before
you can either paint or sing."

Without attempting to enter upon the manifold
artistic teaching of Ruskin, we take the liberty of
quoting his opinion on the nude in Art,—that
delicate and oft-discussed matter. Ruskin is, as
usual, quite decided in his opinion, and healthful as
decided. He thinks that so much of the nude
body, as in the daily life of the nation, may be seen
with reverence, with modesty, and with delight; so
much, and no more, ought to be shown by the
national arts, either of Painting or of Sculpture.
He writes of the Paris Salons, as "costly and
studious illuminations of the brothel," deploring that
so much of the stripped actress is in evidence
there.

Very interesting are his characteristic delinea-
tions of Artists, ancient and modern.

Easily first, as might have been expected, stands
the name of Joseph Mallard William Turner, the
"first and greatest of Landscape Painters." Not
only does Ruskin class Turner with Bacon and
Shakespeare, but gives him the first place in

essential greatness. Bacon did what Aristotle attempted; Shakespeare did perfectly what Aeschylus did partially, but none before Turner had lifted "the veil from the face of Nature."

He is a great admirer of the paintings of Fra Angelico, declaring that the purest and brightest colours are to be found there only; and that in the paintings of the old Friar, the glory of the human countenance reaches actual transfiguration. Salvator gives him the idea of a lost spirit. He writes of Rubens' physical art-power, and of Rubens himself as a healthy, worthy, kind-hearted, courtly phrased animal, with no traces of a soul, except when he paints children.

Ruskin is very severe on Doré. Of a woman who had gone to see one of Doré's pictures, he remarked, that she had better have gone and seen the devil. Doré's pictures, says Ruskin, are "fit neither for the land nor yet for the dunghill." Whistler's Studies, or Harmonies, he characterises as "absolute rubbish." "I have seen," he writes, "much Cockney impudence before now, but never expected to hear a cockscomb ask two hundred guineas for flinging a pot of paint in the public's face."

VII

Ruskin has a Message to all concerned with Religion. The substance of his message is a passionate appeal to the individual and nation "*to be good.*" This, as has been pointed out, was the burden of the sermons which he preached when a boy, and this is also the burden of the more than forty volumes which he has written.

It is surely fortunate for our age that it has, in Ruskin, as a Teacher of the first rank, one whose writings are saturated with the religious spirit. He is no preacher of knowledge for the sake of knowledge, nor of culture for the sake of culture, nor of art for art's sake; but he is a preacher who calls upon man to glorify God, the Giver, sanctifying unto Him every power which he possesses.

The perusal of Ruskin's writings adds a new force to the well-known words,—" Godliness is profitable unto all things." As with a stroke of lightning, he sketches the history of the once-famed Venice, whose transitions were swift like the falling of a star, from "pride to infidelity, from infidelity to the insatiable pursuit of pleasure, and from this to irremediable degradation."

His first article in the Creed of the St. George's Company runs thus: "I believe in God"; and this is his first order to the children of St. George's Company: "Always, and in whatever you do, endeavour to please Christ. Say to yourself after your prayers, 'Whoso forsaketh not all that he hath, cannot be My disciple.'"

It is refreshing, in those days of a pitiful and pitiless Naturalism, to come across such an out-and-out believer in the Supernatural. Ruskin wonders at those who maintain so rigorously the steadfastness of the laws of the Universe, when it is so evident that will—our own will, breaks them

every day ; and sends powerfully home the question,
—If our wills can do so, how much more the Will
of God ?

He is not at all troubled about the miracle of
the sun standing still, when face to face with the
greater miracle of the sun going on.   He fears that
there are some desolate souls, selfish, material, and
unbelieving, for whom " the sun beneath the horizon
stands still for ever,"—those souls, he means, who
are content, so that they eat and breathe their fill ;
content to eat like cattle and breathe like plants,
" regardless of the Spirit that makes the grass
to grow on the mountains."   He writes of the
" Nebuchadnezzar-curse " that sends men to grass
like oxen.   He cannot away with those who
think that this glorious world has been made
simply for the hewing of wood and the drawing
of water ; who imagine that it is to give them
wood to hew and water to drink that " God has
made the pine forest to cover the mountains like
His own shadow, and the rivers to move like His
own Eternity,—the poor vine-dressers and husband-
men, who love the corn they grind and the grapes
they crush better than the gardens of the angels
on the slopes of Eden."

Ruskin believes in Prayer, and is not ashamed to
say so.   As a Christian man, he confesses that he
believes Prayer to be in the last sense sufficient for
the salvation of the town, and drainage in the last
sense insufficient for its salvation.   Not that he is
unconcerned about drainage, but if, of the two, he
must choose between drainage and prayer, " why,

look ye," he says, " whatever you may think of my
wild and whirling words, I will go pray."

Ruskin has also a Message to the Churches.
Although he has taken the trouble to tell us
that he is not an Evangelical, we do not remember
of ever seeing the very soul of evangelical teaching
put better than he himself has put it. We refer
to that sentence in which he says that the root of
every heresy and schism in the Christian Church
has been the effort of men " to earn, rather than
receive, their salvation." He is sure that preaching
would be more effective if people were called on,
not to work for God, but to behold God working
for them.

Amongst other things in the religious sphere,
Ruskin has· something to say on the desire to
beautify churches with architectural adornments,—
painted windows, pictures, upholsteries, and so on.
Having no doubt whatever about the good that
Religion has done to Art, he distinctly questions
whether Art has ever done any good to Religion.

He would certainly like to see beautiful and
costly buildings erected for the Worship of God,
but then he is pleased with such, more as expressive
of the spirit of the worshippers than for any good
which they will do to the cause of Religion. He
is sure that more has always been done for God by
few words than by many pictures, and more by
few acts than by many words.

Attaching very little importance to Denomina-
tionalism, he says it does not matter a burnt stick-

end from the altar, in heaven's sight, whether a
person is Catholic or Protestant, Eastern or Western,
but only whether a person be true.   There is a
fine passage in which he says, that when " Venice
is true to St. Mark, her flag flies all over the
Eastern islands; when Florence is true to her
Lilies, her flag flies all over the Apennines; when
Switzerland is true to her ' Notre Dame des Neiges,'
her pine club beats down all the Austrian lances;
and when England is true to her Protestant virtue,
all the sea-winds ally themselves with her against
the Armada."

Ruskin has something to say on a subject much
discussed at the present time—the Union of the
Churches.   For one thing, with much insight, he
deplores the violent combativeness of the sects of
the Christian Church, sure that such a spirit comes
nearer defying than confessing Christ.   In the
Construction of Sheepfolds — condescending on the
subject of the Union of the Episcopalian Church of
England and the Presbyterian Church of Scotland,
he writes of such a union as both desirable and
possible; maintaining, at the same time, that if
such a union is to be accomplished at all, it must
come about not by absorption, but by compromise.

He uses great plainness of speech.   He tells
those who belong to the Episcopalian Church, that
they must cut the word " Priest " entirely out of
the Prayer-Book, and that they must also throw
out the passages about " Absolution."   Instead of
the word " Priest," he would substitute the word
" Minister " or " Elder," maintaining, wisely as we

think, that the authority of a Christian Minister is that of a King's Messenger, and not of a King's Representative.

He has also something in the way of counsel to those who belong to the Presbyterian Church of Scotland. He thinks that the Scottish Church has no shadow of excuse for refusing Episcopacy, seeing it is in the Bible, and no excuse for refusing a written form of prayer.

We do not enter upon any discussion as to whether the government of the Church by Episcopacy is more in harmony with the Divine Word than government of the Church by Presbytery. We content ourselves with remarking, that Ruskin makes a larger assumption than he is entitled to do, when he says that Episcopacy is warranted by the Word of God. Something may be said for the Episcopal form of Church government as a development in the course of the Church's history, but the claim is ill founded, and acknowledged by competent scholars of the Church of England to be so, when an appeal is made to the Law and to the Testimony.

Were we to discuss the propriety or otherwise of using liturgical forms in the Worship of God, we would be inclined to take much the same line, considering that the *Scriptural link*, a very important one, is the weakest in the whole chain. There is a question asked by a Covenanter that keeps sounding in our ears,—" Where got Jacob his Liturgy, when he wrestled all night in prayer with God ? "

One sentence of Ruskin's settles the question of

Consecrated ground,—as if, writes Ruskin, "any ground could be consecrated that had the bones of rascals in it, or any ground profane where a good man slept."

Ritualism is to him simply childish,—a playing with symbols when realities are so near. He tells us that he has many friends amongst Priests, and that he would have had more had he not long been trying to make them see that "they have long trusted too much in candlesticks—not quite enough in candles, not at all enough in the Sun, and, least of all, enough in the Sun's Maker."

VIII

Ruskin has also a Message in Politics. Here he is a Radical, in the best sense of the word, caring most of all, not for the forms or the fact of government, but for the character of the citizens who compose the nation. His wise counsel is,— "Make the people good; get the good man, and so, get the good citizen."

He has not much to say on the Reform of the House of Lords, one of the burning questions of Politics, but what he has to say is worthy of note. In his opinion, it will not do to say that the House of Lords forms an impediment to business, for the question must be asked, what is the use of them? —they have a use, and that is, to govern the country. If they do so—well; and if not, why then, they must go. "Will they," he asks, "be Lords indeed, and give us laws; Dukes indeed, and give us guidance; Princes indeed, and give a beginning of a true dynasty, which shall not be soiled by covetousness, nor disordered by iniquity?"

On another burning question in Politics—the question of Home Rule for Ireland, he has nothing to say, except this, that he assumes that the purpose of this movement is to see to it that "Ireland should belong to the Irishmen." This, he concludes, is not only a most desirable, but ultimately a quite inevitable condition of things, being the assured intention of the Maker of Ireland, and all other lands.

IX

Last of all, we have Ruskin's Message in Social Economics. His message, scattered up and down his writings, is found in its fullest in *Fors Clavigera*, and embraces almost every department of social life.

All through his words there runs, clear as crystal, the great and saving principle, that man's good, or happiness, does not lie in *anything outside of himself.* Ruskin's gospel, and a veritable gospel it is, is that man's true good, or essential happiness, lies neither in money, nor railways, nor machinery, but in something else;—something simpler, more natural, a something which is divine.

No cheating or bargaining will ever get a single thing out of Nature's establishment at half price. Do we want to be strong?—we must work. Do we want to be hungry?—we must starve. Do we want to be happy?—we must be kind. Do we want to be wise?—we must look and think.

People are, he says, not one whit stronger, happier, or wiser, by the making of stuff a thousand yards a minute, or changing one's place at a hundred miles an hour; for a man's good lies not at all in going, but in being.

The world's prosperity and adversity depend in no wise on iron, glass, electricity, or steam. " To watch the corn grow, and the blossoms set,—to draw hard breath over plough and spade; to read, to think, to love, to hope, to pray,—these are the things that make men happy." Surely wiser words have not been written in our day.

As has just been remarked, Ruskin touches on a great variety of topics in his Social teaching. He has uttered wise words on Love, and Courtship, and words as wise on the subject of Dress. So far as Courtship is concerned, he thinks that when a youth is fully in love with a girl, and feels that he is wise in loving her, he should tell her so plainly, and take his chance bravely with other suitors. He is of the opinion that the orthodox time for courtship is seven years, and should never be shorter than three; and that a girl worth anything ought to have at least half a dozen of suitors under vow to her. He would have the courtship gone properly about, not the mob-courtship of modern times, in a miserable confusion of candlelight, moonlight, and limelight, and anything but daylight.

So far as Dress is concerned, Ruskin will have young ladies dress as plainly as their parents will allow them, but in bright colours, and the best of material. They may wear broad stripes or narrow,

bright colours or dark, but they must not buy yards
of useless stuff to make a knot or flounce of, and
they must not drag their dresses behind them on
the ground. Their walking dress must never, he
says, touch the ground at all; adding, that he has
lost much of the faith that he once had in the
common sense, and even in the delicacy, of the
present race of English women, by seeing how they
will allow their dresses to sweep the streets, " if it
is the fashion to be scavengers."

Like Carlyle, he is an ardent preacher of the
gospel of Work; stoutly maintaining that all,—
high and low, gentle and simple, should work with
their own hands at some sort of work or another. He
is indignant at those who think that it is neither
lady-like nor gentleman-like to work with one's
own hands, setting his seal to the truism, that there
is no degradation in the hardest labour. There is
degradation, as he remarks, in extravagance, bribery,
indolence, or pride. It degrades anyone to be a
knave or a thief, but it does not degrade a gentleman to become an errand-boy or a day-labourer.

He insists on ladies working with their own
hands. "You can," he writes, "make your own
bed, wash your own plate, brighten your own
furniture." To the objection that this is servant's
work, he replies, almost with vehemence, that of
course it is; and asks, Why hopes a lady to be
better than a servant of servants ?

Is the statement forthcoming—" But God made
me a lady "; then at once comes the reply—
" Become one of Christ's ladies, and serve."

But cry the ladies again—"You don't expect us to work with our hands, and make ourselves hot?" Why then, asks Ruskin—"Who, in the name of Him who made you, are you, that you shouldn't?" "Have you got past the flaming sword, back again to Eden? Forsooth, you will make slaves, accursed slaves, of others, that you may slip your dainty necks out of the collar."

But, once more say the ladies—"We thought that Christ's yoke had no collar." Then replies their monitor—"It is time that you knew better."

Ruskin becomes literally fierce when he comes to speak of War—insisting that there is no physical crime so far beyond pardon, so without parallel in guilt, as the making of gunpowder and war machinery. "Two nations," he writes, "go mad, and fight like harlots." "May God have mercy on them"; but he cries out, "what mercy is there for you, who hand them carving knives off your table for leave to pick up a dropped sixpence?"

If our soldiers were dressed in black, like other executioners, instead of in scarlet and gold, the game of War would not be so popular, in Ruskin's opinion.

He has much to say on the Land question. He is appalled at the terrible overcrowding in our cities, when there is so much land to be occupied, so much of God's air to be breathed, and sunshine to be enjoyed;—grouse and black-cock, "so many brace to the acre; and men and women, so many brace to the garret." There is, in his opinion, but one prin-

ciple involved in the Land question, and that is—
" Each man shall possess the ground he can *use*,
and no more." Take care, he writes, of your
Squires. The land belongs to them, because they
seized it by force, long since ; and you have the
same right to seize it now, and that is, none : they
had no right then, neither have you now. The
land, by Divine right, is neither theirs nor yours,
except under conditions not ascertained by fighting.

In the meantime the Land is theirs, by the law
of England. The first duty is to obey the law, be it
just or unjust, until it is altered, if alteration be
needful, by due peaceful deliberation. His last
word on this subject is : " Become diminutive
Capitalists and Squires yourselves."

We have no space to dwell upon Ruskin's founding of St. George's Company, the aim of which is to
buy land, and live upon it, and work it, in simple
ways. Suffice it to say, that this is one of his pet
schemes, giving him much trouble, and costing
immense money.

" We will," he writes, " make some small piece of
English ground, beautiful, and peaceful, and fruitful.
No steam engines,—no railroads upon it,—no un-
tended or unthought of creature about it,—none
wretched, but the sick,—none idle, but the dead,
—no liberty, but instead, obedience to known laws
and appointed persons,—no equality, but recognition
of every betterness that we can find, and repudia-
tion of every worseness. All will go quietly, and
safely. There will be plenty of flowers, and veget-
ables, and corn, and grass. There will be Art.

There will be Music and Poetry.   The children will learn to sing it, and to dance to it."

It is a lovely picture, a winsome social ideal,—John Ruskin's endeavour to realise, on this earth of ours, a bit of that kingdom of Christ which is righteousness, and peace, and joy.

"And the sucking child shall play on the hole of the asp, and the weaned child shall put his hand on the cockatrice' den.   They shall not hurt nor destroy in all my holy mountain: for the earth shall be full of the knowledge of the Lord, as the waters cover the sea."

OPINIONS OF THE PRESS ON THE "FAMOUS SCOTS" SERIES.

Of THOMAS CARLYLE, by H. C. MACPHERSON, the *British Weekly* says :—

"We congratulate the publishers on the in every way attractive appearance of the first volume of their new series. The typography is everything that could be wished, and the binding is most tasteful. . . We heartily congratulate author and publishers on the happy commencement of this admirable enterprise."

The *Literary World* says :—

"One of the very best little books on Carlyle yet written, far outweighing in value some more pretentious works with which we are familiar."

The *Scotsman* says :—

"As an estimate of the Carlylean philosophy, and of Carlyle's place in literature and his influence in the domains of morals, politics, and social ethics, the volume reveals not only care and fairness, but insight and a large capacity for original thought and judgment."

The *Glasgow Daily Record* says :—

"Is distinctly creditable to the publishers, and worthy of a national series such as they have projected."

The *Educational News* says :—

"The book is written in an able, masterly, and painstaking manner."

Of ALLAN RAMSAY, by OLIPHANT SMEATON, the *Scotsman* says :—

"It is not a patchwork picture, but one in which the writer, taking genuine interest in his subject, and bestowing conscientious pains on his task, has his materials well in hand, and has used them to produce a portrait that is both lifelike and well balanced."

The *People's Friend* says :—

"Presents a very interesting sketch of the life of the poet, as well as a well-balanced estimate and review of his works."

The *Edinburgh Dispatch* says :—

"The author has shown scholarship and much enthusiasm in his task."

The *Daily Record* says :—

"The kindly, vain, and pompous little wig-maker lives for us in Mr. Smeaton's pages."

The *Glasgow Herald* says :—

"A careful and intelligent study."

Of HUGH MILLER, by W. KEITH LEASK, the *Expository Times* says :—

"It is a right good book and a right true biography. . . . There is a very fine sense of Hugh Miller's greatness as a man and a Scotsman ; there is also a fine choice of language in making it ours."

The *Bookseller* says :—

"Mr. Leask gives the reader a clear impression of the simplicity, and yet the greatness, of his hero, and the broad result of his life's work is very plainly and carefully set forth. A short appreciation of his scientific labours, from the competent pen of Sir Archibald Geikie, and a useful bibliography of his works, complete a volume which is well worth reading for its own sake, and which forms a worthy instalment in an admirable series."

The *Daily News* says :—

"Leaves on us a very vivid impression."

Of JOHN KNOX, by A. TAYLOR INNES, Mr. Hay
Fleming, in the *Bookman*, says :—

"A masterly delineation of those stirring times in Scotland, and of that famous Scot who helped so much to shape them."

The *Freeman* says :—

"It is a concise, well written, and admirable narrative of the great Reformer's life, and in its estimate of his character and work it is calm, dispassionate, and well balanced. . . . It is a welcome addition to our Knox literature."

The *Speaker* says :—

"There is vision in this book, as well as knowledge."

The *Sunday School Chronicle* says :—

"Everybody who is acquainted with Mr. Taylor Innes's exquisite lecture on Samuel Rutherford will feel instinctively that he is just the man to do justice to the great Reformer, who is more to Scotland 'than any million of unblameable Scotsmen who need no forgiveness.' His literary skill, his thorough acquaintance with Scottish ecclesiastical life, his religious insight, his chastened enthusiasm, have enabled the author to produce an excellent piece of work. . . . It is a noble and inspiring theme, and Mr. Taylor Innes has handled it to perfection."

Of ROBERT BURNS, by GABRIEL SETOUN, the
New Age says :—

"It is the best thing on Burns we have yet had, almost as good as Carlyle's Essay and the pamphlet published by Dr. Nichol of Glasgow."

The *Methodist Times* says :—

"We are inclined to regard it as the very best that has yet been produced. There is a proper perspective, and Mr. Setoun does neither praise nor blame too copiously. . . . A difficult bit of work has been well done, and with fine literary and ethical discrimination."

Youth says :—

"It is written with knowledge, judgment, and skill. . . . The author's estimate of the moral character of Burns is temperate and discriminating ; he sees and states his evil qualities, and beside these he places his good ones in their fulness, depth, and splendour. The exposition of the special features marking the genius of the poet is able and penetrating.

Of THE BALLADISTS, by JOHN GEDDIE, the
Birmingham Daily Gazette says :—

"As a popular sketch of an intensely popular theme, Mr. Geddie's contribution to the ' Famous Scots Series ' is most excellent."

The *Publishers' Circular* says :—

"It may be predicted that lovers of romantic literature will re-peruse the old ballads with a quickened zest after reading Mr. Geddie's book. We have not had a more welcome little volume for many a day."

The *New Age* says :—

"One of the most delightful and eloquent appreciations of the ballad literature of Scotland that has ever seen the light."

The *Spectator* says :—

"The author has certainly made a contribution of remarkable value to the literary history of Scotland. We do not know of a book in which the subject has been treated with deeper sympathy or out of a fuller knowledge."

www.ingramcontent.com/pod-product-compliance
Lightning Source LLC
Chambersburg PA
CBHW030622030726
47497CB00006B/1597